The Expectations

The Expectations

Alexander Tilney

Little, Brown and Company
New York Boston London

Little, Brown and Company
Hachette Book Group
1290 Avenue of the Americas, New York, NY 10104
littlebrown.com

First Edition: July 2019

Little, Brown and Company is a division of Hachette Book Group, Inc. The Little, Brown name and logo are trademarks of Hachette Book Group, Inc.

The publisher is not responsible for websites (or their content) that are not owned by the publisher.

The Hachette Speakers Bureau provides a wide range of authors for speaking events. To find out more, go to hachettespeakersbureau.com or call (866) 376-6591.

ISBN 978-0-316-45037-9
Library of Congress Control Number: 2019932443

10 9 8 7 6 5 4 3 2 1

LSC-C

Printed in the United States of America

For M, D, L, and M

The Expectations

1. Finally

THE NEWBS WERE LINED UP IN THEIR UNDERWEAR ALONG THE FAR wall of the Hawley basement. Ennis Quinn, the captain of the wrestling team and the hardest sixth-former in Hawley House, stepped out from the pack of older kids, and Ben Weeks's shoulder blade met the cool stone behind him. Ben tried to keep his nervous elation from becoming too apparent: he had spent so long waiting through other things to get here. Ennis began to pace in front of the newbs, his eyes forced wide, his paper-bag-colored hair buzzed wrestling short, the tip of his tongue moving over his lips. He seemed built of denser stuff than the other kids.

The older guys in the dorm stood on all sides, now swaying in time together, and because they couldn't let the junior faculty two floors above them hear, they chanted in whispered unison, "A St. James newb is a quiet newb! A St. James newb is a quiet newb! A St. James newb..."

Ben could feel how scared the rest of the new kids were, and he was overcome with a protective pity for them. He wished he could impart to them what his older brother, Teddy, graduated that past spring, had imparted to him. This would just be a glorified pillow fight, it was happening all across campus in the basement of every dorm, it would weld them all together, they had come down here strangers and would leave each other's future groomsmen.

But, now, Ennis paced. Ben kept expecting him to start talking or yelling, to open the ordeal, but he just continued to walk back and forth, and the chanting of the other upper-formers all at once grew stale. They had repeated the words so often that the meaning had gone away in their mouths.

Now it seemed that this could be more difficult. Ennis kept pacing, not speaking, as though waiting for someone else's line to prompt him. Of course they had all been drinking, the upper-formers, but Ben hadn't come close enough to smell it. The newbs remained standing there, hair sleep-askew. Fear began to turn in Ben, new fear about actually getting hit now, and fear that this would be something other than what he had hoped it would be.

Ben's roommate, Ahmed, was the only newb who wasn't staring absently down at the drain in the floor, waiting for this to begin so that it could be over. And Ahmed was the only newb who was wearing a bathrobe: off-white waffle weave with crimson piping. His eyebrows were low and he followed Ennis with his eyes. What had Ennis done to earn this?

Earlier that day Ben had come through the door to the room and met eyes with Ahmed, this brown boy wearing a magnificent plum-colored dress shirt, and Ben had been quietly shocked by what was there in his face, in such contrast to all the other faces he had ever seen at St. James: a pure enthusiasm, a near-complete absence of guile. Now Ahmed closed his fists and released them, close-release, close-release, close-release, close-release. Ben watched Ahmed, and Ahmed watched Ennis. Still Ennis paced, still he said nothing, and it seemed like some mechanism was broken inside him.

Ben had so much to rely on. He took himself back to the living eyes of the crowd behind his court as he faced them, right arm above his head, after winning the last point of the Under-15 Junior National Squash tournament. Ben tried on that triumph again, tried to let it take him. Manley Price, the St. James squash coach, had been waiting for him to arrive on the team. Ben saw his brother Teddy's face, utterly free from doubt, describing St. James's classes, late nights in friends' rooms, afternoons deep in the woods. He saw Hutch's face across the Camp Tongaheewin canoe shed, telling the other kids how sweet St. James was going to be. Ben saw the class photos of his uncle and father and grandfather, all the Weekses who looked like him, all the way back. Fear was natural, fear was even part of the appeal, but he belonged, he belonged, this was the correct beginning for all of it.

"Newbs!" Ennis finally called out in a whisper. "We are going to see who is the toughest among you!"

Again Ennis lapsed into fixated silence, and all of Ben's assurance went away.

"We are going to find out who is the bravest! The strongest! The fastest! The best! The best! The bessssssst!"

Ennis curled his fists in front of himself and lowered his head toward his chest now, chanting to himself, "The bessssssst! The bessssssst! The bessssssssssst!" The morning of that day seemed very long ago.

★ ★ ★

After two hours on the blazing highway, Ben's dad had taken
Exit 20 into Doverton's strip of car washes, mattress stores, drive-
thru banks, the Pizzeria Uno, the Staples, the Boston Chicken.
Ben wondered when the school would build its own exit off
of 93 so you didn't have to drive through all this, the hectic
electrical wires across the sky, the parking lots without a single
car surrounding restaurant-shaped buildings with no glass in the
windows. They passed Doverton's dignified red-brick mental
hospital, the tan public high school, the Citgo station crouched
in its concrete lot.

The road narrowed. Now the houses on either side sagged as
though underneath the clapboard they were built of sodden foam.

Then the forest seemed to unwind, to expel the hasty man-
made things, and it became the kind of forest that people think
of when they think of New England. Ben dried his palms on the
front of his khaki shorts. His real life was so close, but now unexpectedly he wanted to keep driving for a few more hours, to
go out into the woods with his dad and find sheets of lichen over
wide granite tables. At home a few years before, they had walked
through the woods and taken lichen flakes to compare with the
pictures in the thick manual on the library coffee table. Since
then that book had lain there, perfectly undisturbed.

The back of the Volvo station wagon was snug: two hockey
duffels full of clothes and bedding; his three Prince Extender
squash racquets, which Prince had just sent him; half a flat of new
yellow-dot squash balls; Action Eyes glasses with white Croakies;
two pair of Hi-Tec court shoes. He had Teddy's hand-me-down
stereo; a cardboard tube with a Led Zeppelin poster and an
M. C. Escher poster inside; cleats, Saucony running shoes, brown
Oxfords; the red Marlboro Racing hat with the Formula 1 car
on it that Teddy had given him, which Ben had stuffed with two

T-shirts and wrapped in a fleece so it wouldn't get misshapen in the duffel; a Mac Classic; a schefflera tree in a wicker basket; an alarm clock; toothbrush, toothpaste, Old Spice, and shampoo-and-conditioner-in-one. A new North Face Mountain Jacket was also rolled up in his duffel bag, and Ben had cried to get it.

They kept driving now under trees whose heavy foliage blocked out the sky. Ben kept waiting for St. James's front sign. He had come up for so many anniversary days, for squash matches where he had undergone Manley Price's famous handshake, for Teddy's games, for years of Parents' Weekends.

And before that, Ben's father had come up on the train from the old Penn Station; and his uncle; and his grandfather, who on the living room mantel laughed in black-and-white with Bobby Kennedy; and his great-uncle, whose name was on the certificate of incorporation for the Council on Foreign Relations.

And before any of that, in New Bedford, Massachusetts, then still a colony, Samuel Weeks had been a sailmaker, sewing by hand the sails for a single whaling vessel, the *Vulcan*. Soon he ran a thriving sail- and boatmaking enterprise, and his sons thereafter invested in shipping and importing, rising to prominent places in state government.

And so, in order to become equipped to carry on this lineage, twelve-year-old Thomas Weeks had in the fall of 1856 arrived in God's Pocket, New Hampshire, in a surrey carriage behind two overcast-gray horses, for the first day of the first semester of St. James's first year.

Thomas's parents were risking their son's education, and by extension the social standing and future of the family, on a new pedagogical idea. A young minister, the son of a family friend, had decided to establish an intentionally remote, enclosed educational haven in the old-growth forest. At the time, the academies—Andover, Exeter, Milton—weren't boarding schools at all. Their buildings lined each town's main street and students lived with local families or in independent rooming houses. But every family knew a few boys who had come back from the academies with drinking and gambling problems, and this was an error in the system. The point had always been to have a son escape the distractions and temptations of the city in order to become prepared.

So to announce its contrast, St. James chose as its school symbol not an eagle or lion or dragon, but an ant. The school crest was a black worker ant below an open Bible over the motto *Vade ad Formicam*. That impressed the Weekses. All students would live together on campus under the direct supervision of teachers, and together they would undergo the same curriculum of Latin, rhetoric, mathematics, and theology. Students would work on the buildings and grounds. After four years, the risk paid off several times over.

Thomas went on to Princeton and was an early investor in the rubber industry. The Weeks family had contributed to the rubber tire, the sealing gasket, the windshield wiper, the shoe sole, the conveyor belt, the latex glove: modernity itself. Money was not a possession but rather a trust, and the owner simply a trustee, a steward.

Ben had been told this story many times. He had been reminded of the particular worthiness of this origin, but most of the time it was too familiar to be distinct to him. The photo of Thomas Weeks with the six other graduates of the first St. James class hung inconspicuously along the back hallway of Ben's house, and Ben would sometimes look at all of them leaning on the split-rail fence and wonder when it had become the rule to smile in pictures. Almost right away, St. James had been accepted as one of the very few training grounds for America's nervous and changeable aristocracy, and soon several other schools imitated the idea.

But now, in the middle 1990s, this design, this intentional remoteness, was starting to break down, and it would only continue to break down. The majority of St. James kids already had email addresses, and in a few years, the dorms would be wired for broadband Internet. And then hip-hop slang would sound cooler than what had bloomed in this particular Galápagos of Grateful Dead dialect. And the kids would start looking at the same amount of porn as everyone else, Gchat with their friends from home, check Facebook between classes, tend Instagram, and get calls from their parents on their phones every day. And their parents would call their teachers and wonder about that grade on that quiz, or that decision not to start the kid for the second half of the game.

But not quite yet. Still, as Ben and his father drove toward campus, you could go an entire semester without seeing a newscast or hearing commercial radio, and each dorm shared one pay phone in the basement. Even though N.W.A CDs and Peter North on VHS had passed the gates since Ben's dad had graduated, the remoteness still functioned as remoteness; it was still easier to escape distraction here. To what end?

And then the simple white sign between granite posts appeared: ST. JAMES SCHOOL.

Ben's dad braked and pulled off into the spur of the entrance lane. Untrained evergreen hedges grew tall on either side, blocking for a moment the powerful sun, and the car drove slowly between them.

The St. James admissions packet—the sight of its thickness had washed Ben with relief—told him he would have a roommate, but it hadn't given him any information about who the room-mate would be. Ben loved that he would have a roommate. This kid would give Ben a place to deploy the expertise he'd learned from Teddy. When he had visited St. James before, met Teddy's friends, he'd learned that if a kid's last name sounded familiar, it wasn't a coincidence. Yes, *that* food company, that steelmaker, that bank. Ben and his roommate would know St. James slang to-gether, they would have inside jokes, they would go talk to girls together and compare notes after. Ben would let the roommate know how to act at Seated Meal and at the Den, what no one wore, how to make upper-formers think you were cool enough for a newb but not trying to be too cool. When you went to someone's room you never knocked on the door because only faculty were required to knock, and so anyone who knocked was faculty.

Ben and his roommate would know how to get liquor (Ben had no idea how to get liquor, but so what) and other kids would want to come to their room to partake. Ben would hang out with his roommate more than with the guy he knew from Tongaheewin, Taylor Hutchinson—Hutch—and Hutch would want to hang out with Ben because he was kind of unavailable. The Tongaheewin staff had let Hutch go on the Long Canoe Trip even as a 14-and-Under, and during the dance with Loheewo, he had apparently fingered Heather Reese on the tennis courts. This past summer people said they had gone all the way. Hutch was up for Best Camper two years in a row, but he had scoffed at the idea, saying that only suck-ups got that prize.

"But I bet Weeksy wants it, huh?" Hutch said, punching Ben pretty hard on the shoulder. And in fact Ben did want Best Camper, and he blushed, and the rest of the kids at their table laughed and Ben punched Hutch back but it was so light. Hutch had afforded Ben more respect once he found out that Ben was going to St. James too.

Ben and his roommate would steal an industrial-size bag of powdered Jell-O from the Dish and caulk the gap under the door of someone's ground-floor room, then, with a hose through the window, fill the room with a foot of water, pour the Jell-O in, turn the radiator on and stir the whole room with an oar from the boathouse, then turn the radiator off, leave the windows open, and, when the room was discovered with a foot of perfect gelatin across it, be hailed as epoch-defining practical jokers, and Hutch would nod that it was pretty awesome.

Ben already missed his friend from home, Tim Green, with his eternal middle part and his cargo shorts, but finally he would have better, cooler friends, friends for whom he had no hidden pocket of embarrassment.

Now the entry lane hedges dropped away from either side of the car. Playing fields like green lakes opened around them. A barn-red barn sagged slightly to their left, and across the road stood a series of faculty houses in brick and white clapboard.

Beyond a fringe of trees rose the square tower of the school chapel, knotty spires pointing up from each corner. Its liver color seemed to vibrate against the ultra-sincere blue of the summer sky. To call it a chapel had always seemed strange to Ben; it was a full-scale cathedral, and its tower was visible from almost everywhere on campus.

Ben sensed the North Face jacket and the Marlboro Racing hat in the car behind him and almost shuddered with the anticipation of wearing them when the time came. Soon he would feel the right way. If he had come in on the first day wearing the hat, people would think he thought he was cool, but soon he would be able to wear it.

11

Driving in now, Ben saw kids along the paths in their hats, mostly the two-bar Game hats with the names of different colleges across the front, but he knew that his Marlboro hat was better because it was the same shape and structure as the Game hats, but it was distinct, one of a kind, and the curve of the brim was perfect. Hutch would immediately recognize that it was perfect, and Ben wished that Teddy had given it to him early enough to wear at Tongaheewin.

They kept driving, down a slight incline toward Founder's Hall with its bleached-bright columns, then over the nameless brook that ran through campus. Usually his dad talked constantly when they came to St. James, pointing at places through the window and relating things he had done in each place, but now he was quiet, maybe also under the heaviness of his hope. He had been co-chair of the fundraising committee for the new squash courts, so at least Ben knew he would want to go see them. Maybe Manley Price would be there at the courts waiting for them.

Now they came to the parking lot behind the unlovely quad dorms, 1930s institutional Gothic built of brick and sandstone. Ben's dorm, Hawley, did its part to confine an expanse of grass on the building's far side. They parked amid the other cars and got out and stretched in the hot sun, and the chapel bells rang all four Westminster Quarters and then a single bong: one p.m.

The dorm thrummed with kids and parents intent on carrying things in and setting them up. Ben and his dad wore khaki shorts and polo shirts but not sunglasses because sunglasses were gauche. Room 24 was empty. Two beds, two surgical-green rubber-covered mattresses, two desks. Ben and his dad set the first bags on the floor. Three windows on the far wall looked out over the back parking lot and the stretch of grass to the Two-Laner, and then the cinder block gym beyond. Ben knew that if he stuck his head out the window he could see the squash courts just up the rise to the right. The wind pushed slowly through the heavy trees.

On both desks lay the folder with the line-drawn map of the school and the schedule of first days' activities, and on top of that, a small, dark blue leatherette book.

THE ST. JAMES COMPANION

was printed on the cover in stout, gold-embossed letters, and the page edges were stained red. Ben chose the bed and desk on the left, and he slipped the book into the desk's pencil drawer.

Outside, older kids were hugging each other and laughing. Ben carried a standing lamp and his dad carried one bookshelf speaker under each arm. They set up the stereo and hung the Escher poster of ants crawling along a Möbius strip. Ben's dad had given him a three-by-five reproduction of an Audubon drawing of the Great Auk, a sort of penguin that looked like an affronted London aristocrat. The little print was in a worn-out, gold-painted frame, and Ben jammed a thumbtack into the outside of the room's door and hung the frame on the tack. Ben kept imagining a short-haired girl coming to visit him. The last thing she saw before their eyes met would be this quirky, charming picture.

Now in the parking lot it was sweat-hot. The leaves flashed white as they faced the sun. Cicadas ground off and on as though theirs was the noise of the heat itself.

As they made trips to and from the car carrying things in, Ben nodding and half smiling to every new person he passed, girls were doing the same thing, moving with their parents between the cars in the quad parking lot and the neighboring dorms.

Ben looked at the girls but tried not to look too hard. He noticed the pretty girls, but he also saw the cusp-pretty girls. Even in hurried glances with his arms full, Ben could tell which of these St. James girls had been awkward. There had been a couple girls like this at Sidney, his school at home. Their long necks just now belonged with the rest of their bodies, or their eyes weren't quite so close together anymore, and even though Ben couldn't know its precise history, the unaccustomedness was clear.

The always-pretty girls seemed to consume attention as a matter of routine, or even as a nuisance, and Ben couldn't blame them for that. But the cusp-pretty girls had never before been looked at so hard—by boys, by men, and by the always-pretty girls—and it seemed to make them aware of their surroundings in a way that appeared exhilarating and slightly painful for them.

Ben felt kinship with those cusp-pretty girls, slight kinship, because now for the first time people were starting to look at him with a story in their minds too. Because Ben had in the past year gone from being a pretty good squash player to being maybe the best boys' squash player in the country. Even in a world so tiny—he played a sport that most of America would never know about—that new celebrity, the way the coaches and parents and other players actively reassessed him, stood out clearly to him.

Ben loved the feeling that people were going to respect him, that he could lift his shoulders and feel a mantle of dominance laid over them. But to talk too much about oneself was bad, to have too much self-regard, and so when he smiled about winning, lifted his arm above his head as he turned to the crowd—eventually that would feel natural. It was like a demented eddy in him when the triumph that he had wanted for so long, that all the other players around him worked so hard for, that his father was incandescent for on his behalf, didn't feel exactly the way he thought it was going to. Ben could sense that every time these people looked at him, they were trying to assess how closely the real thing lived up to what this Weeks kid was supposed to be. He hoped those cusp-pretty girls were noticing him, feeling him feel kinship with them.

All at once everything was up in the room, and so Ben and his dad decided to go see the new courts. As soon as they walked down the steps at Hawley's back entrance, Ben again expected Manley Price to be there, knowing exactly how long Ben had already been on campus. Slowly they went up the rise toward the new building.

The game of squash—two players in a room the size of a two-car garage hitting a rubber ball off a wall, each trying to hit a shot that bounces twice before the other can reach it—started in England in the 1830s and soon spread throughout the British colonies. St. James, from the beginning almost desperately imitating England in its architecture, curriculum, and pastimes, built in 1885 the first court in the United States. There was no standard court size at the time, and St. James's court happened to be narrower than the ones taking shape in England. St. James, and then clubs and schools in Philadelphia and Brooklyn Heights and Canada, were playing in the winter before reliable heating, and because cold rubber doesn't bounce easily, the Americans developed dense balls that retained heat well and moved fast even when you could see your breath on the court.

But in the rest of the world, a wider, shorter court became standard. A ball developed that you could pinch between your fingers and that wasn't overactive in warmer climates like India and Hong Kong. And so the two games existed in parallel: "hardball" in America and "softball" around the world, and the American game became a strange, isolated variant.

This American game was the version that everyone around Ben played growing up. Ben's dad, Harry, had been on the team at St. James in the mid-1960s and remained a fanatic, playing three times a week at his club. Manley Price started as coach after Harry graduated, and many times out loud Ben's dad had expressed regret that he hadn't been there for the Price era. Harry and his friends at the club wore paper slippers after the shower and cupped their privates in talcum powder and used combs lifted by a metal plunger out of the jar of Barbicide and drank Scotch and played backgammon.

Harry somehow never became true friends with the other men whose families had always belonged to clubs like this, had founded clubs like this. His real friends—and more or less the only friends he had, rather than his wife's friends' husbands— were Chip and Paul, the two guys he played squash with most often. Chip was an engineer from Wilmette, Illinois, and Paul was an insurance executive from Houston, and they had moved to Connecticut to work for United Technologies and Cigna, respectively. Chip and Paul had both picked up squash as adults. Late-to-the-gamers are always the most intense, and they were the only two guys at the club who played hard enough for Harry's liking. The three of them never entered official tournaments; they just played endless winner-stay-on-court games. The three of them dove for the ball, their knees bled, they wore complicated braces, but they never missed a court time.

Even though he would have been ashamed to catch himself thinking it, Harry thought he was the social better of these two men. Partly he enjoyed their company so much because he didn't have to impress them, and because they couldn't accurately assess the nuances of his class and how closely he did or didn't adhere to its rules. When he was around real WASPs, Harry sometimes had a feeling that he'd been wasting his time with Chip and Paul, but he was always relieved to see them again.

Harry used squash as his handle on St. James. It was his way of counterbalancing the influence of his brother, Russell: Russell Weeks, founder and chairman of Landreach Capital. A home at 80th and Park and one in Amagansett. Served on the St. James board, audited the school's books each year, and co-authored the Annual Report. In 1992 Russell had given the majority gift for a major addition to the school's observatory, including a telescope seven times more powerful than the previous one. Harry gave every year too, but he prided himself on spending time: when the SJS squash team played a school in Connecticut or southern Mass, Ben's dad would go cheer and talk with Manley Price about strategy and training approaches.

At Harry's club he and Chip and Paul played the American game, but Chip had first learned to play squash on International courts with a softball while working for Siemens in Munich, and so when he came back to the US, playing the American game felt like hitting a Super Ball in a closet. In a long, patient fit of pique he built an International court out of cinder block and plaster in his backyard, and he called it the "μm Club," or the "Micron Club" after his favorite unit of measurement. He gave Ben and a few other local kids the keys and said they could use it whenever they wanted.

From Ben's house to the country club was a sixteen-minute drive, but it was only a seven-minute bike ride to the Um Club, and so almost entirely out of inertia Ben at age eleven began spending ninety percent of his playing time on the International-size court playing with the International ball. He and the other kids who ended up at the Um Club were generally in better shape than their tournament opponents because a softball is harder to put away. Their points lasted longer, but their timing was off for the American game, their movement not as precise, and so they would almost inevitably lose in the second or third round of any tournament they entered.

On certain weekend days Ben played with the other kids at the Um Club for four or five hours at a stretch, going through three or four changes of T-shirts and socks. And sometimes after school or after dinner or when he couldn't sleep, Ben would bike over and just hit balls, straight long shots ("rails") and drop shots. He would stay there for hours, and would be surprised when he saw the time as he walked off court. Chip would look out his bathroom window while brushing his teeth and see the court lights on, then hear the faint sound of the ball against the racquet and the slightly louder sound of the ball against the wall.

Ben couldn't have told you why he was doing it, exactly; there was just something soothing about the limits of the court, the consistency of that world, just a few walls, and the ball, and the racquet, and he could submit to those boundaries and make only the very few decisions that they dictated.

Ben's mom, Helen, would hear Ben come in at eleven p.m. on a Wednesday, and it occurred to her what a strange kind of worry she felt. She knew he wasn't out doing drugs and breaking windows. She knew he wasn't getting the neighbor's daughter pregnant. Instead he was digging into some deep solitude, some absorption that she worried he wouldn't be able to extricate himself from. Harry told her to let it go; didn't she remember being a kid, being caught in little fixations? She did. Days during the summer when it would have been too much effort to actually begin any real activity—practicing the piano like her mother kept reminding her to do, going to the beach with friends—she remembered taking out all of her jewelry—the thin chain with the St. Christopher on it, the charm bracelet with the flexible fish and the spinning Ferris wheel, the thin strand of freshwater pearls—then heaping everything all together and mixing it around until it was tangled, then untangling it all again. "See?" Harry said. "All kids do that, he's just doing it with squash."

And still, what if this rule-bound thing shaped him to its shape? What if he never felt the pull of rulelessness? And she knew that Harry wasn't impartial about this, that he would have responded differently if the fixation had been something other than squash. So for a couple years Ben played, and he and his Um Club friends stayed toward the bottom of the middle of the pack.

But then, in the early nineties, US squash got tired of being a backwater, and colleges wanted to be able to recruit international players, and so gradually everyone started playing softball on narrow courts. And then when colleges and clubs one by one started renovating their courts, they went International-size, and suddenly Ben didn't have to adjust. When he reached for the ball, his racquet was there, when he forgot himself the default was right. All of the Um Club kids went up in the rankings, but Ben had spent the kind of time that none of the rest of them had spent, and so he could always get to one more ball, always made the better choice, always had the decisive half inch.

Something changed as he started beating the Um Club kids and then going on to win tournaments. Before, they had all just been hacking around, turning up the Allman Brothers and Led Zeppelin on the shitty all-in-one stereo unit behind the Um Club court, clapping for each other during hard-fought losses in the quarters. They had all sat on the thin carpeting of various college gyms and private club lounges, stretching and making fun of each other, folding over gauze pads and taping them to the undersides of their feet where the calluses had pulled off in a flap as thick as an orange rind, eating PowerBar after PowerBar in miniature bites so as never to get on the court too full, pressing sweat-soaked clothes into plastic shopping bags and squeezing the air out, tying them shut and forgetting to open them when they got home, then discovering civilizations of mildew. They made jokes together about the preening kids in the top five whose parents went paper-faced when they lost.

But when Ben started winning, winning by a lot, the faces of the other guys went a little quieter toward him, and soon a kind of lacquer began to come over their eyes when they looked at him. When he was still on court, Ben saw all of them sitting together, showered and in long sweats. Suddenly there were jokes that he hadn't been around to help invent. The only one this didn't seem to happen with was Tim, but then Tim never really seemed to care about squash that much to begin with.

And now when his mom came to see him play, when she saw him beat the other kids, she worried that maybe Ben was getting too used to it. He seemed to expect the awe already; she saw him compress his lips into a smile after coming off court early in a tournament, treating the applause almost as a sudden rain shower. To her he looked so beautiful—thin but strong, those flash-gray eyes—but she truly couldn't tell if this was just a mother's bias or real information in the world. And so even though she rooted for him, when he came off court and looked for her, she could feel herself trying to be a little clay-faced, to stand on the other side of the scale, to convey to him that winning was important but not more so than other things, not more than being respectful and kind and not thinking too much of oneself.

But to see him play, to see his arms and legs moving in such a coordinated way, so soon after he had hardly been able to stand up on his own, to see him brush the slate-black hair out of his eyes, to see him fold a bandanna to the perfect width in a way she had never showed him how to do and then knot it behind his head—all of it, his mere supple existence, sometimes surprised her, made her afraid that he would turn out to be less gentle than his father, less openhearted.

Teddy was out of her hands; she had known even before Teddy could speak that he would be out of her hands. She had to concentrate to remember the times when of his own volition Teddy had treated something or someone gently. But there was tenderness in Ben, and so it worried her when Ben became so good at squash because she knew that tenderness needed tending. There was something of her brother-in-law, Russell, in him that had maybe received too much oxygen when Ben started beating everyone.

Even with his mother's apparent worry, and with the changes in his old Um Club friends, Ben luxuriated in the future waiting for him on the St. James squash team, Manley Price's legendary team, the Tide. The wood plaques in the St. James lounge listed in gold paint the thirty-four times they had won the New England Championships. Eleven times between 1979 and 1991: the Long Streak. SJS number one Blake Perkins had won the Independent School League individual championship four straight years starting in 1984, and twice he had beaten the number two SJS player for the title.

This dominance had two causes. One of course was Price, whose two constantly repeated maxims were now stitched on felt banners in the lounge:

Some Other Team May Beat Us
But They Will Have to Bleed to Do It

and:

Play the Percentages

Price ran sprints with his kids, even into his fifties. He could clearly explain stroke mechanics but stopped before making a player self-conscious. He was a widower and a rumored late-night alcoholic, which gave him a tragic majesty that allowed the kids to build a kind of crusade narrative for each season: the world had wronged their coach and they could rectify that through their own selfless contribution.

The second cause of the Long Streak was the furnace under the St. James courts. Since the forties it had been the pet of Ed Poniatowski, the school's head maintenance man, and he had made so many provisional fixes and had memorized such a vast complex of minute adjustments that when he died in 1976, the furnace left the control of men. The Athletic Director set aside funds to replace it, but Price convinced him to leave it alone and instead coached directly to it.

Eighty percent of the time the heat hardly worked at all, and the St. James courts were almost as cold as the outside air. Squash balls bounce much less when they're cold, and although they get warm mainly by being hit, the temperature of the court determines the pace of the game. Cold courts make the ball slow and so it's easier to win with drop shots but harder to win with power. SJS players wore long underwear and wool sweaters, and they learned to scrape every ball off the floor, pry every shot out of the back corners, and get the ball deep in the court by hitting it high on the front wall.

When the furnace woke up, though, the air quavered over the radiators, and players would set balls on top of them until they were almost painful to pick up. When the court is hot, the ball bounces higher and is harder to kill. St. James players learned to run and run and run, to be patient and not try to force the end of a point, to play for reliable shots instead of outright winners. They learned to lay the ball into the nick— the seam where the wall and floor meet—in order to keep their drop shots from bouncing up too high. They learned to lob gentle balls over their opponents' heads and let them die in the back corners.

People began calling the furnace the Dragon. Because of the Dragon, SJS could play anywhere, but opposing players could almost never play the game dictated by the SJS courts.

Price promised five hundred dollars to any of his players who could beat the slowest member of the crew team in a 2,000-meter erg piece ("twenty-five cents per meter"), and twice he had to pay. No other school brought players into that kind of fitness, and the kids who couldn't tolerate emergency signals singing through their nervous systems dropped off the team.

Success begat success, and the best players from Brooklyn Heights and Philadelphia wanted to play for St. James. Price recruited in a way that seemed to other coaches ruthless and a little pathetic. It was just high school squash, after all.

Price seemed to hover over the school, outside the dull interchange of classes and homework, something more elemental to the school's enduring idea of itself and its cold-water New England beginnings. When people mentioned him, he seemed more like the chapel or library than like a private citizen.

By the mid-eighties the team started calling itself the Tide. Before matches they would huddle together and chant over and over, "You can't stay dry, the Tide is rolling in, the Tide is rolling in, the Tide is rolling in. You can't stay dry, the Tide is rolling in . . ."

When Ben was mediocre at hardball, he had always hoped to be part of the Tide but knew that he would be toward the bottom of the ladder, maybe even JV. Kids at tournaments nudged each other when Price showed up, scouting, and some of them played worse under the pressure of his scrutiny.

Then, at the beginning of Teddy's fifth-form year, the year Ben started seventh grade, a chunk of plaster fell from the ceiling of Court 4 and knocked a player's racquet out of his hand. St. James's American courts went overnight from being classic to being embarrassingly out-of-date, and Ben's dad had found his project. He and a group of other squash alumni promised to raise six million dollars to finally replace the furnace, and to convert the facility to wide International softball courts.

So when the 1994 Junior Championships were at Harvard on International courts, Manley Price came to watch, and after Ben walked off the court after not dropping a game in the semifinals, Price was there at the Poland Spring cooler. Ben nodded in recognition and smiled but he was still too out of breath to say anything, almost thankful that nervousness didn't have anywhere inside him to reside. He filled a paper cup with water and sipped from it as Price stood right there wearing a small, extremely intense smile.

Ben stepped a bit away from the cooler so that the two of them could have a thin buffer of privacy. Price clearly wanted to say something, and Ben looked at the man's face, dug through with creases, his wheat-colored sweater with holes at the hem and right forearm, his sticking-up hair like a cropped tassel out of an ear of corn.

Price took two fingers and poked Ben in the chest.

"You," he said.

Ben pretended to be still too winded to speak. He just smiled as though there had been some good joke and sipped from the water cup again.

"You have it. The Long Streak is going to be a preamble to you." Ben smelled Price's breath, like leaves long on the ground. Price hadn't taken his eyes from Ben's, and Ben nodded curtly, hoping it looked polite, appreciative of this thing Price had said that Ben was now realizing was extravagant praise, praise almost beyond imagining. It felt like the kind of reality-dream you have just between wakefulness and sleep.

"You can kill, can't you? Right now they're just dying for you, so it's hard for me to tell. You have to answer this for me: If there's someone just as good as you are, or even a little better, can you go right to the inside with him? Can you go there and kill him?"

Ben nodded because that's what was being asked of him and Price smiled, all the lines in his face coming together, his eyes gleaming slots.

"Take care of yourself—start that application." And then Price turned and walked away as though he had forgotten about Ben completely.

Did Ben know how to kill? It had really only been six months that he had been winning, when overpowering his opponents felt inevitable. If he could have described it, he would have said that he loved letting some energy pass through him as unopposed as possible. Was that killing? Was murder part of that energy? The other Um Club kids came up to him. What did Price say? What did he want to know?

That night after winning the final—turning to the crowd and seeing them all looking at him, not even hearing their applause but taking the weight of their gaze—Ben told his dad that Price had said hello.

"Was he excited?" Ben's dad asked.

"Yeah. He was really nice. I mean, I think I might play pretty high up there."

His dad hugged him and Ben could feel him restraining himself from hugging too tightly. Ben wished Teddy had been there to see it. But, also, he was glad that Teddy was with friends spring skiing in Vail.

And so, as though it were blossoming just for him, the new St. James squash center was finished the summer before Ben's first year: twelve International courts, ASB brand, the building's interior totally remade without changing the staid brick exterior. When the architect had finished the plans, Ben's dad spread them over the dining room table and the family ate in the kitchen for three weeks. He would finally and permanently hold his own against his brother Russell.

And now on the first day of school, as Ben and his dad in a medium sweat set down the last box, they nodded to each other in agreement to go look at the new courts. Ben had expected his dad to be shuddering with excitement, but still he was quiet, and Ben guessed that he was worried about leaving, or maybe he was afraid of meeting an experience that he'd anticipated for too long.

In the bright heat they walked up to the giant furnace, furry with rust, now bolted down on a ten-foot-by-ten-foot concrete slab in front of the courts building. It looked like the sire of ancient mechanical bulls. Below it, on a sloped granite block, a bronze plaque.

THE DRAGON

1935–1993

ST. JAMES SQUASH

The two of them went inside the courts, still not speaking maybe from reverence, and after they had admired the two stadium courts below the bank of carpeted steps, they came back out into the obliterating light and walked very slowly to the dorm amid all the other students and adults moving around them. Ben realized that part of him had expected that Price would be living in the courts.

"Parents always stay too long on the first day," his dad said, smiling to Ben. "That's the problem." So there on the Hawley doorstep, with two kids carrying in a futon frame behind them, Ben hugged his father goodbye. They came apart and his dad had his lips pressed together, and then the Volvo accelerated neatly out of the parking lot, and Ben's connection to the outside world was broken.

2. These Spotted Tigers

Bᴇɴ ᴛᴜʀɴᴇᴅ ʙᴀᴄᴋ ᴛᴏ ᴛʜᴇ ᴅᴏʀᴍ, ꜰᴀᴄɪɴɢ ɪᴛ ʙʏ ʜɪᴍꜱᴇʟꜰ ɴᴏᴡ, and then considered his roommate. Just conceiving of the two of them sitting together after check-in, talking about wherever the kid was from, dulled Ben's sudden pervading homesickness.

Ben's Old Boy, the student assigned to shepherd him through the first few days, showed up with a firm handshake and introduced himself as Avery. He was sorry he hadn't been there to help move stuff. Avery was a rower with acne that was going to scar, and he seemed somehow proud to be sweating. They went over to the rectory to shake hands with Mr. Aston, the school's new Rector. (Aston would have been called the Headmaster at another private school, but St. James had kept the word "Rector" from its religious beginnings.) Then Avery took Ben to get his school ID made. Avery dropped him back at Hawley and said he'd see Ben at Seated Meal that night.

Ben walked into the dorm. He pushed open the second-floor fire door with its broad chicken-wire window and walked down the hallway, looking at his ID and moving his thumb over the photo. He wished he weren't so thin; there were light shadows under his cheekbones. Ben didn't know that his nickname in Juniors was "the Sliver."

As he put the ID in his pocket, he saw that the door to 24 was slightly ajar. Even though he didn't hear anything, he anticipated that the kid would like the Allman Brothers and so he almost seemed to hear the Allman Brothers. But then he saw that the drawing of the Great Auk was gone from the door. From inside the room he now heard a drawn-out, grating metallic screech and a rhythmic pounding. He came up to the room's threshold and saw that the door was held open with a gray rubber wedge. He stood looking into the room for several seconds before anyone noticed him.

The dark-skinned boy in a plum dress shirt sat at one of the room's desks, his dry lips slightly parted, looking down at the welcome-packet map of the school. A bed was in pieces against the far wall, and two very slim, short men in dark coveralls were building something. One man knelt over a chop saw cutting a two-by-four and the other nailed a piece of two-by-four to the wall.

As Ben looked at this boy's face, it seemed entirely clear, easy, and Ben realized that his own face, which he was trying to keep so implacable, was instead every moment betraying his doubt and fear, his desperate anticipation, and his tremendous effort to conceal his doubt and fear and anticipation. Even as Ben knew with finality that this was his roommate, he was also convinced that this kid was in the wrong room.

The worker kneeling over the chop saw noticed Ben first. He looked up, then stood and let his hands come to his sides in a vaguely military way. "Hello," the man said very deliberately to

Ben while looking at the boy at the desk. The other worker turned around and automatically held the hammer in front of him with both hands.

The boy lifted his gaze from the map and looked at Ben as though he had just come out of a cellar into the warm sun. Most of the time, when Ben met new people, it didn't occur to him right away whether he liked them or not; he almost always only thought of whether they liked him. But Ben knew that this kid was going to like him, and even without any intention to take advantage of that fact, he felt cruel. The boy stood up quickly and the chair teetered on its back legs. The nearer worker made a move to steady it, but after an instant it rocked back upright.

"Ben! You are Ben! I'm Ahmed! Ahmed Al-Khaled."

"Ahmed, hi!"

They shook hands, and when the time came to let go, Ahmed kept holding on with a grip that was at once tight and girlish. He was plump but not heavy.

"I looked at your picture in the student directory." His accent was British, but lightly so, as though each word had just come out of its packaging.

"I composed letters to you but I could not finish them properly." Ahmed vocalized his p's slightly so that they sounded more like b's, and there was a slight flutter in each of his r's. "You are just the roommate I had imagined, just what I had hoped for."

Ahmed saw Ben's stillness, his gray eyes and careful smile, and it seemed so much more appropriate than the overflowingness of home. But also there was surprising worry in Ben.

"Good, yeah," said Ben, and finally managed to get his hand free. He looked at the workers and what was happening to the room, and Ahmed followed his gaze. He looked back to Ben and then seemed to realize that something needed to be said. "Ah— Ben, this is Hector and . . . Benito?" The man who was Benito nodded, and both workmen smiled to reveal compromised teeth.

Then Ben saw them looking past him toward the door. Ben knew immediately that it was something bad, and he turned to find three kids at the doorway looking in with incredulous smiles. Ben turned back to the room and saw what they saw. Framed photos of the school—a bright red maple tree in front of the chapel, the main Kuyper Library from across the pond at sunset, a crew shell in the early morning mist—hung perfectly centered on each wall. Ben's NAD stereo components and Klipsch speakers had been moved, and in their place stood a black lacquered stand with a sleek Bang & Olufsen slide-apart CD player on it, flanked by chest-high pole speakers.

The picture of the Great Auk was laid on top of Ben's stereo components. There was no mistaking that Hector and Benito were servants.

Ben turned back to Ahmed, whose expression of happy anticipation had hardly changed, and who now looked to the doorway as though to welcome everyone. Ben expected the other kids to just walk into the room and take things roughly in their hands and laugh. One kid in a green UVM hat pointed and said, "Oh my god, look." Ben looked. It was a gargantuan burgundy tufted-leather sofa with bright brass upholstery nails. He imagined Hector and Benito carrying it up the stairs with Ahmed giving a fountain of directions while the tendons in their necks stood out. Two more kids appeared in the doorway and began to gawk.

Ben turned to the kids and put on a dismissive smile, then kicked the wedge away and closed the door. He turned back around and gestured toward the tools and two-by-four pieces. "What's this stuff for?"

"You lift the bed and you can put the desk underneath. We can have maximum space. We can do the same for you," Ahmed went on, gesturing to the workers with a short sweep of his hand as though presenting them to Ben as a gift. His smile seemed to ache with the effort of making everything ideal.

"I'm . . . okay. Thanks, though."

Ahmed's smile was extinguished. "The work is unpleasant. Perhaps we can go to the Den and sit and get to know each other better while the work is finished." He smiled again.

"Why did you take down my poster?"

"These photographs are beautiful."

Ben looked at the two workers, whose faces were at once anxious and disengaged. They wanted the interaction between the two boys to end so that they could finish the work.

"Perhaps we can go to the Den and get to know each other better while the work is finished," Ahmed said again. Ben knew that the Den's snack bar would be closed now and the room deserted.

"I think I'm just going to walk around for a while and say hi to some friends." Ben didn't want to look at Ahmed's face as he said this. He pretended to look all around for anything he might need before he left. "I'll be back at five to get dressed for Seated, so . . . " He didn't have the brazenness to say, "so everything better be finished by then." Ben nodded to Hector and Benito.

"I am so looking forward to this year," said Ahmed.

Again there seemed to be only sincerity in his face. Ahmed smiled, and he saw Ben place the gift of this smile to one side.

"Me too," said Ben. He turned away.

Ben turned the door handle slowly and peeked out. The hallway was empty.

When Ben was out in the hall, with its smell of commercial

cleaning products and hardly noticeable mildew, he was taken over by homesickness. He wanted to live with someone like Tim Green; it would have been fine not to be really that cool. He imagined a whole year sharing a room with this person, and the prospect of never feeling at ease made him come close to crying. He had the right to feel at ease.

At the end of the hallway he shoved open the fire door and let gravity take him down the stairs in two- and three-step drops. He started walking toward the school's power plant at the far southwest end of campus. Someone was playing the carillon in the chapel tower, and Ben could just decipher the plodding tunes. Between hymns came waggish versions of the *Inspector Gadget* theme and "I Saw Her Standing There." When Ben passed anyone on the path he looked straight down at the toe of each shoe as it came forward. Every time he looked up or came around a corner he thought it would be Hutch.

Ben couldn't remember how Tim Green had joined the Um Club crew. He was from the neighborhood right next to Chip's, two-level Colonials one after the other. The differences were there. Tim and Tim's dad wore T-shirts from 5k runs, there were pitchers of sun tea on the front walk, no one came to cut the lawn or mulch the garden beds. There wasn't enough room in Tim's backyard to really huck a Frisbee, and so they walked to the little reservoir near the house or stood on the quiet street.

Once when Ben's mom was dropping him off at Tim's house, she said, "I can't stand houses this close together. Everyone can watch each other's TV." And in fact one time after dark when Ben and Tim were walking back from the reservoir field, Ben saw synchronized changes of light through the darkened windows of three adjacent houses.

Tim was a good guitar player and Ben had taken piano lessons, and so when they were tired of playing squash they'd migrate back to Tim's house and jam in Tim's bedroom, Ben on the shitty Casio keyboard. None of it really mattered, and so it was the easiest time. Ben had thought that all those shapeless hours would be redeemed when he met the kid who would become his best friend at boarding school.

It occurred to him that he still hadn't seen Price, either, and even though Ben had only been on campus for a few hours he had a mild guilt and a companion sense that Price knew he had arrived, knew his location, even, and was deliberately withholding his presence until the most correct occasion.

When Ben came back to Hawley about an hour later, all the construction equipment was gone, a Persian-style carpet covered the center of the floor, and Ahmed's bed hung five feet up the wall with his desk underneath.

Ahmed sat on the leather couch, which had been set beneath the room's windows. He was wearing white boxer shorts and a white undershirt snug around his belly. Ben looked from Ahmed to the other end of the room and saw that his bed had been lofted as well.

"Wait, why did you do that to my bed?"

"You said it was okay."

"I said I was okay without it!"

"It is better."

"Ahmed, where are you from?"

"From Dubai. I hope you will visit!" As he said this, Ahmed worried about the idea of Ben actually visiting.

Ben stuck the tack back into the door as hard as he could and rehung the Great Auk. He went off to the shower, and through his rage he worried that some upper-former would want the shower. He had never heard the word "Dubai" before. He returned to the room, and Ahmed went to the bathroom in his waffle robe and thong sandals (Ben couldn't imagine him calling them "flip-flops"), carrying a wire basket of shampoos and soaps whose brands Ben didn't recognize.

When he came back, Ahmed started to lay out his Brioni suit, his John Lobb shoes, one of the shirts he had had made on Jermyn Street, the blue-and-pink Hermès tie. As each item came out he expected Ben to nod and commend him on his knowledge and discernment, the same way you hope a record-store clerk will nod at the albums you bring to the register.

But Ben silently pulled on his khakis slightly frayed at the cuffs and a blue Oxford shirt, picked out the red tie with small blue paisleys, and from his duffel unfolded the blue blazer his mom had gotten him at Marshalls. He slipped on his dark brown docksiders.

Ben couldn't have named the brands Ahmed was wearing, but he felt a mixture of tenderness and disdain that Ahmed was so flagrantly overdressing. Ben had a sense of proportion. Things were abundant with his family and their friends—houses with wide terraces or a folly cupola, tennis courts, a swimming pool here and there—but there was always a sense that they were minor-nice, that Greenwich and New York City were serious fancy in a way that Sudbury, Connecticut, would always be looking up to. But there was also pride in this, the pride of understatement, of the just-less-than-shiny genteel. Some important connection needed to be maintained to the Calvinist Yankee, the reuser of tea bags and the constant lowerer of the thermostat. His uncle Russell was a little too much. Caviar and good wine were correct for Ben's family once or twice a year as a celebration, but besides that there was intentionality in Triscuits and Cabot cheddar.

Ben's family had rented a house on Nantucket for decades, but the bigger and bigger houses that had started to grow there were bad, vulgar; even the idea of owning a thing that you only used for three weeks a year was dangerously wasteful.

And still, it had been important for Ben and Teddy to experience London and Paris and Rome and Athens, and so they went. It was important for Ben to learn the piano, and so they had a Steinway and weekly lessons before he let serious piano fade away. Even if you were able to afford a Mercedes or a BMW, anything more than a Volvo or maybe an Audi was gauche. It was important to the Weekses to have their sons know the difference, for Teddy to go to Gold & Silver if he wanted to, but also for Teddy to work as a landscaper in the summers to learn the value of an education. The Weekses ate Ben & Jerry's Heath Bar Crunch, cooked from *The Silver Palate*. They had a cleaning lady, but the idea of live-in help was from an earlier time; it would be a bad error now. Ben's day school had put off repairing the roof of the auditorium for two years, but they still insisted on a semiformal dress code every day including Fridays, and so Ben now tied his tie with hasty facility.

When Ben slid its knot lightly against his collar button and pulled on his blazer, Ahmed was still standing in bare feet with each sleeve of his French-cuff shirt extending past his hand like a neutered dog's plastic cone. He used a lint roller to remove specks of sawdust from the charcoal pinstripe suit jacket he had hung over the back of his desk chair.

"We've got to go, Ahmed."

"Yes—I will just button these"—he raised both cuffs—"and I will be down."

All the Hawley third-form boys—ninth graders in the outside world—waited in the common room to walk over together to the

Dish for Seated Meal, and no one talked. The Head of House, Mr. Dennett, stood near the entryway in a boxy blue blazer and thick-soled shoes. Dennett tried to hang jokes on the students closest to him, but they just laughed politely.

As far as Ben could tell, almost everyone in the dorm was there and Ahmed was still missing.

"Hey, are you Teddy Weeks's brother?" This was whispered to him by a tall blond kid whose collar left a half-inch gap all the way around his neck.

"Yeah?" Ben whispered this, too, but the kids close to them could obviously hear, and Ben thought that if they could just speak in normal voices then other people in the room would start talking and everyone would have more privacy amid the general noise.

"He graduated last spring, right?"

"Yeah?"

"So he's your brother?"

"Yeah."

"I heard he wrote like a five-hundred-page novel in two weeks and then had to be institutionalized."

"No, that's not true."

The blond kid frowned at Ben as though he were in no position to disprove stories about his brother. Having Teddy as a brother was an asset; Ben should have felt like Teddy was an asset. All of the kids around them were listening now.

Another blond boy leaned in from where he stood next to the faux-wood-sided television. "I heard he got two girls pregnant in two weeks and the school had to pay for secret abortions." The boy was slight enough to look like a grade schooler. "Is that true?" he asked Ben.

"I don't know. I never heard that."

The first blond again: "I heard Teddy unscrewed his Lava lamp and poured the wax blob in some newb's plant, and when the kid asked what it was, Teddy told him the Head of House's daughter had given herself an abortion in the bathroom and stashed the deformed fetus in the plant."

"No shit?" said the smaller blond, laughing, and by now Mr. Dennett was looking over at them. Dennett's face was now either blank or edging into a scowl. Was he upset that they were talking? Or did he hear "Head of House" and think the kids were talking about him? Or was he looking at Ben just because he was potentially as big a personality as Teddy? Ben wished he could just make it known that he was number one Under-15.

"Who's missing?" asked Dennett, and he counted the boys in pairs. He looked down at his clipboard and then up at Ben.

"Hey, Ben, looks like Ahmed is the last one. Can you go bring him down? We gotta go in exactly"—he looked at his Ironman digital watch—"one minute if we're not gonna be late."

"He said he was going to be right—"

Ben sprinted up the stairs with hatred coursing through his legs. He hauled open the fire door and smacked down the hallway in his hard shoes. He pushed the door open and beheld Ahmed, sitting on the couch still in the undone shirt and boxers, patiently feeding a cuff link through the holes in the shirt's left cuff.

He looked up and nodded, then leaned back over his work and said, "Sometimes it goes through right away, and sometimes it is like threading a needle with a noodle." He looked up again and smiled at the assonance.

"Ahmed, what are you doing? Everyone's waiting for you downstairs!"

Ahmed snapped straight, and with his cuffs flapping, he hurried to the trousers over the back of his chair. Ben sprinted back down the hall and through the fire door, then leaned over the banister and shouted down, "He's almost ready, we'll be right there!"

Dennett called back, "Listen, you know where the Dish is, right? You're at table eight in the Middle Dining Hall and Ahmed is table fourteen in Lower, okay?"

Ben wanted to keen and run after them, but the idea of Ahmed wandering alone through the empty campus pained him. He ran back to the room to find Ahmed with a long shoehorn gently lowering his heel into a light brown shoe. Ben looked out the window and saw the thinning troops of girls in white and black moving across the grass and out of sight.

"Ahmed..."

Finally they were going down the stairs. Ben hit the crossbar of the exit door and they moved out into the slow air. The bottom edge of the sun was at the tree line. The campus was as empty as a public square after a bomb scare.

"Oh, it is so beautiful here. My brothers should be able to see this place!"

With each step, Ahmed seemed to savor pressing up onto the ball of each foot. His right hand swung away from him as though he were a farmer in a poem casting seeds into a furrow. Ben walked faster and almost pulled Ahmed along as they headed onto the path around the pond. The trees closed in around them.

"I am sure they would not start without us."

"Five hundred people are not going to stop dinner for the two of us, Ahmed."

Ahmed had to break into a two-step trot every ten steps or so to keep up. The early-dusk light reflected off the pond through long, slim evergreens, and it was as though the scene were mocking Ben with its placidity. They emerged from the path and jogged up a short set of stairs onto the brick path leading to the Dish. The Dish—officially the Dining Quarters but no one called it that—resembled the quad dorms in its English Gothic style and brick-and-stone complexion, but it was forty years older and forty years more refined. Slate roofs reached down into sleek gargoyles, the windows were tall grids of small leaded panes, and the tunnel passage to the entrance went under a two-story archway. The two of them came to the twelve-foot-high oak entry doors.

Ben took hold of the wrought-iron hoop handle—as thick as a garden hose and as big around as a small pie plate—and leaned his weight back against it. The wide hinges moved smoothly and Ahmed stepped through. They jogged down the long hallway to the dining hall, shoes clacking on the smooth brick floor, past Gothic-arch windows on one side and oak panels listing graduating-class names on the other. Fingers had passed over the famous names until they had been rubbed shiny. Soon they heard the surf of dining hall voices.

Ben reminded Ahmed where he was sitting and went to find his own table, where they were already halfway through the main course. The other kids and the two faculty members smiled to him, but Ben was warm with embarrassment and tried not to make any more of a spectacle of himself.

In the common room after dinner Ben searched the thrumming, glossy crowd, and finally over by the coffee tureens he saw Hutch's lion head.

Hutch had the conviction of his own rightness around him, and Ben made his way over, leaving the other kids from his table as they all looked for somewhere else to adhere to. It seemed to take Hutch a second before he recognized Ben, almost as though he were performing the delay, but then he smiled and they clasped hands and hugged briefly, shoulders only.

Hutch felt Ben's dense, thin torso, which had always seemed off to him. Was Ben just kind of blank or was some important part of him elsewhere, someplace he judged better than this place? Hutch had occasionally wondered whether Ben thought Tongaheewin was kind of lame.

They both got coffee from the high silver urns, then Hutch walked back to the group he had been standing with and introduced Ben to Evan, his shorter, dark-haired roommate, who had gone to school with him in Locust Valley on Long Island. Their parents had called and arranged for them to room together. Soon there was a group of six—Todd, Mark, and Kyle were all in Woodruff with Hutch and Evan. They had all heard about Ahmed's servants, and that was all they wanted to talk about.

"Who fucking does that?" Hutch seemed to be asking Ben directly, asking Ben to join in his outrage. Ahmed had violated something important to Hutch, and it was important to him that everyone agree.

Evan provided the necessary idea. "Does he think this is his fucking fiefdom?"

Ben wanted to tell them about the clearness of Ahmed's face, how little guile...But instead he opened his mouth to start describing the couch and the pictures and the stereo. Before he could start speaking he felt a sharp hand at his elbow.

Ben turned, alarmed that it could be Ahmed, but even from the firmness of the touch he knew it wasn't him. He found instead a boy just shorter than him with dense red freckles all across his face and hair the color of his freckles. The boy wore a blinking smile. It was Rory, from Juniors, a year older but not a great player and not cool.

"Ben!"

41

Ben smiled and raised his eyebrows, feeling behind him the other group of guys waiting to see if this new conversation was worth their time.

"Hey, Rory."

"I was so worried that SJS was going to suck this year because we're switching to softball! And Cole Quinlan got in a car accident at grad parties. But I saw you at Nationals. Dude, we can still keep the Tide rolling."

Ben began to cherish the idea of the other guys being impressed by his squash reputation before Hutch had a chance to laugh at it.

But he couldn't turn around to explain, and Rory made no overture to the rest of them, and then Ben heard Hutch start talking confidingly to the others, and that group closed up behind him and it was just this kid and Ben now.

"Is Price here?" Ben asked. "I haven't seen him yet."

Rory half laughed. "Price only comes to Seated Meal when he wants to come to Seated Meal. He'll find you, don't worry." Ben gave a small smile. "Dude, we're starting captain's practices tomorrow. I can't wait to see you play. I can't fucking wait."

★ ★ ★

After Aston turned his Vespers address to the first-year students—"Being new can be difficult, but being new also allows one to see things more clearly than at any other time . . ."—Ben receded into his thoughts like an animal into its own fur.

Here he was, finally. Rehearsal was over. The chapel was easily four stories high, its ceiling vaulted in deep, dark wood, chandeliers hanging down like giant brass thistles, each wall an acre of stained glass. How could you depict the crease at the corner of a lamb's mouth in glass? Long parallel wooden pews ran the length of the building on either side of a center aisle facing in, letting the school see itself. New students in the first row, more senior students on the elevated rows behind, faculty along the walls in shallow mini-thrones. Ben knew that Price was in here somewhere but he couldn't see him in any of the seats along the far wall in either direction. Maybe Price was sitting behind him.

The huge space was illuminated for this first night by white candles on slender wooden posts that fit over the slanted hymnal rests in front of each pew, and the points of flame formed lines that seemed to converge down the length of the space. When the student body had grown beyond the capacity of the chapel in the 1930s, the school didn't cram folding chairs at the end of the nave or decide to take fewer students. Instead it broke the back wall free, mounted it on railroad tracks, rolled it back thirty yards, and built the necessary connecting walls and ceilings and stained glass and pews. Wealth hadn't needed to explain itself to anyone.

Coming in, Ben had been handed a slim unlit taper with a paper hilt, and now he held the candle across his lap. All the third-formers, the newbs, looked indirectly at each other across the aisle, seeing the nervous and the self-assured, the girls like ships and the girls like finches. Which will be my friends? Which of the boys could be the boy?

If Ben just stayed on track, took the challenges presented to him and prevailed over them, then he would be on the correct course. It felt like he was still watching himself be here, but all he had to do was wait and it would feel right. This place was for him. All the times at Sidney when he had almost overcome his discomfort and surrendered to their dances or running down the hallways, he had reassured himself about his hesitancy, his withdrawal, by reminding himself that all the same stuff would happen at St. James, and would happen better there, with all rightness.

In the low plush light of the chapel he looked at and away from the pretty girls and again at the cusp-pretty girls. Would they come watch him play? There was Hutch in the front row down toward the Rector's place.

They paused and sang "Our God, Our Help in Ages Past." Ben thought about God. Hymns like this didn't do anything to convince Ben of God's reality, but he loved them anyway. Even if so much of his life had been spent getting the plain cheese at Park Ave. Pizza in the strip near their house, or driving by the sound barriers and sumac along I-84, or at Strawberries looking at CDs, or at TJ Maxx with his mom looking for dress shoes, these hymns seemed to arise from where his real life should have been spent, in the forest or collecting blackberries near the red tobacco barns, and he recognized the rightness of these hymns in a way that made him resent having to experience the tawdry, good-enough things of the 1990s. The hymns felt sewed into the clothes of his personhood, their texture not only the best-feeling on his skin but also emphasizing the plastic fibers of Blockbuster and *A Current Affair* and Milli Vanilli against his neck. He sang this hymn, quietly yes, but with a pang in his chest.

As Aston went on, the candleglow seemed to induce prayer hypnosis, but Ben hadn't ever really known what people meant when they said "to pray." It seemed like sitting in the lap of the grandest imaginable shopping-mall Santa, asking for things.

Ben looked up and imagined the workmen carving all this wood, setting all the glass, hanging the massive doors, moving the bricks from the truck. That work seemed real. It seemed real for a kid his age to lift bricks into a wheelbarrow.

The prayers and the hymns blurred, the light like warm snow.

One of the Chapel Wardens approached Aston with a lit taper, and Aston held his candle wick above the flame, then turned and lit the candles of three students and the nearest faculty member. The flame was passed from one to another, and slowly the light spread until it came to Ben, and soon all the candles were lit, a meniscus of light swelling up into the deep space. Ben thought he heard Aston making some metaphor about spreading light. Aston asked them to stand and line up together to walk out, oldest students first. He asked third-formers to remain. He made more comments about discovery and self-discovery.

"Have a wonderful year," Aston said to them. "Go out into the school that is now yours!" They filed toward the exit, Ben smiling to the kids around him and keeping an eye out for Price but with no one saying anything. The doors opened into an alley of old students, who whooped all together as the first girls left the mouth of the chapel entrance into the night. Everyone walked out, and the shouting older students plunged into the line of newbs to hug them and lift them off the ground. The air was cooling fast but it still had the day's warmth in it, and after the chapel's stillness, just the turning breeze seemed wild to Ben. He thought he felt what he was supposed to feel. The older students were hamming it up, screaming and jumping up and down, but they meant it, too, and Ben wanted to be part of this, where it would matter if you were missing. Ben saw a line of wax run down a boy's blazer sleeve.

Several students away, he saw Hutch, whose tawny head rose and fell with all the other students jumping around him. Ben started jumping up and down too.

★ ★ ★

Ben climbed the ladder to his lofted bed as Ahmed finished putting away toiletries. The rungs the workmen had made were narrow and they hurt Ben's feet. He lay back on the sheets, familiar from his bed at home but new over this plasticky mattress.

"I feel so good," said Ahmed from his bed across the room. "The people at my table were so nice." They had let him know that none of the dishes contained any pork.

Ben didn't respond.

"You know the only thing that is missing here?" Ahmed asked.

"Hm?"

"There is no swimming pool."

"We have all the ponds."

"But there should be a pool. For the winter."

"I guess."

"Ben?"

"Yeah?"

Ahmed wanted to say that his father would be overjoyed if he knew that someone like Ben was Ahmed's roommate. Someone so able to demonstrate the right ways to be.

"Please remind me to tell you about Mr. Underhill."

"Okay."

"I am happy that we are roommates."

Soon Ahmed went still.

The light was still on. Ben was about to call out to Ahmed, to figure out a system of who would turn out the light on any given night. But instead Ben climbed back down the ladder and went to the wall by the door.

In the darkness Ben realized he would need a clip lamp at the end of his bunk. He kept his hands out in front of him and his steps were slow. Already he couldn't remember what the room looked like.

When he was back up in bed, feeling what he supposed was homesickness but also without any desire to be back in his parents' house, he thought he saw slight phosphorescence hanging in the air above him. He couldn't tell whether he was seeing it or whether it was leftover spots on his retina from the ceiling light. He reached up and was touching the ceiling far before he expected to.

He stroked his fingertips along the glowing spots, and the texture was like crumbs. He realized that some earlier kid had stuck glow-in-the-dark stars up here, and some later kid had done an incomplete job scraping them down.

He saw that first person—maybe it was a girl; this had been a girls' dorm once—early in the semester, imagining the wonderful scene that all the stars would create. This girl lifted her hand to Ben when the upper-formers came for them later that night.

*   *   *

"The bessssssst!

"The bessssst, the bessssst, the bessssst!" All the other upper-formers were looking at Ennis now too. Ennis stopped and went quiet but was still hunched over.

"Newbs!" whispered Ennis, then finally straightened up. He paused again; he seemed to be dragging his tongue along behind him. "Tonight we're going to see who is the toughest among you! All-out combat, last one standing wins."

Ennis walked closer and stood in front of each newb one by one and looked hard in his eyes, and each newb kept his gaze down. When it was Ben's turn and he smelled Ennis's breath, he lowered his eyes but tried to give a little smile in the meantime, a nod that he was on board with all of it. The fact that he was

47

Teddy's brother, and that he was going to dominate the squash team, of course those things were known to them.

Ahmed seemed confused, and Ben half wished he had explained what was going to happen before they had come down here. But another part of him was happy that Ahmed would have to learn this way. Ennis approached Ahmed and stared at him, and Ahmed returned the stare but pulled his head back to keep a civilized distance away, his hair touching the wall, and after nearly half a minute he finally closed his eyes. As Ennis passed to the next kid Ahmed looked after him angrily.

Finally Ennis reached the end of the row and hoarsely called out, "Give them their gloves."

The softer sixth-formers handed out pairs of synthetic-leather hockey gloves and nylon mesh lacrosse gloves. Ben received a pair of hockey gloves, which felt dense and rigid and good for landing a punch.

Ennis went on. "You think we would just have you fucksticks maul each other? We're better than that! We have a twist." He held up a red bandanna that had been folded into a strip. Ben saw that it had been folded the wrong way, with the diagonal edges showing, instead of with the triangular tip folding in. Ennis walked up behind Jed Beck, the tallest and most solid newb, eventually the football team's starting tight end, and tied the bandanna over his eyes. The movements were rough and jerky, and Jed's head moved with them.

Several of the sixth-formers had bandannas and each approached a different newb, and quickly almost half the group was blindfolded. Hideo Nakamura moved his blindfold down a little so that it better covered his eyes.

But when one of the sixth-formers got to Ahmed, Ahmed pulled his head away.

"I do not want it," said Ahmed.

"I don't care." The sixth-former went to lift the bandanna to Ahmed's face again.

"No," replied Ahmed.

Everyone without a blindfold was watching them.

"I would prefer to leave," Ahmed said.

Ennis walked right up to Ahmed and again brought his face very close. "If you leave, Ahmed, life gets much, much harder for everyone else."

Ahmed shrugged and let his shoulders fall. "That is your choice."

Ahmed stepped around Ennis and padded out of the cellar in his flip-flops. Everyone looked after him and then turned back to the sixth-formers. Ben felt sorry for them.

Ennis looked around at everyone, his eyes moving quickly from face to face.

"Your friend Ahmed just made your lives a lot, lot harder." His head swung around like an unlatched gate in hard wind. Ben could see him searching for a punishment. Second after second went by, and the blindfolded newbs began to pull their bandannas down.

"Get those fucking blindfolds back on!" Ennis shouted. Ben worried the faculty would hear them. With their clumsy gloved fingers the newbs pushed the bandannas back into place.

Ben looked toward the emergency exit door and saw several gallon jugs of Deer Park springwater along the wall. He lifted his chin and caught Ennis's attention. Then he jutted his chin toward the water jugs, and Ennis turned and saw them, then turned back to Ben and smiled. Later Ben wondered what the jugs had been doing there. Was the school pathetically preparing for a power outage?

And so each of the newbs was forced to drink a gallon of water, and the blindfolds went back on. The upper-formers pushed them all into the middle of the floor and they stood loosely together as though at a middle school dance. The skin of Ben's upper arms and back came against the moving skin of the other boys, and he heard the flat sound of a glove against flesh, and the fight had started.

Even through the blindfold and around his painful swinging belly, Ben tried to project the magnanimity of the generous conqueror. Although he would prevail now, it wasn't anything personal, it was all in the service of greater fellowship. This was exactly the kind of thing he had never done at Sidney.

But then padded fabric grazed his chest and something hit him in the neck, right in the widest part of his windpipe, and he wrenched his upper body away from the source of this, the impact stopping his breath. He heaved but kept it down. He crouched low. The water was so heavy in his stomach that it almost seemed to pull him forward. He thought for a second about shuffling off to the side and out of the scrum, but then a shin met the side of his head and he was taken over by anger, outrage that his unspoken attitude of generosity had been disregarded, and so with his left arm he swept back and forth, then lunged with his right every time he met anything solid. He heard the ragged breathing of all the newbs around him, the hoarse whispered shouting of the upper-formers. He smelled someone's metallic breath for an instant, and they smelled his metallic sweat.

In a later era, when anyone could have quietly recorded this and posted the video, it would have been an artifact, something that wouldn't go away, but even the start of the ordeal was now a decaying memory for all of them. A bolt of numbness under his chin, and his front teeth clacked together and he felt a floating speck of tooth with his tongue and he went hard to his knees. He reproached himself for not continuing on but he pawed his blindfold down and went on all fours back to the wall, where now about three quarters of the newbs sat. Josh Yost and Hideo had vomited into the storm drain. Ben looked around and there were three kids left, not directly facing each other, and then two of them smacked heads together by accident and leaned away and sat down. Jed was declared the winner.

The newbs went back upstairs inside their own hoods of quiet. Ben found Ahmed sleeping in his high bed.

Ahmed was facing out toward the room, profligate with trust, and Ben could tell he was deep down and without dreams. Ben climbed up to his bed now and wondered if he had had so much water that he might wet the bed. He ran his tongue over the small new roughness in his left front incisor.

With his belly spreading on either side of his spine, Ben again looked up at the very slight phosphorescence. He imagined his girl again, peeling the backings off each star and moon and ringed planet. Ben lay there looking at their remains, trying to stay awake until he needed to pee again.

3. Thermocline

Ben woke up; his bed was dry.

After morning Chapel, they had a day of orientation games. Ahmed loved the ha-ha game, where each person rested his or her head on the last person's stomach and then tried not to laugh as the "ha"s came down the line, but he declined to pass oranges from neck to neck because it seemed too intimate.

The next day was Monday and every student received a thick three-by-five card with his or her schedule printed in a grid of days and hours. The newbs racing from building to building, trying to look like they knew where they were going, upperclassmen giving them good and bad directions as the spirit moved them. Ben saw the other kids from the Hawley basement, looked at them and nodded, and they gave each other half-smiles but turned toward getting through school. Ennis and the other Hawley upper-formers stood outside the Schoolhouse, laughing conspicuously as though newb boxing had been such a success that they hardly remembered it.

Ben sat in English, relishing the use of his new notebooks and pens. At lunch he sat with Hutch and Evan, and he was glad they had recognized him even though he knew that was stupid. The two of them laughed when Ben told them about the previous night; for them it had been Rock 'Em, Sock 'Em Newb, where the upper-formers carried them on their shoulders and they punched from there. Ben showed them his new little chipped tooth.

Ben met briefly with his advisor, Mr. Markson, who was teaching English and philosophy. When Ben came for his appointment, Markson was at his desk wearing a beyond-insouciantly wrinkled blue blazer and a maroon knit tie with a square end. Ben couldn't tell why anyone would ever wear that kind of tie. Markson had a ginger, armpitty beard and ginger hair long enough to pull into a ponytail but that he tucked behind his ears as he looked at Ben's schedule. He said it seemed pretty balanced.

He asked if they might take a walk for the rest of their meeting; he had been cooped up all day. They headed out across the playing fields. Markson was six-six at least. He had a constant bend in his posture, but the hunch didn't convey defeat as much as a willingness to listen to shorter people without forcing them to exert themselves to be heard.

There was strong sun and a constant breeze, the kind of day that seems almost coercively upbeat. They watched a heavy staff member go by on a riding mower.

They walked near the tennis courts, and just to make conversation Ben said, "They're having captain's practice for squash already."

"Oh, right, you're a squash player too," Markson said, and Ben almost wished he hadn't known. "I played a tiny bit in college. My roommate junior and senior year was a phenomenal player, though, an Indian guy. It's a great game."

Ben suddenly understood it was Markson's first semester as a teacher.

"Did you go here too?" Ben asked.

"Yeah, it's taking a little time to adjust, actually. I'm still looking at all the teachers and wondering if they're going to find me doing something wrong."

Ben wanted to tell him he was going to do fine, but instead they came back around to the Schoolhouse, where Markson said Ben would know where to find him. Ben nodded and was about to head inside when Markson held up his hand and said, "Hey, Ben, please feel free to come talk to me. Obviously I'm faculty, but it's not hard for me to remember what it's like here. And if you need to talk about home stuff"—Markson stalled here, smiling—"just, whatever, I'm happy to talk."

Ben nodded again, hoping he looked sincere, and Markson released him with another wave.

Ahmed turned out to be in Ben's Approaches to History section, and he seemed untouched by the night before, quietly delighted to be in class, nodding along with the cadence of the teacher's words. Hutch and Ahmed were in bio with Ben, Evan in geometry, no one in Latin. Harry made his boys take Latin because it was a prerequisite for being a Western man.

Ben was shocked by how much work each class immediately assigned. He pinched the total pages he was supposed to read by Wednesday for Approaches; it was as thick as the side of his hand. He had to read half of *Oedipus Rex* and he had a twenty-question problem set for geometry. Conceptually he had known that St. James would have classes on Saturdays, but now the reality of it bore down on him. He left his last class at three thirty and thought he was going to have to work for the rest of the day and night.

But Hutch and Evan said they were going out to the boat docks with some guys because afternoon sports started Tuesday and everyone was going to the docks today. St. James was entirely traversed by water, and almost anywhere on campus a stretch of water reflected the surrounding buildings, trees, and sky. Even after the crew team had moved to Long Pond, a mile off campus, the school kept a dock on Sluice Pond, which extended directly away from the chapel, to give students a place to swim. From the back of the Dish you could make out the hunter-green boathouse, decommissioned now, and the plain wood dock extending down over the water.

Ben, Hutch, and Evan saw small groups heading into the woods on a path that started opposite the chapel. The three of them didn't speak as they stepped from the grass of the chapel lawn onto the white-pine needles carpeting the path, each with a towel over his shoulder.

Ben felt the beauty of the forest—shifting coins of light over the rocks and tree trunks, air fragrant with pine sap and the slight cooking smell of leaf cover in the hot sun—but he was a little worried about what it would be like out on the docks, how he was going to get his work done, and something else further out, harder to name. He was having to put effort into feeling how beautiful it was. Was this beauty the way he thought it would be? Hutch and Evan did not seem to be expending this kind of effort.

The boys kept walking for what seemed like a long time, and just as Ben wondered if they had overshot, the woods yielded up the back of the boathouse: green clapboard with crumbly yellow catkins clinging to the eaves and small windows. They could hear girl-laughter on its far side, and then the light fizz of conversation, and finally the dock itself creaking up and down with the miniature pond waves. The path passed behind the boathouse and then along-side it, allowing no view of the people sitting out there, until two stone steps led directly up onto the main platform.

As Ben climbed the steps, he had a brief vision of catching the toe of his flip-flop on the edge of the deck and sprawling out in front of everyone, slapping his face down against the pressure-treated wood. Ben startled himself; he hadn't expected these scenarios to play out in his mind at St. James.

But he placed each foot surely and took his first step onto the dock, and instead of all the conversations zipping closed and every face turning toward them, a few people looked over but mostly kept talking or lazily looking down at textbooks. Ben saw two people smoking and just made out the high burning smell. Three groups of guys sat against the front wall of the boathouse, and other groups of threes and fours had established encamp-ments farther down the dock. It was pretty crowded, but with no threats that Ben could see right away.

The pond was tea-black against the corrugated band of trees around it. The sun was just hot enough to make Ben's skin tighten. Evan, Ben, and Hutch headed for an open spot on the dock right out in the sun and spread out their towels.

Once they had settled themselves, Ben looked at a group of three girls lying facedown to their right. In the time it takes to blow out a match he took in the all-over downy fuzz, the secret moles, the ridges along the Achilles tendons, the twin dimples at the small of the back, the unbroken expanse of skin from the top of one girl's neck all the way down to the waistband of her bikini bottoms: she had unclasped her top. He saw the crease of flesh where her breast swelled out below her shaved armpit.

Ben remembered himself almost immediately and looked back down at the rainbow terry cloth conforming itself to the gaps between the planks of the dock. But he looked back at that little fold, desperate not to get caught looking, then away, then back again. This girl had a neck so beautiful that Ben wished English had a better word for it than "neck."

Hutch laughed. "Jesus, Ben, it looks like you're trying to see through her."

Ben couldn't tell if the girls had heard it; none of them moved. Slowly Ben turned toward Hutch, and when there had been no reaction from the girls' group for long enough, he lunged over and punched Hutch as hard as he could in the middle of the thigh. Hutch fell back and hooted with laughter, and Evan pounded Hutch's other thigh, and Hutch hooted again, and Ben was happy and worried they were making a spectacle of themselves.

Hutch and Evan took off their shirts—Evan's chest was almost concave—but Ben left his on for now. He didn't want to get a farmer's tan, but he was self-conscious about how thin he was. He hoped some imagined onlooker would understand that he had a strong body for squash: lanky but whip-supple on his right side, solid legs and hips. But who notices anyone else's hips? Everyone would likely just see a person so thin that his somewhat-tallness couldn't be much of an asset.

Ben tried to look anywhere but at that fold of flesh and his eyes fell on the corner of the boathouse roof. Before he had ever seen the boat docks, he'd heard the story of Teddy doing a backflip off the boathouse roof into the water. This was almost unimaginably dangerous, Ben had been informed, not only because the water was only about two feet deep where a jumper could reasonably reach from the edge of the roof, but also because there was this big white-pine tree just to the left of the ideal flight path, and so you had to pass within a few inches of the tree if you didn't want to go too far to the right and land on the dock itself.

Now Ben saw that very pine tree, with its ancient sap stains running down from the holes of missing limbs. It was thinner than Ben had imagined it, and its back side was browning unevenly as though hosting a parasite. Ben realized that on his earlier trips to SJS he hadn't seen the whole school—or even the majority of it—but he had built a complete version in his mind, and now that he was actually here everything seemed to have conspired to be slightly different. The idea of climbing up onto this roof, let alone jumping off it, would never have occurred to him—not even an inkling—if he hadn't known Teddy had already done it.

And then Ahmed's face appeared over the steps and he climbed up and stepped onto the dock. Ahmed carried a caramel leather Coach satchel and wore clompy white basketball mid-tops. He had one of his dark brown, dense-as-carpet bath towels draped over his shoulders. Already once when Ben was alone in the room he had pinched one of these towels between his thumb and forefinger; it was a very serious towel.

Ahmed was glad to see that Ben was at the boat docks; it meant that he had made the right choice to come here after hearing about it in maths. So far the beauty and pace was almost blinding. His advisor had said, "Ask for help if you need it."

The kids around them looked over at Ahmed. "Oh, Jesus," said Evan softly. The three girls next to Ben turned their heads to see. Ahmed waved to Ben, but instead of coming over he headed to sit with Hideo, who was sitting by himself over toward the edge of the dock.

Ahmed greeted Hideo, laid down his towel and straightened it carefully, then took a large Nikon SLR camera out of the satchel and began taking pictures of the dock and the trees. The auto film advance was loud across the dock. He pointed the camera straight up into the blueness of the sky and took a picture. He took a picture of Ben and then placed the camera on top of the satchel.

Ben just lay back on his towel and closed his eyes, and the sun glowed red through his eyelids. Hutch started making conversation with the girls next to them. Ben heard they were from Paige House, and it became clear that Paige was the dorm where the good-looking girls who controlled fates lived. When Ben opened his eyes again he saw that the girl had reclasped her top and was sitting up with her arms loosely hugging her knees.

"Weeksy, you comin in?" Hutch looked over and pulled his feet out of his flip-flops.

"Gimme some time, I want to get really hot before I go in."

"You, my friend, are never going to be hot no matter how long you stay in the sun."

"Go drown," Ben said, and he thought it sounded pretty cool. Ben was starting to see how he would soon feel easy with them. Hutch and Evan walked down to the end of the dock and dove in, the only ones in the water.

Ben reclined again and closed his eyes. When he had started winning at squash he had expected that suddenly his body would change, that he would look more like a man.

"Hold on, 'Weeksy'? Are you Teddy Weeks's brother?"

Ben opened his eyes again. From the encampment to his left, another girl was looking at him.

She had a weakish chin and brown-green eyes that were slightly too close together. She was wearing a lightweight blue sweatshirt even in the heat but wasn't sweating, and she sat up hugging her knees like the other girl had done a few minutes before.

"You're Teddy Weeks's brother?" she said again.

"No." Ben had been working up this line for the last few days: "He's *my* brother."

"Wait, what?"

"Well . . . I just, why can't *he* be *my* brother instead of me being his?"

"I don't . . . follow." The other girls next to this girl were listening now, one Asian and one blond-ish, neither of them particularly good-looking.

"Why do I have to be defined by him, I guess is what I'm saying."

"Oh, good, because I was going to say he was an enormous asshole, but because you're not defined by him, I don't have to say that," she said. "But you two were, um, born from the same woman? Who was impregnated by the same man."

"Yeah."

"Okay, so, what's your name, Not-Teddy?"

"I'm Ben."

They reached to shake hands, and Ben saw why she was wearing a sweatshirt. As she leaned over to him and extended her hand, the fabric went taut with the weight of her breasts. It was all Ben could do not to look down at her chest.

"Alice." She let go and had to lean back slightly to bring her chest behind her legs again.

"I'm Ben."

"Yup, you said that."

The breeze turned and her smell came to Ben and then went away so quickly that he wasn't sure it was hers. He understood that if he didn't say anything the conversation would fail.

"Did he really jump off the boathouse roof?" Ben asked.

"Who?"

"Ted—"

"—I'm not sure who you mean, this 'Teddy' person . . ."

Ben laughed. "All right." He looked back to the front of her sweatshirt but now it just looked like a collection of fabric. Another pair of girls came up the steps onto the dock, laughing easily. They spotted the blond girl sitting in Alice's group and rushed over and hugged and laid their stuff down and started talking about their summers. To make room for them everyone had to move over. And then Alice was closer to Ben, almost as close as if they had chosen to sit together. Unmistakably now her scent came to Ben, of her shampoo but also of her skin. Later in the dining hall, Ben would pass Vanessa Bates and have her good smell pass over him, but Vanessa's smell would be like a clean, empty room. Here on the dock Alice smelled, if Ben could have articulated it, slightly like fingers gummed in rosemary, slightly like freshly dried saliva, slightly like overturned sand in a few minutes of sun, slightly like clothes worn for a few days after washing. Ben was unequipped for it.

Alice's scent reminded Ben of Nina from home, and thinking about Nina he winced there in the sunshine. Ben had liked Nina so much, and after he had won Nationals he had tried to put his hand up Nina's shirt even though he knew she didn't want him to.

Upstairs at his house, with his mother down in the kitchen, he and Nina had pretended to play pool on the miniature Brookstone pool table on the landing until finally he leaned over and kissed her, and she kissed him back. Ben didn't necessarily need to put his hand on her chest; he was amazed just to be kissing her. But he wanted to have done it. His fingers found the seam of her button-up shirt. As soon as the back of his hand was against the skin next to her navel she, still kissing him, put her hand on his chest as though to caress it but with her elbow cleared his arm away. Pretending to take her false caress sincerely Ben brought his fingers back to the hem of her shirt. Again without ceasing to kiss him this time she pinned his hand against her abdomen with her elbow and he couldn't pretend anymore. He had thought to himself, *The girl at SJS is going to want me to do this.* Ben realized now that much of his drive to put his hand up Nina's shirt was from hearing about Hutch and Heather Reese that summer.

Again now he caught Alice's scent, and then he couldn't remember what Nina's had been like.

"You okay?" she asked.

"Sorry?"

"You settling in okay?" Alice asked him.

"Yeah, so far so good."

She laughed. "Liar."

Ben laughed. He quickly looked at her face again, trying to make it pretty.

"What form are you in?" he asked.

"Fourth."

"So it was tough getting used to it, like homesickness, or what?"

"It's a year in and I still feel like I'm trying to get used to it."

"Huh."

"Do you have a roommate?" she asked.

Ben lowered his voice. "See Mr. Smooth over there with the orthopedic shoes and the camera and the freaking satchel? That's my roommate."

Alice turned to look, then smiled to Ben without warmth, and he worried he was coming off churlish.

Alice studied Ben as he sat there on his towel, his flat-black hair and his long, smooth, almost snakelike body.

He was too unsure to fill out his looks, but Alice knew that soon he'd get over his self-consciousness. Soon he'd build up some ease—he'd get a few quizzes back and realize he could hang with the work, he'd see girls smile to him after Seated even if his joke wasn't so funny, whatever team he was on would win a few games, he would wear his shoes the right way—and then he'd disappear into that ease. Alice had seen so many of them make the same change, from glowing with discomfort along the walls of a dance or drifting back from the football fields under planetary helmets, to folding into the language, draping themselves across the chairs in the Dish Common Room, hooting and shouting in the dining hall when a group dared each other to say "penis," each louder than the last, going with the hunch that if they leaned in to kiss that girl she would likely reciprocate.

They would launch into speaking during class, trusting that cogency would emerge along the way, letting the act of talking itself lend shape to their thoughts. She could almost feel it happening in Ben moment by moment there beside her. She wished occasionally that she could break off a piece of this confidence, sneak up on one of them and snip it off like a lock of hair.

Alice looked again at Ahmed, then returned her eyes to Ben.

"Did he really have two servants helping him set up his room?"

"You know about that?"

"Everyone knows about that."

Ben suddenly was convinced that Ahmed had overheard them, but when he turned to check, Ahmed was looking the other way at a few other kids who were coming up the steps.

"Oh well. You win some, you lose some," she said. "How'd you chip your tooth?"

"A Hawley newb is a quiet newb," he said.

She didn't laugh.

From behind them now, three upperclassmen stood up and ran to the end of the dock waving their arms over their heads and screaming ironically. They stopped short and fell into the water like felled trees. Hutch and Evan had been hanging on to the side of the dock but now they pushed off and swam in a group with the older kids. The pack of them headed farther out diagonally from the left front corner of the dock. As they moved through the water they gave the expanse a human scale, and Ben was aware of the volume of air across the entire pond.

The group slowed down, spread out, then seemed to move in insistent, slow zigzags. Finally one of them stopped with an abruptness that didn't seem possible in open water and shouted something. The rest of them swam to him as he seemed buoyed up with his back toward the sky. Then, unbelievably, he straightened up until he was standing out of the surface of the water, covered only to his lower ankles.

"Look!" said Ahmed. "Look!" Ben turned and raised his eyebrows to acknowledge that he was looking, and Ahmed lifted his camera and took several photos.

"Well, the Jesus Rock has been discovered again for the first time," said Alice. Now four of the kids who had been swimming were standing up in the water—not Hutch or Evan yet. The kids huddled close together, and the surface of the rock looked to be about as big as the top of a large refrigerator.

Alice went back to talking to her friends, and several more kids stood up and dove in. Over the next twenty minutes different people exchanged places on top of the rock. They stood close and shivered even in the warm air, so near to each other with so much open skin.

Finally Ben shifted and reached for his towel.

"I'm jumping in." He looked over to Alice. "Anyone else?"

"Go ahead," Alice said. She hadn't changed position from leg-hugging.

He stood up and wriggled out of his shirt, desperate to bury himself in the water so that neither Alice nor anyone else would see his pallor and his thinness; he had a passing image of himself as the ball-chain hanging down from a ceiling lamp. He wanted to run full speed but the uneven planking was too steeply sloped and here and there a nailhead jutted up, so he had to walk down to the end of the dock through the burning of his visibleness. Finally, he leaned into a short, slow dive, crunching into the water, streaming through, the flesh between his toes distinct as the liquid passed over it, then turning over to emerge on his back. He saw everyone facing him from the dock, and it looked like they were spectating his swim. For a second he wondered whether Alice would be impressed that he was swimming, and then realized how stupid that was.

He lay back into a kind of modified backstroke. The water was just perfect, almost the same temperature as his skin, and for a moment it was hard to tell where his body ended. He looked up at the skeins of cloud set absolutely still across the sky. He felt good.

After the upper-formers had had their fill of climbing up on the rock and jumping off, they swam back to the dock to sit in the sun again, and the rock became available to newbs. Hutch and Evan were the first, and they stood up there and presented their chests and set their fists on their hips and looked up into the brave future like mountaineers posing for a summit photograph.

Ben looked back to the dock, and his eyes met Ahmed's for an instant. He immediately regretted it; it was as though the impact of his gaze had lifted Ahmed to his feet. Ahmed came down to the end of the dock, still with his T-shirt and shoes on. His torso looked like a cake decorator's icing bag. Ben realized he had been convinced Ahmed couldn't swim. Without taking off his shoes or shirt, Ahmed leapt into the water with his arms reaching out in front of him as though bracing for a fall, and then his head came above the surface of the water and he started wriggling forward. His face had the determined look of someone cleaning something foul.

Ben rolled over and took several hard strokes toward the rock with his eyes closed, then picked his head up and saw he was a few feet off course. He corrected his direction and took several more strokes, hoping to get out there before Ahmed could come close. Hutch and Evan were still the only ones up on the rock.

The sun reached a place that was suddenly late afternoon, and Ben looked across the water to the library and chapel glowing their different shades of umber. He swam to the edge of the rock, looking up at the two other boys, the water turning their blond hair dark, both of them with the first long hairs starting to grow off their chests.

They cleared a space for Ben, he set his hands on the top surface and started to twist his way up, and Evan took him by the upper arm as he came to standing. Ben steadied himself. He could just see the lighter surface of the rock below the water, and it was slick enough under his feet that he had to keep his knees bent to hold his balance. He looked around at the black plane all around him and the surrounding trees.

And out farther, rising up from the roof of dense green foliage, was the rounded silver dome of the observatory where his uncle Russell had given the telescope. The last time they were all together, in Palm Beach, the family had been reminded more than once that although Russell could have had it named after himself, he had refrained.

Despite Ben's repelling him with his mind, Ahmed swam

implacably to them. As he came closer, all three of them turned to face him. He reached the rock and set his hands on the edge. He was breathing hard but not panicked, and Ben wondered whether this was the farthest he had ever swum. Had he ever been outside a pool?

"I love swimming," he said, looking up to them a little too out of breath to smile. Hutch and Evan laughed, and Ahmed now smiled through his breathing but Ben could see that he knew Hutch and Evan's laughter wasn't kind. Ahmed pulled his chest to the side of the rock and leaned onto his hands to begin to climb up.

"No newbs," said Evan.

"Sorry?" said Ahmed, looking up in the middle of his effort.

"He said, no newbs," Hutch said, "especially no spoiled brat newbs."

"You are new."

"Your servants going to carry you up here?" said Evan.

"You going to buy the Jesus Rock all for yourself?" said Hutch.

"Maybe build some condos on it, some time-shares, maybe a casino, maybe a mall?"

Ahmed laughed a laugh with no humor, only shrugging off what they had said, and went again to climb up.

With his foot Hutch reached out and pushed Ahmed's right hand away from the rock. Just before Ben's foot moved to nudge Ahmed's other hand away, Evan had already done it. Ben could still in his imagination almost feel the softness of his skin meeting Ahmed's, and he suddenly worried that Alice would see them being mean to him.

Ben expected Ahmed to look up at him with supplication, but Ahmed didn't look up at all, and instead just pushed off gently and began to wriggle back toward the dock.

As Ben looked up, he saw the gray-blue fingernail of Alice's sweatshirt move out of sight around the side of the boathouse.

★ ★ ★

The sun came to the tree line and Ben, Hutch, and Evan decided to head to the Dish. With towels around their waists their group came up to the Dish's side entrance, and a couple other guys from Woodruff, Hutch and Evan's dorm, approached them. Ben was already keeping an eye out for Alice, feeling a miniature rise and corresponding dip each time he saw someone who could have been and then wasn't her in his peripheral vision.

And then Ben saw Manley Price walking up from an adjoining path. Just an older man, by himself, a little stiff in the knees, clearly with no awareness of Ben's whereabouts. But something about his uprightness and indifference to being alone suggested the highest evergreen tree on a mountain slope. They met eyes, and Price made just the smallest gesture, his hand remaining by his waist, and Ben began to slow. The other boys looked back but seemed to know to let him go.

Finally Price came near. "I heard you weren't at captain's practice today."

Ben flushed with embarrassment and a sense of moving to the end of a line. "I completely forgot. Everyone was going to the boat docks."

Instead of chastising him or even shaking his head, Price smiled and leaned in close as they continued to walk to the dining hall.

"I remember your brother."

"Oh yeah?"

"Teddy, correct?" Ben was astonished that Price would be uncertain of Teddy's name, and he nodded to confirm Price's memory.

"What a waste of a body. Every time he came to the court it was like the first time he'd ever played. He just had no love for it. You could always see that he'd rather be anywhere else. A couple times I tried to kick him off the team but he would always come back."

Hutch and the rest had gone through the double doors out of sight, and now Ben and Price came up to the same doors, and Ben opened the left one and Price stepped through without changing his pace. Once they were in the corridor with the name plaques and the stone arches and the other kids going to dinner, Ben expected him to talk in a more private tone, but Price's voice continued on just the same as before.

"The last time Teddy came back to the team, his fifth-form year, I think, we had a good team but not the best I'd ever had, and we had a shot at the title but it was going to be close. And just every day when Teddy showed up, he'd bring his mildew energy with him, and I finally told him that if he infected the rest of the team, if I sensed any shrinking from the pain of the work, I'd make him pay for it."

Price turned toward Ben now as they walked. "Your opponent is always going to want to avoid pain, but you run toward it, you go looking for that pain. Then you're not afraid, and you win." He turned to look ahead again.

"But I could tell that to excuse himself, Teddy was going to start rolling his eyes. I knew he was already doing it even if he wasn't doing it in front of me.

"And so I made sure he never came back, and we won."

"Made sure?"

Price smiled. "I told the rest of the team that if I saw Teddy within twenty feet of the courts, all of them would have to row a two-thousand-meter erg piece. Then the slowest three would have to row another two thousand meters, and then the slowest one of that three would have to row yet another two thousand meters. And I never saw him there again."

As they came into the high common room Price stopped, so Ben stopped. Price looked full at him. His eyes were pale and he had outdoors skin.

"You think that's cruel. But it's the best thing I could have done for him. Teddy thought that someone was going to be happy because he was playing squash—your father probably— but that wasn't true, and he was spending hours of his life doing something he didn't like. No one should ever do that. I just made him make a decision that he wasn't strong enough to make on his own. And everyone on the team was happier, and he was happier."

"What did he end up doing?"

Price pulled his head away and frowned. "I don't know."

After a moment Price stepped closer and put a closed hand on Ben's shoulder. Again Ben smelled his vegetal breath.

"Don't worry, Ben. I know you're scared. I'm going to put a lot of pressure on you. But you have the love. I've seen how much pleasure you get from playing, and that pleasure gets even better when you go through a few curtains of pain. When you can go through the last curtain and your opponent can't, that is a kind of living that you'll never be able to find any other way.

"So. Go to the boat docks, go play soccer or some other nonsense this fall, but then after that, it will be time."

Price walked away as if in that instant he had entirely cleared his mind, and it took a moment for Ben to shift himself and take a tray and get in the food line.

★ ★ ★

After the Jesus Rock Ben was nervous to see Ahmed again, so he went to the library that night instead of working in the dorm. At a low table in the two-story reading room, with windows looking out over the pond, two boys were taking a break from reading by playing backgammon.

Ben remembered that last day in Florida with his extended family. They had all been trying to relax at the covered bar looking out over the green-clay courts at the Bath and Tennis, especially Saturday afternoon before everyone had to fly out.

His father and uncle started a game of backgammon. Russell knew how much Harry hated it when he took a long time to roll, and so Russell shook the dice in the felt-lined leather cup, going to turn the cup over but then holding it upright again and continuing to shake.

In the humidity both of their faces were red with sun and piña coladas. Ben's dad didn't lose every game, but his face was so different from his older brother's. For Russell, this was a way to unwind, to pleasantly occupy the parts of his mind that were under strain at work and home, letting a thoroughbred out into a lush pasture so it could feel its legs.

But Harry was full on. He held his head and upper body over the cork board, slightly moving his lips as he counted the heavy, smoky-plastic pieces from point to point. Russell shook the dice and held them, shook them and still held them and smiled, and Harry tried to smile back. Ben always thought of his dad as a success until he saw him with Russell.

Ben found an unoccupied armchair and started reading. When he came back at check-in with so much still left to do, Ahmed smiled to him, how easily he couldn't tell, and Ben was glad he hadn't been the one who pushed Ahmed's hand away from the rock.

With no hesitation, Ahmed said he thought he would play club soccer—the first practice was the next day—but he wasn't sure if he would be able to do that and keep up with all of the work.

"No, it'll help you," Ben said. "You'll get to run in the afternoon and then you'll be more ready to concentrate afterward."

Ahmed broke into that basking smile.

"Ben, with you I will learn just how to be."

4. The Sacrificial Element

THE NEXT MORNING DURING HIS FREE THIRD PERIOD, BEN SAT ON a wooden bench outside the office of the Dean of Students on the third floor of the Schoolhouse trying to get further through his Approaches reading. After Chapel that morning, Mr. Dennett, Hawley's Head of House, had handed him a note asking him to come see the Dean, and so here Ben was, wondering if he had already done something wrong. Had Ahmed complained?

The Dean of Students' office was on the same third-floor hallway as College Admissions, the Athletic Director, and the Bursar, and the name of each department was painted on each door in dull gold outlined in black. The walls up here were bare of student posters, and the smell was different too: dripped coffee burned off a warming plate, toner from a big copy machine, the perfume of the women who ran the offices. Ben heard low voices from inside the Dean's office but otherwise the floor seemed empty.

Ben sat across from the open door of the Bursar, looking in at a front desk covered with paper and jars of pens and an electric typewriter. There was no one inside. Quietly from a little boom-box on top of a file cabinet came the saxophone of a song that Ben thoroughly recognized but couldn't have named, "Careless Whisper" by George Michael.

He wondered whether the Dean, Mr. Phelps, was keeping him waiting out here on purpose. He looked again into the Bursar's office with some tip-of-the-tongue feeling, as though the solution to his wait could be found on that desk.

He heard footsteps coming up the stairs and saw the head and body of an older woman, and as she came toward him, Ben had the feeling that she would recognize him, that she was coming to sit at this empty desk in this office and that she knew all about him.

But then the door to the Dean's office opened, and Mr. Markson beckoned him inside.

Ben sat in a spoke-back chair in front of Bud Phelps, the Dean of Students, whose desk was clean. Mr. Dennett with his cushiony face sat in the chair next to Ben, and Markson perched uncomfortably on the radiator cover next to the windows. Ben both wished Manley Price were here and was glad that he wasn't.

"So, you were there for the initiation fight?"

Phelps was a New Hampshire native with a slight, persistent Up Above accent and silvering hair still in a high-and-tight. He was rumored to have earned a Silver Star in Korea. He smiled to Ben with the lines on his face folding together. The office was simple: tan carpet and built-in bookshelves, wire document baskets with neat stacks inside, the same swing-open windows as in the Schoolhouse classrooms. Ben wondered why Phelps had agreed to work at St. James with all these soft-handed WASPs. He drove an immaculate, all-business Ford F-150 that dozens of boys winced with desire for. Ben wasn't sure whether the politenesses and small jokes that worked on other adults would work on him.

"You were there? In the basement?"

"Initiation fight?" asked Ben.

Phelps smiled again and didn't say anything, seeming to prepare himself for a long wait. This smile was less warm.

Ben wondered who had told. He considered Ahmed for a moment but that didn't feel right. In fact, Leon Carey had been comparing notes with Reid Pillsbury from Gordon House, where the newbs had just had an egg-and-spoon race while upper-formers sprayed them with Super Soakers. Reid had in turn told Fraser Grossman in his stairwell, saying out loud that two Hawley kids had thrown up, and the junior faculty member in Gordon had overheard it and gone to Phelps. The administration didn't like throwing up.

"We know it happened, Ben, so we just need more information. No one's going to get in trouble, so just help us understand more about it." Phelps had stopped smiling.

Ben paused. Phelps's face didn't look angry, but rather sincerely anxious, and Ben felt some thrill of power over these adults.

Ben cleared his throat. "I would definitely help you, but I think there must be bad information out there. Someone said the newbs were fighting each other?"

Phelps continued not to smile. This was only Phelps's second year as Dean of Students after thirteen years as chemistry teacher and hockey coach. As a scholarship boy (Class of '49) and as a new enlistee, Phelps had known what it was like to be at the mercy of other young men, and he had no nostalgia for it. The administration had implemented the hazing talk in dorms the previous year, but Phelps had known it wouldn't change anything. He understood why hazing endured.

Phelps looked at Ben, so transparently filled to the top with the knowledge of what had happened in the basement, so full of admiration for himself for not telling. Ben brought to mind the knee joint of a young horse. Phelps had seen boys built just this way pressing themselves into shelterless hillsides.

Phelps knew a great deal about Ben: his family, his brother, Manley Price's hopes for him. As Phelps laid out the hazing question, he thought about the conversations he couldn't have with Ben. Like most St. James students, Ben didn't appreciate how much effort it took to secure his well-being.

Phelps prayed with sincere intention in Chapel, in the middle of all the student and faculty daydreams, and he often asked God for the forbearance to treat well those who thought he was stupid, including now the new Rector. Aston was trying to make his mark, showing that he rejected the laissez-faire attitude of the previous administration, and so he badly wanted Phelps to just deal with this hazing issue correctly and have it pass away. Phelps needed enough detail to bring in the Hawley sixth-formers and make them think he knew everything, to play the role of the drill sergeant that everyone wanted him to play, and then they would be back on the beam. The Board of Directors wouldn't find out. Neither would other schools, the *Doverton Sentinel*, the *Boston Globe*.

Phelps and the other two adults in the room also had two specific events in mind related to this hazing, history that Ben had heard about but didn't think to apply to this moment.

Two years before, the wrestling team at the Horatio School in Rhode Island had won the ISL championship in a huge upset over Belmont Hill. To celebrate, five members of the team had convinced a fifteen-year-old sophomore girl to give them blow jobs and then to swallow their ejaculate out of the ISL championship trophy. Talk of the incident had spread, and when the local paper ran a front-page story on the moral decay at the school, the girl had decided to withdraw and the wrestling seniors were expelled. Over the next two years, Horatio's applications declined by twelve percent.

The year before that, a new student at Philadelphia's St. Luke's School had been forced into a metal garbage can and rolled down the stairs of his dorm after making fun of his roommate's permanent-press dress shirt. Halfway down the stairs, the student's front teeth met the rim of the trash can and flattened against the roof of his mouth. All the other kids in the dorm believed they had justly punished snobbery and so none of them would admit who had been responsible, and the student's family had sued St. Luke's and settled out of court for an undisclosed sum.

In both cases the administration had been slow to respond, hoping that handling things discreetly would make them go away unnoticed, but discretion had been seen as indifference, and was in fact partially indifference, and so the incidents became not only scandals but signs that the souls of these schools weren't right.

Phelps—the entire St. James administration—knew that over the decades scandals just like these had caused the undeniable decline of other schools that had once been in the top tier. Almost all of these selective secondary schools had once had first and second forms, equivalent to seventh and eighth grades, but in the 1950s, at the Halyard School outside Washington, DC, and at Vernon-Brighton in western Massachusetts, both top-fifteen schools at the time, several incidents of teachers exercising their power over younger boys became widely if quietly talked about. Eventually first and second forms were phased out; by third form, it was thought, boys are not as attractive to a certain kind of older man. But a stain stayed on Halyard and Vernon-Brighton, and slowly their alumni giving suffered, and they began to send one or two fewer kids to Princeton and MIT each year, and their admissions yield forced them to accept more and more mediocre students, and now both schools were ranked in the low thirties.

St. James still traded positions in the top five year after year, but the era when the school had without a second thought moved back that chapel wall was far gone. St. James's carrying costs were much higher than those of most colleges, they had extended more and more financial aid to try to diversify the student body, and the St. James endowment was healthy but somewhat sleepily managed. Several other schools were making savvy investments in technology and energy and had alumni who had prospered in the mid-nineties economy, and those schools had been able to build planetariums and concert halls and dorm rooms with duplex living spaces. In 1950, sixty percent of all students who applied to Ivy League schools got in; now it was closer to ten percent and only getting tougher. For the previous two years, St. James had had an uncomfortable admissions season.

It was exactly this combination—scandal and slippage—that had eroded other schools just as prominent as St. James was now. The new Rector, David Aston, had been brought in from a California boarding school founded in 1980 by an Andover alum. The board sensed that St. James was far from invulnerable, and so they needed Aston to inject the vigor and historylessness of the West Coast, with Phelps providing East Coast ballast.

Sometimes scandals made alumni feel embattled, galvanized, could in fact stoke their loyalty to a school. But Phelps had no appetite for risk. And most of all he didn't want a scandal to distract from what he saw as his slightly subversive mission to fold some kernel of idealism into these students before the world heaped them with wealth and position. Society thought that places like

St. James created unfairness, and of course that was true, but Phelps saw himself as a laborer in the vineyard, and he and many of his fellow teachers took seriously the task of creating ethical leaders. So to preserve the good he thought St. James could accomplish, Phelps was in the unfamiliar position of needing a certain outcome.

Phelps stayed quiet and looked at Ben. The other adults stayed quiet. Ben felt an urge to fill the silence, but then he realized that Phelps was creating this silence to make him say something, and so Ben settled back to wait, and Phelps seemed to know this immediately and cleared his throat to speak.

"You want to protect the older kids. I understand that. But who's protecting the other new students? What if something had gone wrong down there? What happens when it goes wrong next time? That's what you have to think about, Ben. If something goes wrong next time and you could have prevented it, how are you going to feel?"

Even though Ben was still enjoying his intangible advantage, it now seemed slight, and he felt guilty, exactly as he knew Phelps wanted him to feel.

"I'll let you know if I hear about anything like that."

Ben felt the possibility of the adults not being disappointed with him drain out of the room.

"I should probably go. I still need to get books from my room for next period."

"Well," said Phelps, "you change your mind, come back." Ben nodded, but then worried that the nod would be interpreted as an admission of guilt. Then he stood up and nodded again.

When Ben came out into the hallway, the door to the Bursar's office was closed. Ben started down the quiet stairs back into it all, but he heard a door open behind him, and when he turned he saw Markson taking a few jogging steps to catch up. Ben waited, and Markson came down two steps.

"Hey, thank you for coming in, I know that was intense."

"Not the end of the world."

"Nothing gets a school more scared than hazing. But I understand what kind of position you'd be in with other kids." He smiled.

"Maybe it happened in some other dorm, but—" Ben smiled as well, and the two of them seemed to duel with weary smiles for a moment.

"Listen, I've been working on this project—maybe it's a little hokey, but just in the context of all this, I thought you could help me."

Ben raised his eyebrows and compressed his lips.

"Aston has asked me to rewrite part of the *Companion,* and I'm trying to find out what students think about it."

"The *Companion?*"

Markson laughed. "Exactly. You know the little blue book they gave you the first day?" Ben immediately saw where it was in the pencil drawer of his desk. "There's an essay in there on decision-making—actually called 'Decision-Making'—and it's been the same forever, since before I went here; it still refers to students as 'boys.' So I'm redoing it. Take a look, then let's talk over what you think."

"Okay, sure, yeah, will do." Ben paused. "Hey, I would totally say something if there was anything—"

Markson raised his hand to his waist and made a brush-away gesture. "That's not—listen, whatever you want to do. I just also wanted to say . . . it may have seemed this way, but don't think this has anything to do with the tuition situation."

Ben tried to say something but instead lifted his eyebrows again.

Markson closed his eyes briefly, and when he opened them he was looking down toward the far side of the stairs. "Like, don't think they're trying to put pressure on you with that. It's between your parents and the school."

Then the tip-of-the-tongue feeling resolved as Ben remembered the mail that spring as he had waited for his admissions letter. Every day the mail would come and Ben would scour it for anything from St. James, anything on that ecru paper with the ant insignia in the upper left corner, worried that it wouldn't be the thick packet.

And three times he had felt a thin-envelope pang, only to feel relieved when the letter turned out not to be from the Admissions Office but from the Bursar instead. Something was also not right with that, he knew what a bursar was, and the RESPONSE REQUIRED above the addressee block stayed with him like a raised stitch at his collar. But that worry was down under the heaviness of his desire to get into St. James, and then the thick packet came.

But the memory of those letters from the Bursar wouldn't burn away as Ben anticipated coming to school. Something was off with how he had arrived. When he had come in previous years to help Teddy move in, there had been so many people—friends and younger kids and their parents—and so much laughter, hugging, swagger, feigned and genuine disbelief. Ben had hoped the quiet of his arrival was just because it was his first semester, with no one to come back to, but he knew that those Bursar letters were alive in the quiet driving onto campus with his dad.

And the letters had been there the day before the drive up to St. James, when Ben and his dad stood in EMS, the outdoor equipment store, engaged in a strange, quiet argument. Ben had lost his raincoat at Tongaheewin, and they were there to replace it. Ben loved outdoor stores; all the gear sat there ready to do huge, dangerous things. He wanted all of the bright sleeping bags and the tents with their curving poles and the rock-climbing harnesses with all the important metal clipped on and the kayaks and the boots and the folding knives in the glass case and the vacuum-sealed food in the shiny plastic envelopes.

They went to the jackets section. Each of the brands had its own rack, and each rack had four sloping studded bars so that the tops of the jacket fronts could be seen: North Face, Patagonia, EMS brand, Columbia. Ben stepped over to the North Face rack, but his dad picked up and started inspecting an EMS brand jacket.

Ben explained Gore-Tex and breathability. The snow skirt that snapped together under the hem of the jacket. The reinforced fabric at the shoulders and elbows, where contact with pack straps and ice axes demanded durability. *His dad had never needed any of that—he wore a yellow slicker when it rained and a parka skiing.* You couldn't really go mountaineering without a jacket like this. *When did Ben climb mountains?* But Ben wanted to do that. He had always wanted to do NOLS. Ben had been taught not to waste money on cheap things. He would be ashamed to be seen in an EMS jacket.

"It's not worth three hundred and eighty-five dollars, Ben."

"You know how cold it gets up there."

"It's not even insulated! It's a windbreaker!"

Ben looked at that correct jacket, hanging there in all its authority, in hunter green, his favorite color. With those square shoulders and the pipe-shaped hood, the North Face jacket looked like a sentry, like you would have no choice but to be ready whenever you put it on. The EMS one was like a plastic bag.

"I'd rather just wear a fleece than have something that's not serious."

"I don't understand the need to be *serious*."

Ben started to walk away toward the hiking boots section, to the sloped plastic ramp molded into rock shapes.

"Ben, stop."

Ben had been very near tears, both struggling not to cry and letting himself verge over. He tried to remember whether his dad's eyes had looked scared about actually giving up the money that the jacket cost. There in EMS, Ben had thought it was just about the principle of frugality, of not spending too much on a piece of clothing. It had never once occurred to him that $385 could meaningfully subtract from the total amount of money his father had.

But those thoughts must have been there. His father must have been having those thoughts all during the drive, as they carried bags up to the room, as they went to see the squash courts—

—and as they walked to the courts that first day. Ben had put his hand on the Dragon's side for a moment and looked up. His father should have been wearing a calm smile, suppressing delight at this beautiful thing he had brought into the world, his own thing that he wasn't going to name after himself. But Ben instead knew he would see a tautness across his father's face.

No landscaping had been done yet, and so the earth around the long, low brick building was still yellow mud molded into the shape of bulldozer treads. Stacks of bricks were covered in partially tied-down Tyvek sheeting, and dusty tree roots stuck up from the mud at hectic angles.

They passed the Dragon and walked through the soft dirt to the building's entrance. The courts would probably be locked, but Ben decided to try anyway, and the door's thumb latch gave. Ben pulled the door open and the two of them smelled the off-gas of new carpet and fresh paint. They stepped inside, first Ben and then his dad.

The red glow of the vestibule's EXIT sign created the feeling of being somewhere late at night. Ben pulled open the inner door and they went in and looked down from the top of the gallery. Courts 1 and 2, the marquee glass-back courts, sat side by side at the bottom of a carpeted bank of stadium steps. For an instant Ben remembered what they had looked like in the architectural plans, but then this reality crowded out any other version. The walls of the gallery were bare drywall with the seams and screw heads plastered over blotchily. The lines of the courts seemed almost hallucinatorily straight.

Ben could see a burr of dust over everything. The Manley Price Courts.

"What do you think?" his father asked.

"They look amazing." Ben missed the water stain on the ceiling of the Um Club court, the mismatched carpet remnants in the little lounge. Chip had sprung for a glass back wall, but you had to wedge it closed with a wooden shim after the latch had broken.

"They do look amazing."

The two of them didn't move. Ben didn't know what they were supposed to do now. He realized he should have been a little surprised that they hadn't brought shoes and racquets to hit with.

As they stood there looking down, not going farther in but not turning around to leave, Ben thought that maybe his dad was so subdued because he was going to miss having Ben at home.

Ben's dad took in a breath, exhaled, and said, "I hope they're worth it."

Now, in the stairwell with Markson, Ben tried to remember

with more specificity just what it had been like at the courts. How much of the quiet there had been money quiet?

Markson looked at him, the act of his compassion there in his eyes. "And of course, listen," Markson said, "I know what financial trouble at home can be like. My family went through a rough period when I was in college. It's stressful."

Ben kept nodding and nodding.

"So, again, if you want to talk about any situation at home, I'm much more than happy to."

Ben had never thought of himself as someone who would have a situation at home to talk about. But now Markson was concluding, looking in his face, asking for some acknowledgment.

Ben thanked Markson. Markson smiled with genuine warmth, so much so that Ben felt afraid his problem was serious enough to demand a smile this warm.

★ ★ ★

After making it through geometry, then bio, Ben walked back toward Hawley. He just wanted to get under the covers and pause his life for a few minutes before JV soccer tryouts. Ahmed had told him that morning that his father had agreed a swimming pool was necessary, and they were getting board approval now before beginning to interview architects.

As he went down the slope toward the little bridge to the quad, he saw Hutch and another kid from Woodruff, Kyle, coming up toward him.

"Weeksy!" said Hutch, and Ben couldn't resist blooming.

"Fellas," he said, and clasped hands first with Hutch and then with Kyle, which was awkward as he and Kyle had only barely nodded to each other before now.

"We were just talking about your fucking roommate."

"Oh yeah?"

"Did he really walk out of newb boxing, too?" This from Kyle, who Ben could see was sort of playacting his outrage.

"A Hawley newb is a quiet newb," Ben said, smiling, and the other two laughed, and Ben was almost frightened by how gratifying their laughter was. He didn't mention the pool.

"Dude," Hutch said, "come to our room tonight before Seated for crank time."

Ben knew it would seem cool to have another thing to do that could prevent him from agreeing to this.

"Sure, definitely."

"And tell your roommate to go fuck himself in the meantime," Kyle said.

Ben came around the corner to Hawley's back entrance, catching sight of the Dragon up the rise. He walked up the stairs, desperate for a few minutes of sleep, but when he came onto the hallway, he saw a chrome wheeled clothes rack next to number 24. Ahmed's shirts, back from Thomas & Ridgelow Cleaners, were draped in thin plastic and hung on wide-shouldered wooden hangers. The hangers filled up the shirts as though there were a patient torso in each one.

Ben went into the room, sat at his desk, beyond sleep's reach. He knew he needed to work.

Instead he opened the wide shallow drawer and almost to his surprise found the book there, the *St. James Companion,* just as it had been. He looked at its leatherette covering and the dry red of the page edges, then flipped through it. He had a craving for objects like this: small, talismanic things that seemed to collect wisdom regardless of what was printed in them. He wished his father wore a watch so that it could be passed down to him.

He wished his family had a vellum book from the Middle Ages in the collection of some archive somewhere. These stout gold letters on the cover had never experienced a moment of self-questioning.

He opened to the ant insignia over *Vade ad Formicam* on the flyleaf, then to the motto on the next page: "To serve man and to glorify God." He read the next section, entitled "Expectations."

> The school expects that a boy will never present the work of others as his own.
>
> The school expects that a boy will never take the possessions of other boys, nor those things belonging to the school.
>
> The school expects that a boy will never use intoxicants of any kind, nor bring intoxicants onto campus for any reason.
>
> The school expects that a boy will...

He flipped through the rest of the book and found the prayers for use in school life. "An Intercession," "For a Right Spirit," "The School Prayer," "For Guidance," "In the Evening," "When Busy," "Examinations."

> **Sports**
>
> Lord, you have said that the glory of the young is their strength; grant me the strength of mind and body to play my part on the field of sport. Give me the will to strive with all my heart, to play fair, and, in victory or defeat, to give honor where honor is due. *Amen.*

And then Ben came to the last section, the one Markson was working on, a code of conduct written by the third Rector of the school, William Beech.

Decision-Making

Above all else, a St. James education teaches a boy to make selfless and courageous decisions.

As he considers his actions, a boy must ask himself,

First: Does my action accord with God's will?

Second: Is my action to the benefit of the other boys at the school?

Third: Would I be proud of my action if it were known to all?

If you can answer these questions with a peaceful and steadfast heart, you will know you have made the right choice.

Always apply these questions faithfully and you will be a man of high ethical standing. You will be an asset to your country, to the world, and to your God.

★ ★ ★

Ben was ready for Seated, out of the room, and almost to Woodruff before Ahmed had showered. Hutch and Evan's room was right. The couch was covered in a purple paisley tapestry, the posters on the wall were *Are You Experienced* and lacrosse. Ben sat and joked, and he heard his jokes and wondered if they betrayed that his parents hadn't paid his tuition. He had been so close to losing thoughts like this.

Crank time was the half hour before Seated Meal when you could play music as loud as you wanted to. Hutch and Evan's second-floor windows were all swung wide open. Evan had hefted one of his big blond-wood KEF Q80 speakers, and with its back resting against his chest he was now setting its front edge facing out on the narrow windowsill. Ben was glad he already owned a decent pair of speakers.

"We're going to fry everyone walking by," Evan said. With one foot he slid over his CD tower and set the back edge of the speaker on its top, then very gingerly tested the balance and removed his hands.

"That's one!" He moved back to the amp and carefully lifted the bundle of speaker wire for the other speaker out from behind the component stack.

"I wish we had some wetness," Hutch said.

"I almost pulled some of my parents' stuff," said Kyle, "but like three days before school my dad told me he was watching all the levels."

"Shit, I totally could have gotten some from my parents," said Ben, thinking of the neglected bottles at the back of the cabinet under the sink in the den, wondering if they could afford to lose it now. A boy will never use intoxicants; answer these questions with a steadfast heart. "I know there's a bottle in the way back they've never scratched."

"Oh, dude"—Hutch turned to Ben—"how could you not tell us that Ahmed walked out of newb boxing!"

"Ugh, Jesus," Ben said.

"It's like," Evan began, "how much further does it go? If he's doing shit like that and nothing happens, then that becomes totally fine, and then..."

"And then," said Hutch, "fuck that."

"Fuck that," said Evan, before crouching down and hefting the second speaker.

Evan's body went still as he began to place the front edge of the speaker on the sill, and Hutch looked at Ben and Kyle and grinned. Ben felt cold. Hutch held his finger to his lips, stood up from the stuffed chair, and silently began to move toward Evan. He turned to Ben and Kyle and beckoned with his hands for some conversation so as not to have Evan suspect anything. Ben's mind was empty and then he said, "They've got to have a bottle of Beefeater about a decade old. They mostly drink wine and that shit's for cocktail parties, but when was the last time they had a cocktail party?"

By this time Hutch was within arm's reach of Evan, and he carefully extended his arm, then bumped the heel of his hand into Evan's elbow. The speaker moved a crucial four inches, less teetering than cascading out the window, but Evan lunged forward and got his fingers around the far edges, scraping his forearms against the inside of the window frame. The speaker went still again. "You motherfucker!"

Hutch folded back on the chair in laughter, and Evan shakily set the speaker on the carpet. He took the few steps over to Hutch, and Ben could see him weighing how much he should let out. He punched Hutch's arm lightly enough that Ben could tell that if he had punched harder, he wouldn't have been able to control himself.

"Motherfucker!" Evan said again, his voice embarrassingly high, and then, because there was nowhere else to go, he laughed too, and the four of them sat there laughing. Then Evan went back to the window with the second speaker, turning around again and again and show-glaring at the other three, and then it was in place and they played the Allman Brothers live *At Fillmore East*. Evan kept looking around the speakers to see if there was anyone below them hearing it.

"Yo," Hutch said to Ben, "I think we're going to town Saturday."

"Oh, cool," Ben said, trying to remember how much money he had in his checking account.

"Where should we go?"

For a second Ben had no idea why Hutch would be asking him this—Hutch's face showed no vulnerability in not already knowing where to go—but then Ben remembered about Teddy, and he searched his memory for the places Teddy had talked about.

"Escobar's is good. Um, the Lamplight has buffalo wings—"

"Buffalo wings, yes!" said Kyle.

Hutch nodded quickly, as though he had decided on this beforehand and was glad they had arrived at the correct choice, and then they saw that they were going to be late to Seated and pulled the speakers out of the window, tying their ties as they hurried down the stairs.

★ ★ ★

Coming back from Seated, Ben felt pulled down into a trance of fatigue, and he was almost on top of a person sitting on the Hawley stoop.

"Whoa, slow down there, pard." Alice was sitting at the bottom of the entry steps in the late dusk wearing this time a green fleece jacket over a lemon-yellow dress from Seated Meal. They looked at each other, and Ben wanted so badly to step close enough to smell her. She really was so close to being pretty, especially here in the departing light, but some balance in her face just wasn't there. She was hugging her knees again.

"What's up, not-Teddy?"

"Ha, right. Um, not a lot. What are you up to?"

"Waiting."

"Ah, okay."

"You seem perturbed, Ben."

He laughed. "I guess I'm a little perturbed."

"What about?"

A few kids were walking behind them across the little stretch of grass, and Ben tried to come up with something that could unspecifically sketch what was going on. Again he saw the silhouette of the Dragon there across the slope. "My dad's just being a pain in the ass."

"How so?"

He hadn't planned on her caring to the point that he would have to make up anything significant. "Well, he doesn't know if he wants me to stay here."

"Really. Lucky you."

"He says he thinks it's a bad influence."

"A bad influence how?"

"Um, I guess things were a lot more strict when he was here? He thinks it's too far away from being like a Spartan training ground for young men." He wondered if his dad had read "Decision-Making."

"Oh, right, girls will corrupt the boys."

"I'm not agreeing with him."

She laughed. "Oh, no, I'm sure you're not."

"It's just, you know, the Spartan part." Ben didn't know if he could keep this going. "He wishes we all showered in cold water or something."

"How much does he know about Sparta?"

"He was a classics major..."

Alice shifted around on the step as though to face Ben even though they were already facing, and the breast closest to him pulled against the jacket for a moment. "I heard this story about a Spartan warrior."

Ben nodded.

"So there's this young soldier in training, right? He catches a wolverine for food, but the trainees aren't allowed to have any food other than the rations they're given. So he catches the wolverine right before roll call one day, and he doesn't have time to kill it before he has to line up, and he's standing there as the sergeant or whoever is yelling at them and giving them orders."

She was suddenly very excited about the story. "And he's holding this wolverine and the wolverine is like thrashing around and biting the soldier in the stomach. And rather than scream and drop the wolverine and expose what he did, he tries to endure the pain, and just before the end of roll call he falls over dead without having made a sound." She paused as though waiting for him to react with some gesture of wonder. "That is serious discipline."

"Rations must have been grim to want to eat a wolverine."

She laughed again. "Yes. But I guess I don't really see your dad's point. Life doesn't seem soft to me here at all."

"No?"

"Just the *work*. And I mean, my family has this guy I'm already supposed to be doing college applications with."

"A guy?"

"Yeah, like a consultant. I had to sit down with him before coming back and like review the classes I was going to take, the sports, the extracurrics, to see if it all 'presented a coherent narrative.'"

"What does that mean?"

"That's exactly what I said. He said I had to think like a college admissions officer. What kind of profile would I want to see come across my desk, what kind of student would stand out, how would this person fill out a freshman class?"

"You're already applying to college? Aren't you in fourth form?"

"'*College applications start the first day*,' says Dale. And my father went to community college, my grandfather didn't go at all, so they've been trying to get me into Princeton since I ate my first Cheerio."

Ben decided not to mention that his dad had gone to Princeton, and they seemed to be at an impasse.

"Anything else your dad objects to?" she asked.

Ben tried to think of things that dads usually objected to. "He doesn't like the fact that kids drink and do drugs here. I actually think he'd be fine with the drinking part, it's just the drugs he can't deal with."

"Why, do you do a lot of drugs?"

Ben laughed. "I'd be cooler if I did."

"Really?"

"Oh, come on. Kids who do drugs are all mysterious and dangerous and are having all kinds of amazing mental experiences while all the rest of us are having our regular everyday experiences."

"Yeah, that's true, I suppose."

"Do you do any drugs?" he asked, hoping she would say no, definitely not.

"I dabble." She looked at him more intently. "Are you being a nice person to your roommate?"

"I'm sorry?"

Just then Ian Richardson, a broody upper-former from newb boxing, came out the back door, and Ben moved to make room for him to pass.

"Hey," Ian said to Ben. He turned to Alice. "You ready?"

"Yup, just shootin' the breeze. You ready?"

"Yup."

Alice got up and gave Ben a little two-finger salute.

"Viva Sparta," she said.

"All for one and one for all," Ben said. He watched the two of them walk across the Two-Laner, Ian's shoulders pulled up slightly toward his ears. The streetlamps pushed back the new darkness, and they walked past the gym into the cover of the woods.

★ ★ ★

An orange molded-plastic chair on chrome legs was set next to the pay phone in the basement laundry room, and Ben sat there, trying to move himself to call home. This was adjacent to the storage area where newb boxing had happened, and Ben tried to smell throw-up but didn't think he could make out anything other than fabric softener and dust and the massive foundation. Ben felt again in the late-late summer the foundation's coolness.

Ahmed had come back that night from the Dish and said that the news of his father donating the pool had become known, and at lunch a group of kids had brought him bowl after bowl of Jell-O, bowing and asking him if they could be of any further service, until he had dishes of Jell-O stacked all over his tray. Ahmed had asked Ben what that meant, and Ben had told him it was just a prank.

Now in the basement, the phone resting in his lap, Ben looked across the room at the wall. It was built of irregular chunks of limestone bonded together with ashy mortar. Ben fixated on the shapes, seeing them as individual rocks and then again as parts of the wall.

At last he put the pleasurably heavy receiver against his ear and dialed the long calling card number. He imagined calling Alice, being able to tell her things without having to worry about the way she would see him looking at her.

"Hi, Mom!"

"Little bird!" Genuine excitement and unmistakable tiredness. "Tell me everything. So, you got there..." Ben forgot to be resentful that he was the one calling them. He relayed an edited version of events since his dad had dropped him off.

She laughed, and Ben almost curled up with the pleasure of hearing her laugh. Eventually he came up to the present day. "Is Dad there too?"

"He's out getting stuff for dinner."

Her voice knew. Ben outlined what Markson had told him. When he was done there was quiet between them.

"What's happening, Mom?"

"I'm sort of finding out now." This was the tone she used with adults; Ben had wanted her to talk this way, but it had come so quickly.

"And?"

"It's been happening for a little while."

Ben waited.

"Some investments he made started to go bad—the parking garages, and there was some mining, I think. And so he tried to bail a couple things out with inheritance money, hoping they would turn around? But that didn't work, I guess. And now I'm learning we've been living on the rest of the inheritance, sort of putting things off, hoping some real estate investments were going to get going. So he's been...sort of stuck for the last little while."

Ben flushed with the pleasure of these adult confidences. But the information also demanded that he know what to do with it, and he had utterly no idea.

"He's still working, though?"

"He works in his office at home, but the partnership dissolved a few years ago."

"A few *years*?"

She didn't say anything.

"Are you going to have to drop out of the program?"

"At this point in a PhD it's mostly grants. But I'm not exactly a help. And anthropology isn't the most lucrative field to have chosen."

"Fuck."

She didn't reprimand him.

"And the squash courts?"

"He contributed some, but almost all of it he raised from other squash alumni." She stopped, and they each heard the hum of the connected phone line.

"But he's been talking about this new opportunity on the West Coast. He's invested in a piece of property out there and waiting for the right time to sell it. Which would be soon. It's a big investment, a fairly big risk, but he's excited about it. So let's let him concentrate on that. He's worrying about all this, he's trying to plan. But he's embarrassed, too, obviously."

Ben tried to hear where her patience with his dad ended, that closing off that always seemed available to her. Ben remembered a long drive to Cape Cod when his father had the flu, had to stop every few minutes and dry heave with his head out the back door, and even though no one could blame him for being sick, Ben's mom seethed nevertheless and drove with ruthless consistency. But Ben didn't know if he could sense it now; maybe that impatience had become a luxury.

Ben stayed quiet for a few moments, and he wondered whether his dad was telling his mom the truth about whatever it was on the

West Coast. He had never considered the possibility that his dad could lie. Dads in movies who acted slippery seemed as fictional as cat burglars.

Now it occurred to Ben that he had hardly ever even been embarrassed with his dad, let alone suspicious. When he was young the two of them showered together every morning before school. Ben tried to remember any strangeness about being naked with his dad in the shower and simply could not. It had been simple. Sometimes Ben had stood under the stream of water with his head tilted forward, letting the water hit the top of his head, letting it fill his hair and then flow down and gather above his forehead and stream down. Ben would often hold an empty shampoo bottle and direct the stream of water from his forehead into the bottle, filling it with water and pouring it out and filling it with water again.

What was his father thinking as he saw his son do this strange thing? Didn't he have to get to work? Ben remembered no sense that he was being watched, but now it seemed impossible that his father hadn't been looking down at him, baffled that this little boy who hadn't existed a few years before was caught in this purposeless ritual.

After one shower, as they were toweling off, Ben had asked his dad about his pubic hair.

"What do you mean?"

"How doesn't it get in the way?"

"How?"

"Where does it go under your underpants?"

"It just stays flat."

"Flat?"

"Yeah, you don't feel it. It's just under your underpants and you don't feel it at all."

"It's not itchy?"

"No, you get completely used to it. It comes in a little at a time and you don't notice it at all."

Ben was confused, almost disappointed that this utterly foreign thing really didn't make any difference.

"So let's let him concentrate on that, okay?" his mother repeated on the phone.

She was surprised the school had said something to Ben; Harry said he had talked to them about more time. She wanted to be up there with Ben, to lean their bodies together in an easy hug, but she also wanted to convey enough bright, brisk indifference that he wouldn't worry. She wanted to convey that to herself.

"How are you guys handling Kenyon?"

"He's working on it."

Ben stayed quiet.

"It'll be okay, Ben."

He didn't say anything.

"In a year you'll hardly remember this."

They said I love you.

5. The Tiny Island

CLASSES WENT BY IN WORRY, HOURS AND HOURS OF READING, soccer practices, Seated Meals in the High Dining Room and cafeteria lunches, and even though Ahmed seemed not to have let the Jell-O incident touch his serene enthusiasm, he didn't eat Jell-O at the Dish anymore.

Ahmed loved the rain. He loved the cool greenness. The pool construction was imminent: his father told him they were almost done with the plans.

Rory told Ben about another captain's practice, but for some reason Ben had no interest in playing. After seeing the boiler on its block every day when he came and went from Hawley, he wanted to do anything but play squash.

In bed every night he would watch the glow-in-the-dark stars fade as he tried for sleep. But every morning he looked forward to Chapel. He hadn't come any closer to believing in God, but he loved singing the sturdy inevitable hymns, he loved inhaling the five-story air, and he loved the light that erased the cames in the colored glass and traversed the room. The light found such traction in that air.

Ben still hadn't worn the Marlboro Racing hat. Each time he had thought to put it on, he had envisioned the person wearing that hat blazing with self-regard, and he knew he couldn't make that bid for coolness unless he was better situated. He felt grateful that the stream of school was there to distract him. He would catch himself getting absorbed in throw-in drills, the Siege of Yorktown, the endless vocab flash cards, the swing of his grade school compass. Twice that week he and Alice happened to pass on the paths while walking alone, and each time she stopped and talked to him for a minute or so as though she were inspecting a strange, lively puzzle. They would laugh and wave goodbye and Ben would be left still strategizing how to lengthen their conversation and get close enough to smell her smell. He had learned how to pick up the scent of other girls: you let your breath out as you passed shoulder to shoulder and then you inhaled in their wake. It was wonderful, and he would leave Alice wishing he could both talk to her and let her pass by.

But then he'd notice a wrought-iron chandelier with triple-twisted supports for each bulb, an owl carved in wood on top of the banister post to the Rector's Chapel seat, the rows of computers in the language lab, the tubes and tubes of cerulean blue in the Art Building, and it would occur to him how much each must have cost. He walked into Chapel every morning, nodded to Markson and Dennett, and wondered what all the faculty knew and thought about him, about all of the students. The teachers sat there, not-quite-completely-awake just like everyone else, and their eyes landed on distinct faces as they streamed by. *Spoiled, Asperger's, slut, parents can't pay, druggie, spoiled, monotone jock . . .*

By Saturday a month in the air had become tight with cool-ness even at noon, and at lunch Hutch was excited about dinner in town.

Ben had $11.90 in his checking account. Already at the table he knew that Tyler, Todd, Mark, and Kyle were in, and inevitably Evan would be going too.

"Lamplight, for sure," Ben said, and they all nodded. They'd grab a cab from in front of the gym after everyone had showered after practice. Ahmed was going into town with a couple kids from club soccer and he had asked Ben if he wanted to come, but Ben said he was going in with Hutch and those guys but thank you.

Ben spent all of soccer practice worrying how he was going to cover the cab there, and the meal, and the cab back. Hutch had said they were going to buy a handle of Jack Daniel's somewhere, and even though Ben doubted they could pull it off, he had to have the money to contribute if they actually managed it.

And so Ben walked the slowest back from the field, and he took the longest shower, and after he dried off he waited in the little vestibule between the shower room and the main locker room until he didn't hear anyone left. He waited there longer, and through the high windows he saw the bottom edge of the sun meet the tree line, and finally he put his face to the window in the gym door and saw no more taxis in the parking lot.

He walked out of the gym in the early dusk. He knew in the cab they were joking about the driver or someone's early attempt at scoring a betty, already their togetherness was galvanizing, and his steps were slow as he approached the dorm.

The lights were off. He sat on the leather couch. What would "Decision-Making" say he should do now? He couldn't bear to do more work, and so he went back outside. He started walking. Looking into the windows of the Den, he saw that a lot of the black and Hispanic kids were still on campus too. It was strange to see them in full possession of the pool tables and the stereo. They were playing the music that Ben only heard as background noise during the summer, and they looked easy with each other. They had lost the formality that they always seemed to carry.

What was Alice doing? What if the two of them could just sit alone?

Without student voices the campus was loud with the friction of the wind through the drying trees. He tried to savor the coming stars and the air and the streetlamps; he knew just what kind of impression this was all supposed to make on him. The carillon began playing, again that version of "Inspector Gadget," and Ben hated whoever was playing it. He kept finding another route to take from one end of the campus to the other. Out near the hockey rink, fluorescent pink tape marked the trees to be cleared for the pool. The chapel bells rang the quarter hours. He walked around the track twice, feeling the springy give in the red shredded-rubber surface.

★ ★ ★

Eventually it rang ten thirty, the time he had set for himself as okay to head back to Hawley before check-in at eleven. As he passed the other dorms he saw kids getting out of cabs with the airy melancholy of coming back to school. He avoided making eye contact in case it was that group of guys.

Ben walked into Hawley and came into the common room. Leon and Hideo were sitting in front of the TV watching *Fletch;* Chevy Chase was playing tennis. Mr. Tan, the school's Chinese teacher, was on duty, and Ben waved to let him know he was in. Mr. Tan made a mark next to Ben's name and nodded and smiled to him as though Ben had supplied a word in a stubborn crossword puzzle. According to the microwave, which had by now spread its smell through the common room, it was 10:37. If Ben stayed here until eleven, everyone coming in would know that he had checked in this early. As he climbed the stairs, Ben strangely envied Mr. Tan; how nice and simple it must be to be an older dignified Chinese man, how clear the ways you're supposed to act.

He looked at his Great Auk as he opened the door. The room was exactly as they had left it, the comforter twisted up on his bunk, smoothed out on Ahmed's. Ben wondered whether Ahmed had servants at home, and if so, how he had learned to be so fastidious. It smelled like Ahmed: Polo cologne, that tangy body odor. Ben opened the window to the air.

The older guys, Ennis and his roommate, Fitzy, had already started bringing newbs up to their room to drink. The two of them lived in the Chute, a third-floor room so named for its long, narrow shape and slanted eave ceilings. It was the most desirable room in the dorm because it was the farthest away from the faculty apartments, and Ben couldn't figure out whether Ennis and Fitzy had gotten the Chute because they were cool, or whether they had become cool because they had drawn the Chute in the housing lottery.

If the Chute had him up to drink, then maybe that would spark something, and then maybe he could start wearing the Marlboro hat, and then maybe it would take off from there even if he couldn't afford to do certain things. Other than Rory and a couple other guys on the team, no one seemed to care about him and squash, really. Maybe even at St. James squash was kind of a niche sport, or maybe he would only get credit for it once the season started and he started winning. He hoped that his becoming cooler would somehow mean that the school would be less likely to ask him to leave. He was also slightly bruised that Ennis and Fitzy hadn't yet invited him to drink. The fact that he was Teddy's brother alone should have been enough, so maybe he had already started acting like a kid who couldn't pay.

He sat down into his desk chair and set his elbows on his knees. The kids that Ennis and Fitzy had chosen to bring up to the Chute were an odd assortment. They hadn't had Jed up, but they'd invited Jeremy Cohen, who was right on the edge of being pretty lame.

He wondered whether Ahmed was back from town yet. He imagined what the common room downstairs would be like right now. Slowly, kids would be coming in from the outside air that had started to cut in earnest, and one by one they would sit back into the stiff fabric couches with something like an old man's sigh.

Tomorrow was Sunday, the empty day, when everything you did was a decision not to do work for Monday classes. The kids down in the common room were enduring a temporary reprieve, aching for time to move slower. Here was their gap of a few hours after the end of Saturday classes and games but before school loomed again, the few hours when nothing was expected of them. Even deciding what to do—to go up to someone's room and talk, to play video games on the illicit Nintendo, to maybe just go to sleep early—any of those definite actions would mean the end of possibility and the death of their reprieve. So they delayed, and just sat in the common room doing nothing.

Ben looked down at the linoleum tiles on the floor of his room and tried to find any kind of repeating pattern in the darker green and lighter green spots. He didn't want to be in the common room, but he didn't want to be in here alone, and he definitely didn't want Ahmed to come in and find him here alone. He went down to Jed's room once the clock read 11:02. Jed was there, peaceful with his black buzzed hair and hawk's nose, reading a *Punisher* comic book while his roommate, Gavin, played *Minesweeper*. Jed had gone into town with a couple of guys on the football team, and Ben said he'd had to stay in: there had been a bit of a family emergency, nothing serious, but he had had to be on the phone and had missed Hutch and the other guys. Ben realized he hadn't had any dinner and was abruptly tense with hunger, and Jed had some Doritos and Ben ate those. At 11:33 Ben decided to go to sleep just to close the door on the day and get up tomorrow and start new.

When he came back to his room it was still empty, and he was surprised. Ahmed should definitely have been back. He went to get his toothbrush and toothpaste out of the cup on his dresser.

The door opened, but it wasn't Ahmed's voice that said, "Hey, Weeksy."

Ben looked up and saw Ian Richardson, the upper-former he had seen with Alice, staring intently into the room through an opening just wide enough for his face. Ian did a quick scan of the place.

"You all right, man?"

"Yeah," said Ben. "Yeah, just got in. What's up?"

"Here, come upstairs."

Ben looked around for anything he might need.

They hurried down the hall as though they were already doing something against expectations. Ben thought of the little blue book, and somehow it seemed in support of what he was doing. Ben tried to think of something to say, but nothing came to him as they hit the hall door and took the stairs two at a time. He realized that Ian had already been drinking; Alice liked him in part because he could get wet.

As they came onto the third-floor landing, Ian pulled open the fire door into the Annex, the small hallway where two single rooms were situated along with the Chute. As soon as they came through, Ben could already smell the difference up here. It smelled like older guys. Right Guard spray deodorant, Salvation Army furniture, light patchouli, and the slightly nauseating off-brand Lysol that the cleaning crews used, which smelled almost more like hairspray than germicide. The guitar solo from "More Than a Feeling" wafted faintly out to them. Ben felt his chance; maybe everything wasn't lost.

Ian opened the door to the Chute without knocking, and the twin guitars approached their apex. The lighting was dim. Boston was actually a pretty lame band, unless the Chute was listening to it ironically, which was hard to tell. Directly in front of them stood a bookcase that hid what was going on in the rest of the room; furniture used for this purpose was called a delay. The bookcase had been pushed against the left wall and its top corner sawed off to conform to the eave. Ben and Ian stepped around the delay into the main part of the room, and Ben took in at a glance the people there: Ennis, Fitzy, and Jed. Ben remembered how they all had looked during newb boxing, the fully dressed older kids divided so sharply from the newbs in their underwear, but now Jed seemed piled alongside the others, not quite comfortable, but a member of the same species. Even though he had been in Jed's room just a few minutes before, it felt like Ben hadn't seen him in a day.

They were sitting on parallel couches along each wall. A single standing halogen lamp pointed directly into one of the eaves, and a red lava lamp sat on an overturned milk crate next to the arm of one of the couches. Posters clung to the eaves in a slight catenary, but the angled light cast glare across them and Ben couldn't see what they were of.

"Weeksy!" said Ennis with a wide-open grin. "Take a seat, man."

Ben sat next to Fitz, who was blond and round, always slightly breathless and with his khaki pants almost falling off his hips. His roundness reminded Ben of Ahmed. Ian pulled up one of the desk chairs, turned it around and sat in it backwards, and looked moodily at Ennis, and all at once he knew: among sixth-formers, these guys weren't considered very cool. Hawley House in general was considered kind of lame. Ben wondered whether Teddy had made these guys' lives hell. He felt a tiny, slightly disappointing power over everyone in the room, and he smiled. "What's happening, guys?"

"Not a lot, man," said Fitzy, whose eyes seemed unable to open more than halfway. "What's up with you?"

"Not a lot."

"You up to wet a little?"

"Um, yeah, definitely."

Everyone laughed, and Ben laughed too.

"Set him up," said Ennis. Fitz leaned over the far arm of the couch and did something down out of sight. Ennis smiled at Ben. "What's goin on?"

"Not much, just, you know, work and stuff." This felt lame to him, and now he worried that they would want him to pay for the liquor, but then he told himself that this was ridiculous.

"How's Teddy?"

"Ah, pretty good, I think. He's liking Kenyon. I actually haven't talked to him in a while."

"He was a fucking legend."

"Legendary," said Ian.

"Crazy, man, I remember," said Fitzy, sitting back again and looking into the past, "some of the shit he used to do, I for sure thought was going to kill us."

They went on for a few minutes with Teddy memories.

"Did you ever wet with Teddy?" Fitzy asked.

They all looked at him, even Jed who had maybe never heard of Teddy before now, and Ben felt how much they wanted him to be Teddy in that moment, to deliver something mythic and undeniably right into their lives. And he wanted to do that so badly too.

"Um..."

"Is it set?" Ennis looked at Fitz, who nodded.

"Switch with him, man."

Ben got up and they switched seats. The CD changer clunked and spun, and Hendrix, "The Wind Cries Mary," came on. The Chute had done a sound check with Dennett and there was a mark in Wite-Out on the amp dial that showed the maximum allowed volume.

"Oh, I love this song," said Ben.

"Glad to accommodate you," said Ennis, laughing.

Ben looked down behind the arm of the couch. A Snapple bottle three-quarters full of what looked like tea stood next to a little brass cup. From above, it was hard to tell how big the cup was. He reached down and was surprised to find that it had a stem and a pedestal; it looked like an Indian oil candle. He picked up the cup and held it in front of his face to inspect it.

"Don't hold your shot, man. Take it," said Ian.

"What?"

"Don't hold it!" said Ennis. "Drink that shit."

Ben put the rim of the cup to his lips and tasted what was there. It was like warm paint thinner. He tipped it all into his mouth. His gullet clenched against it, he gripped the little cup around the stem, but he stayed still and managed, after many seconds, saliva flooding his mouth, to get it down.

"Wow, that looked smooth," said Fitzy. Everyone laughed, including Ben, genuinely. He felt better. "Hoo," he said.

"Is this firsting?" Ennis asked with wonder.

"It is, yeah." Should he have made up a story about stealing gin with Tim Green?

"Yes! Oh, that is so great," said Ian. "Sketching Teddy Weeks's brother! All right, set one up for me and then we're going back to you."

Ben opened the Snapple bottle. He poured out the whiskey, making sure the liquid came out just as wide along the rim as before.

He stood up and switched with Ian, who clapped Ben on the shoulder so hard that he had to step over a little to keep his balance. Ben sat in the turned-around chair and looked at Jed again. They smiled at each other.

Ben knew what song would come on after this one ended, and sure enough, "Fire" came on. He looked at the poster above Fitzy's head—the *Hindenburg's* elongated egg devoured by black-and-white flame. Here he was. He tried again to make it feel right.

It was his turn again. He took another shot—this one was much easier. He poured one. He switched with Jed.

A copy of the Student Directory, which everyone called the scopebook, lay on the table, open toward the middle, and Ennis picked it up.

"Oh, dude, Danica Morales," Ennis said.

"She's awful, Ennis," said Fitz.

"Fuck you—it's not a good picture. Tell me you haven't seen her ass and wanted to deep the shit out of it."

"Yeah, but she's friends with all the track guys."

"Have you guys seen Lily Jarvis?" asked Ian.

"Who's that?"

"She's this newb in Paige. She's so tasty, she's got this little blond haircut. She could just tuck it behind her ears while she's..." Ian demonstrated the hair tuck and laughed, and Ben never would have guessed he could be so playful.

Ennis flipped two pages back. "Yeah. Wow, yeah." He took a pencil off the table and brought his knees together to serve as a desk. Ben expected him to lick the point of the pencil before he started writing: "Get...your...lips around...my pole." Everyone laughed. Ben thought he felt good.

"How about Nicole Berger?" Jed said.

"Who?"

"You mean Nicole Rieger," said Ian.

"No, Berger, the fourth-former." Everyone was quiet for a second.

"Yeah, she's all right," said Ennis.

"She's cool," said Ian. Everyone nodded.

"Or the girl with the huge artillery," Ben started, glancing at Ian. "She's not like scary pretty, but her boobs are just...Alice... Help me here."

"Alice Morehead?" asked Ian.

Ennis, Fitzy, and Jed all said at once, "Aaalice Moooorehead! Yes!"

"Jesus, those things are epic," said Ennis. "Right, dude?" He leaned over and punched Ian in the leg. "You gotten pounded with that artillery yet?"

"Fuck off," said Ian, scowling.

"Benny boy, write what you feel." Ennis handed the book to Ben.

He wrote, "These guns will end the Battle of the Bulge."

He handed it back to Ennis.

"Ha!" Ennis read it to everyone, and they all seemed to think it was okay.

"I hear she wanted to maybe get them reduced," said Fitz.

"No!" Ennis moaned. "Ugh, what a crime. A crime against humanity, seriously." Ennis turned to Ian. "So what's your deal with her, man? You guys scrumping yet?"

"We're talking," Ian said. His shoulders were back up and tense. "I don't know. I just wish she was better in the face. Just like, she's so close." Everyone nodded, and Ben detested him.

Ennis turned to Ben. "So what's it like to be roommates with *Ahmed*?"

"Um, it's pretty strange." He laughed and expected everyone else to laugh, but they didn't. Ben wanted to describe how Ahmed smelled but he thought that would sound racist. He wondered what Ahmed would do if he were in this room with alcohol around him. He realized he had never seen Ahmed pray. Weren't Muslims supposed to pray all the time?

"He's a happy person, I'll say that. He keeps asking me questions about how to act here. Sometimes it's like I'm his sherpa."

"Huh," said Ennis. This seemed to have lost them, and Ben wanted them back.

"I just want to show him how to be easy. You know?" Ben took a breath. He wanted to have easiness. He wanted the older guys to need him.

"But I can't believe he just walked out of newb boxing..." Their eyes moved with discomfort, and some small power returned to Ben. "Did Phelps have you guys in to talk?"

"Yeah, it was fine," Ennis said, and the rest of them nodded and kept nodding. All of them had sat in Phelps's office and wondered aloud how the rumor could have started that Hawley had done newb boxing. They had all listened to the same talk about you think it brings everyone together, culture of fear, St. James stands against that.

"It is bullshit, though," said Ian. "You don't just walk out."

"But just," started Jed, "Ahmed just seems completely clueless, you know? Even just like getting food at the Dish. I saw him talking with the dining hall lady who puts chicken patties on buns, and like twenty people are piling up behind him. It's not that he's trying to go *against* anyone, he's just like . . . like an absolute beginner. He doesn't know anything about how to act." Jed looked like he was advertising cereal as he said this, his dark buzz cut over his ruddy face and the cliffs of his forehead and cheekbones.

"I guess," Ben went on. "It's just, how do you learn that stuff? How are you taught to handle yourself?"

Fitzy rolled his face over to Ben. "Totally."

"It's true," Ennis said. "It's total bullshit. Newb boxing was going perfect until he pulled that shit." He stared at Ben and Jed, bulling his face at them. "Right? You fuckers were terrified."

Ben nodded emphatically. And he was close, he almost had something. "And I guess it's just, like, how would Teddy handle that, you know?"

"It's true," Ennis said. "Just cause he's a foreign kid, just cause he's so clueless, doesn't mean he gets to do whatever. And now his dad donating a fucking pool? It's like, be here more than five minutes. And acting like you own the school, deciding whether or not you newb-box. We'd never let them"—Ennis pointed his chin at the two younger boys—"we'd never let them get away with it."

"Yeah, that's all I'm saying," said Ben, and then committed to shutting up for good now.

"It's true," Ennis said again. "It's total fucking bullshit. As though we can't run a group of fucking newbs."

The Hendrix album ended and the changer moved again and Ray Charles started singing "Georgia on My Mind," which no one wanted to hear, and Ennis told Fitzy to pour him another one while he found something good to play.

Ben had another shot, and then another. He wondered vaguely what time it might be, whether his father was sleeping or awake. The digital clock on one of the desks said it was 6:07 p.m., which he knew it wasn't. The rotation went around again. When he looked at the Snapple bottle, there was just a rind on the bottom, and Ennis went to fill it up again from the closet. They finished that one too. Ben took another shot, he should have been counting, and stood up to let someone else go, and when he dropped into the couch, his head flopped back and met the wall. It sounded like an apple against the kitchen floor, and incandescent amoebas floated in front of him for a second. Everyone said "Ohhh!" and pain clapped into him and he laughed in pain and tried to make his vision go back to one copy of everything.

And then he was on the stairs with Ennis under his arm on one side and Ian under the other, and his legs felt like long heavy socks. And then he was in his bed and he saw Ennis's silhouette in the doorway against the fluorescent light of the hall, and Ennis was saying something to Ahmed, whose voice sounded very clear for someone who, Ben thought, must have just been woken up.

And then Ben picked his face up from something sticky and the smell made his body flex again, and his head felt like there was another head inside it, a head relentlessly expanding. He looked down and saw that one of Ahmed's thick brown towels lay over his pillow. He let his head rest against it.

And then light fell through the window like a pillar. Ben was irreversibly awake. It was 6:40 a.m. The side of his face stung from where it had marinated in his vomit. He heaved again and

114

nothing came out, but his body didn't unheave for moment after moment, and when it finally relaxed he heaved again, and then was able to lie still for a while. He clung on to whatever rung of experience he was on now, because whatever was below it seemed capable of extinguishing him.

★ ★ ★

After a while, it seemed to Ben that he was involved in some devotional act, as though he were remaining motionless to placate the animal who controlled his pain. He wanted to make that animal read "Decision-Making." Had the Chute done this to him intentionally, to pay him back for something Teddy had put them through? Had he already forfeited what little edge he had gained by going up there? Ben went into and out of an exhausted trance, lying again to Phelps and again having no financial claim to be here, and finally he woke up and noticed that the brown towels were gone and that there were newer black ones under him. The door opened and he saw Ahmed backing into the room carrying something. Ben wanted to turn toward the wall but couldn't bring himself to move. Ahmed turned around and Ben saw that it was one of the orange dining hall trays with two tall, hard-plastic glasses along with what looked like a couple plates and a teacup. It was against the rules to take cups, glasses, plates, trays, or cutlery out of the Dish.

Ahmed set the tray down on Ben's desk, pulled out the chair, then picked the tray up, stepped up onto the chair, and put the tray on the mattress next to Ben. The smell of cooled tomato minestrone put the texture of overcooked pasta in Ben's imagination and another heave came up in him but subsided. "I can't eat, Ahmed." Speaking hurt his throat and he was surprised by how low his voice was.

"You cannot be the whole day without food."

"I can't."

"Drink. The tall ones are water."

Ben was afraid that if he moved, the mattress would shift and the tray would spill, but slowly he pressed himself up to one elbow and reached for a glass of water. He looked at Ahmed, whose face was grim. That Ahmed had brought him this food made Ben want to weep. Ben wildly wished he hadn't said those things up in the Chute. Ben tipped a water glass to his mouth and just wet his lips.

He would make sure to wash all the towels. He would find out what brand they were and buy Ahmed new ones. He couldn't buy new ones. He would apologize. He could taste the faint chlorine in the water and it nearly made him retch but he knew that the only way to feel better was to have some water, and so he took a sip and felt the liquid pass over his ragged throat. He took another sip. He saw the plastic packets of saltines—he wished they were oyster crackers—and tore one of them open with his teeth. When he put the corner of a cracker in his mouth, the flood of saliva was exactly like the one before throwing up, and he heaved hard but kept everything down.

"I can't eat with you looking at me, Ahmed." Ahmed stepped down off the chair and sat down at his desk. He turned on the little lamp and began to mark down answers to a math problem set. "Thank you," Ben said, and Ahmed turned to him and smiled briefly and turned back to his work. Ben looked down at Ahmed's back, and then took another bite of the cracker and the salt tasted delicious. He finished the cracker and started another one.

★ ★ ★

When the sun was starting to set, Ben finally felt steady enough to leave his bed and go to the shower. He still hadn't done any of his work for Monday. The hot water made his head hurt for a minute and then everything seemed to relent, and relief washed through him. Moneylessness couldn't touch that feeling. He went back to the room hoping he wouldn't run into anyone.

"I'm going to bring this stuff back to the Dish," said Ben after he got dressed. "Can I bring you anything?"

"No, thank you."

"Anything from the Den?"

"I have everything I need."

"Okay, I'll see you in a bit." He paused. "Hey, where were you last night?"

"Oh. I signed out and went to Boston for dinner."

"Oh."

"It is not far."

"Yeah. All right, see you soon."

"Okay."

Ben walked out into the clear dusk with the high scraping clouds still lit bright. The lamps along the paths came on, immediately darkening the trees and buildings. Ben's body felt exhausted and relaxed and full of joy.

★ ★ ★

That same Saturday night after coming back from town, two Woodruff boys were caught checking in drunk. Jason Bowman managed "I'm in" when he came through the door and made it upstairs. When Mr. Rawlins, the Head of House, went to check on him, he found Jason passed out on his bed with all the lights on.

Rawlins then went to the room of Jason's best friend, Brett Tamor, who had apparently been lying on his couch listening to "Blue Sky" by the Allman Brothers loud enough that TJ Adkins across the hall had almost gone over to turn it down.

Rawlins picked up a red plastic cup by the couch, smelled it, then looked in Brett's closet, where he found two plastic half-gallon bottles of S.S. Pierce vodka. Both boys went before the Disciplinary Committee the following Tuesday evening, and while Jason was given six months' probation, five sessions with a substance abuse counselor, and three days of work duty, Brett, whose closet had actually contained the vodka, was expelled. Everyone was shocked. When Aston read the announcements in Chapel, he described the beginning of a new policy. "If a student is known to have abused alcohol or drugs, that student will get help. But if a student purchases drugs or alcohol, brings them onto campus for themselves or others, he or she has knowingly damaged the fabric of the school, and has forfeited his or her place here."

In the secondary school market, it was clear that St. James now wanted to appeal to parents looking for a stricter atmosphere. Students were quiet but resentful. The new sixth-formers had waited their turn to be able to get away with the things sixth-formers had always gotten away with. Several girls cried when Brett's parents picked him up and drove away.

Meanwhile, Jason didn't go to classes for three days, and instead served work duty with the school's grounds crew. The general resentment toward the administration mixed with an envy of Jason.

When you showed up for work duty, you were issued a pair of gloves: white leather palms and finger grips, red fabric backs and reinforced cuffs. Each glove had your last name written in Sharpie on the cuff. The grounds crew guys were Dennis and

Terry instead of Walker and Ian. Most boys reporting for work duty suddenly appeared in double-kneed Carhartt pants.

When kids on work duty came into the dining hall at the end of the day, still holding the paper coffee cups they had been given at the 10:15 a.m. break, still smelling of woodsmoke and the cold afternoon, they folded the cuffs of the gloves and slipped them in their back pockets, the empty fingers sticking up. They moved more slowly than the other kids. They had put in their hours and had something to show for it—the stones from a collapsed border wall regathered, a lawn leaf-free, a baseball infield raked—and now they owed no one any further effort.

They would feel nostalgia for that work-duty time, not only when they returned to the constant anxiety of being a student, but also when they graduated from college and went into their working lives, always with the option of working more, but with the connection between work and reward never sharply defined.

The school never had a student slop out the trash enclosure behind the dining hall, or dig up a collapsed drainage pipe, or take down a broken bough still hanging in a tree. No dishwashing, no dorm cleaning, no laundry pickup. Nothing in the power plant, nothing with machines (in the mid-eighties a branch being pulled into the teeth of a wood chipper had kertwanged out, smacking the shoulder of a student who had been caught making fake IDs), nothing on ladders. No electrical work, no plumbing, no hammers or nails, no prolonged heavy lifting, nothing around the ponds and streams, nothing that involved going off campus or outside the theoretical view of a faculty member.

Despite all his exploits, Teddy had never gotten busted, and he had talked about his blemishless record with a mixture of pride and regret. One late night out cruising to see his girlfriend, Teddy had spotted Snake Eyes, the overnight security guard and Vietnam veteran, commando-crawling through the under-brush by the gym to keep his skills sharp. When Teddy was a third-former, a sixth-former in his dorm, Liam, had gotten busted ordering a margarita at Escobar's, his third offense. On the day a student's punishment is read, that student is excused from Chapel, not only to avoid direct shaming, but also in certain cases to enact the temporary forfeiture of the student's place at the school until he or she has served work duty. But Teddy said that Liam was the only student ever to see his own funeral: on the morning his deed was read aloud, he had managed to get a key to the chapel tower, and he climbed out along the gang-plank over the wooden panels in the chapel ceiling and looked down through an open panel to witness it. When the Rector announced that he was getting kicked out, Liam gave a rebel yell that echoed all throughout the chapel.

Getting in trouble for something glamorous, working with your hands, having a justified grudge—all of it seemed to Ben like the best way to be. At the same time he couldn't imagine doing anything against the rules. How wonderful it would be to get kicked out for actually doing something, not to have to wait.

6. The Queen's Guard

W<small>HEN MAIL CAME IN TO THE</small> S<small>T.</small> J<small>AMES</small> P<small>OST</small> O<small>FFICE AT TEN</small> thirty, the fence across from the PO was the place to sit to see the school come to check mailboxes. It had been this way since the little cylindrical pump house had been decommissioned and reopened for this purpose in 1931. Third–period classes were over and the Dish hadn't yet opened for lunch.

Ben sat there with Hutch and Evan. Even in the full sun the air now was like tearing paper. Not that anyone really cared with Brett's expulsion so fresh, but Ben had explained away not showing up to go into town by saying his mother had gone to the hospital with a heart murmur and so he had needed to stay by the phone in case anything happened; luckily it had turned out to be nothing. Ben had also told them about drinking in the Chute and they seemed to afford him some respect for it, but still, here in the bare air, he had imposter's skin. Every new minute, the administration could call him in to tell him he wouldn't be asked back.

The PO late-morning was also the best place and time to watch ladies. In the Dish common room people could get in the way and girls were maybe close enough to hear. But here in front of the PO boys had a clear view and they could say quietly but clearly that Laura Schwarzman had a better ass than Julie Mason. Their friends might say they were wrong and blind and crazy, but they could still say it.

And so because everyone was there and watching, people nonchalantly planned to make an appearance. All of this made it a little risky for the three of them to be sitting there shivering on the chain fence, and without the other two, Ben never would have dared. It wasn't the senior couches in the Dish, but it was a privileged spot.

The site for Ahmed's swimming pool was now being cleared, and the hiss of chain saws was audible everywhere on campus. When they had found out about the pool Hutch and Evan had just shaken their heads and laughed in fury. Ben had seen Manley Price twice from afar on the walking paths and managed to avoid him both times. Squash should have made him feel powerful and rooted into the school, but every time he thought about it he wanted to move his thoughts to something else. He waved to Markson whenever he saw him, and had started carrying the little blue *Companion* in his backpack all the time. He liked seeing it there when he pulled out his notebooks.

Now Rosie Barton and a friend no one really ever noticed came up the path from the Schoolhouse, walked around to the front of the PO, and went inside out of sight. Everybody held a different opinion on Rosie. She was extremely pretty, with light hair and a good face, and she definitely had a decent pair, but a lot of guys thought she had no sex appeal. She had never had a boyfriend and she seemed girlish in a slightly blank way. To

Hutch and Evan, it was a waste for such a good-looking girl to be someone sex just never occurred to. Ben was sort of ginning up his agreement with them but he didn't really care.

Hutch had already started hooking up with Tara Oliver, but they hadn't seen each other in a few nights. Now he was talking to Ursula Childress, but her *name*. Evan had been going to Emma Ponsolt's room but hadn't made a move yet.

"What's up with you, Weeksy?" Hutch turned to him. "Where's your beaver, man?"

"Playing the long game," Ben said.

"You're not that long," said Hutch.

"How would you know?" said Evan, and they laughed routinely.

Ben looked for Alice. He found himself waiting to see her most of the time now and trying to calculate what he would say. Sometimes Ben would get the pang of recognizing her from far away, but then it would turn out to be Laurel Oppenheimer, who had similar coloring and posture. Ben now hated Laurel.

He couldn't imagine what he would ever say to Alice, and when he did see her across a lawn or at the end of the Schoolhouse hallway, she was always wearing her baggy green fleece with her arms crossed in front of her. Her shoulders hunched forward and her spine curved as though she were trying to suck her breasts into herself. Ben saw her with Ian a distressing amount. Once she was riding piggyback while he wove back and forth through the staked saplings in the Dish courtyard, and once they were standing near the rear entrance of Paige and she seemed unhappy.

Now Ben and Hutch and Evan were watching intently for Rosie to come back outside, and so they all saw Ahmed when he moved out of the PO reading a postcard. He was wearing a loden-green cashmere sweater and a long crimson scarf. Ben saw him squint as the card came into the bright sunlight. Everyone liked physical mail, but it seemed to be a delicacy with Ahmed, who cultivated a number of pen pals around the world.

Ahmed stopped there in the doorway so he could concentrate on the postcard, and two girls—not Rosie and her friend—came up behind him, unable to leave the PO until he moved. He just drifted a few steps farther forward, and finally the girls split and moved around him, turning annoyed glances on him as he continued to study the postcard.

He began to turn it over to look at the photo. Ben had the feeling that Ahmed couldn't move in such an unguarded way without something happening to him.

Ben had forgotten to keep looking for Rosie, and then he saw a person in a gray hooded sweatshirt move quickly out of the Art Building's side exit toward Ahmed. A shot of guilt passed through Ben; the dense body was indelibly Ennis's. Ben decided to hope it wasn't Ennis. The figure wasn't running; he took long low strides with his arms held by his sides. He reached into the kangaroo pouch of the sweatshirt and came out with something short and black—for an instant Ben thought he was going to stab Ahmed. The figure closed the remaining distance in the time it took Ahmed to flip the card back over again.

Ennis stepped up behind Ahmed, reached his free arm around his neck, and pulled back snug. The PO crowd turned and Ahmed's mail slid across the ground. Ahmed tried to pull the arm down, but it didn't move and he gurgled shortly. Ennis brought the black thing in front of Ahmed's face and switched on the wireless hair clipper. Ben heard the faint buzz as Ennis brought it gently against Ahmed's forehead. He slid the clipper up. Hair fell over Ahmed's face and shoulders, and Ben saw it drift down onto the mail.

Ennis released Ahmed, letting a sheaf of hair fall from where it had collected across his forearm. Ahmed went to his hands and knees. He had saliva down his chin. Ennis took the same long smooth strides down the path toward the Schoolhouse, and then he passed into the woods out of sight.

Several seconds passed, and then Ahmed reached out to sweep a letter toward himself, and this seemed to break everyone out of their collective trance. The girls closest to him went to help him up. Still the bored, annoyed sound of chain saws. As Ben walked to Ahmed, remorse resounding through him for what he had said in the Chute, he nevertheless clenched his jaw with the same shiver as when he had put his flip-flop over a hobbled bumblebee in the dorm bathroom, feeling the resistance of its exoskeleton and then its sudden collapse. Hutch was behind him, but Ben knew exactly the look of triumph that would be in his face. As he came to Ahmed's side, he saw that the front of the postcard showed two furry-hatted guards at Buckingham Palace.

★ ★ ★

Even though Ben was hardly touching Ahmed, just lightly holding his upper arm, he felt like he was dragging him up the stairs. They pushed into the room and dropped their book bags and Ahmed came down into his desk chair. He looked totally blank, as though he were coming out of sedation after surgery. His longer hair lay over the bare strip, but there was a disturbing lack of volume there, as though Ahmed's head had a deep dent in it. Ben had expected the Chute to put something disgusting in Ahmed's bed or throw mugs of ice water on him in the shower.

"Stay there." Ben left and came back with Jed's hair clipper. "We have to do it all the way."

Ahmed saw the clipper. "No—"

"We have to. How are you going to go around like that?"

"It is not meaningless! In Islam there are only certain times for that. And if my father sees—"

"He's not going to see you. We're going to cut this now so that it looks even, and then you'll have months to let it grow in before you go home. It'll be fine. And you never pray anyway."

"But I should!"

"You have to cut it."

Ben imagined Ahmed walking into the dining hall, trying to maintain that uprightness with this dent along his head. He pulled Ahmed to his feet and walked him over to stand in front of the full-length mirror on the back of the door.

"Look, Ahmed." Hairs lined Ahmed's collar and lay trapped in the fibers of his sweater.

Ahmed held back his hair so he could see the entire empty swath. He knew he looked just as foolish as they had wanted him to look. His forehead, cheeks, and lips grew heavier. It was painful for Ben to see.

"Well." Ahmed paused. "If there is a reason."

Ben folded back the corner of the carpet, then moved the chair to the bare floor in front of the mirror, and Ahmed sat. After a moment of thought, Ben draped one of his own towels over Ahmed's shoulders to catch the hair. He plugged the clipper into the low outlet by the door. Ahmed's face had set. Ben flipped the switch on the side of the clipper and it whirred warmly. Ben set the plate of the trimmer against the right side of Ahmed's forehead, and as he pushed the blade through, the hair fell away with thrilling ease. Ahmed's eyes were closed as the hair passed across them.

It fell onto Ahmed's shoulders, his lap, the slim edge of the chair behind his back, the floor. The machine was quieter when there was hair in it, and so it got momentarily loud when it passed through the empty patch.

Ben saw that he had to shave against the grain to get the proper shortness, and he worked the edges of the clipper around Ahmed's ears like getting the knife in the leg joint the one time his dad let him carve the turkey. He made several passes over the back corners of the skull, where the hair grew in a swirl and longer pieces kept sticking up no matter what he did. The skin was getting red where he had worked it over again and again.

Ben finally had to accept that this was going to be Ahmed's hair. His inability to make Ahmed look better, less haphazard, made his throat close. He pictured Ennis laughing jaggedly with Fitz and Ian.

Ahmed looked like a tired monk wearing someone else's beautiful sweater. Ben switched off the clipper and Ahmed touched his head gingerly, as though it might burn his fingers, then with new familiarity. He passed his hand over his scalp, back and forth, and even though his face stayed grim, Ben thought he had to partially relish the new sensation.

"I'm sorry, Ahmed."

"Usually I like having my hair cut." He kept feeling his head. "The air moves."

They both stayed quiet, and Ahmed turned to look at himself from the left side, then the right, then left, then right again. Already he had grown incrementally more used to it. Finally he moved his eyes from his own face to Ben's eyes. Ben looked ashamed.

"Have I been doing a bad job?" Ahmed asked.

Ben tilted his head to one side.

"A bad job of knowing how to be?"

Ben thought about how to put it.

"Please help me improve."

"You're doing better, Ahmed."

"Please help me."

Ahmed had endured enough for one day. "You're doing well, really."

Ahmed undressed to take a shower. In his towel, with his back turned to Ben and his bare shoulders covered in short hairs, Ben saw what he would look like as an older man.

Ben got the broom from the staff closet and swept up the hair. He moved the smaller and smaller piles onto a manila folder and then into the trash. When he was done he stared into the wastebasket, and it looked like Ahmed's proud head was down in there.

★ ★ ★

When the soccer vans pulled onto Turnbull's campus later that day, Ben still had Ahmed's hair on the cuffs of his shirt and in the eyelets of his running shoes. He was trying to get through *Tartuffe* but he couldn't concentrate. The varsity team was in the van behind, and it felt strange to have JV in the lead, coming onto the campus first. Even just twenty-five minutes farther south from St. James the trees hadn't started to turn. THE TURNBULL SCHOOL, EST. 1893 was in white letters on a broad, powder-coated orange metal sign. Ben knew that the JV soccer game didn't matter at all, especially that day, but still his hands were sweating as they always did and the van was quiet.

Turnbull's lawns were so green that it looked like they had cannibalized other lawns, and the rails of the fences suspended between granite posts had been painted almost iridescently white. All the signs—for each building and intersection—were the exact same orange powder-coated metal with white typeface. Ben realized that each sign at SJS was slightly different and kind of ad hoc. They passed an enormous glass cube with a sign, ALSTEAD LIBRARY, in backlit stainless steel letters on a marble block in front.

As they pulled up to the Turnbull gym, Ben was amazed at the twisting shape, the smooth slate-gray exterior, the three-story windows. The St. James gym was just a cinder block rectangle; this looked like a contemporary art museum. The team walked into the gym lobby and enormous banners of the Turnbull school clubs moved in the air conditioning above them, along with a suspended crew shell which had, according to a bronze plaque on the wall, won the Henley Regatta in 1966 and 1971. A helical staircase led them up to the visitors' locker rooms, which were bright and clean and had row after row of wide lockers painted Turnbull Tiger orange.

Both SJS teams changed into their uniforms and put their bags away. Only a few kids had remembered to bring combination locks but the idea of anyone stealing their stuff here was beyond imagining.

Coach Johanssen gave them a talk. They went down the back stairs out to the fields, an ocean of grass marked off into discrete rectangles. They passed the Wong Swimming Pool, a dome-roofed brick building with another set of enormous windows. Wide water was divided by blue-and-white lane lines, and there was a separate diving pool with two springboards and two platforms, like the Olympics. Ben could understand Phelps's fear, Aston's fear. Ben kept his head turned toward the windows and saw an Asian girl step to the edge of the high concrete platform, turn her back to the empty space, and after an impossible pause, hop backward and tuck her body into a single forward flip before elongating again and slipping out of view behind the windowsill.

Varsity lost 1–0 and the JV game was a 2–2 tie. Ben had acquitted himself with a couple good stops. Both teams walked back to the gym, and Ben showered as quickly as he could. He walked through the hallways before they had to get back on the bus. All the equipment in the weight room was the same brand, and the padding on the benches, armrests, and ankle bars of the weight machines was a consistent Turnbull-orange vinyl. They had an annex with four basketball courts and a three-lane running track around the outside. Ben passed a door with a sign on it that read FILM/VIDEO REVIEW. It was locked.

And in a little vestibule outside a door marked DIRECTOR OF ATHLETICS, on a coffee table between two very new fabric-stuffed chairs, a fan of magazines was spread just so. Second from the top was the Turnbull Annual Report, which Ben slipped into his bag before jogging back to the bus.

★ ★ ★

Ben again sat in the spoke-back chair in front of Phelps's desk, now with Markson in the chair next to him, but no Dennett. There was no warmth in Phelps's face. They would have smelled Ben's bad breath if they had been close enough.

"You need to be honest this time, Ben."

Ben wanted to be able to say he had been honest last time, but he just nodded.

Aston had already brought Phelps into his office, and they had talked over game plans if papers picked this up. Aston had tried to call Ahmed's parents twice but had only been able to reach the sheik's chief of staff, a Mr. Rafsanjani. Phelps knew they had very little room for error on this.

In Hutch and Evan's room, the two of them hadn't been able to stop laughing about it, knowing it was mean, but still, there was no other option. The way Ahmed had been so placidly looking at the postcard just before: it was perfect. Maybe Ben had suggested something in the Chute . . . Something about how walking out of newb boxing was bullshit? The last thing he would ever do was take credit.

But out of sight Ben had started to say to Ahmed, how about a pair of running shoes instead of the cordovan monk-straps? How about *Hot Rocks* or *After the Gold Rush* instead of the busy, wavery-voiced, string-and-cymbal stuff he listened to?

"Students protect each other, Ben," Phelps now said, "but this isn't just putting a bucket of water over someone's door. Force-shaving someone's head is brutal."

"Whoever it was had the hood of his sweatshirt up. You couldn't see his face."

Phelps sat back and looked out the windows. Markson shifted toward Ben as though to help him reconsider what he had said. Ben abruptly felt angry. Why should they make him responsible for telling on Ennis? Why was that his problem? But the freight of it, the value of what he knew; Ben understood distinctly that he needed to hold on to that advantage. The school had already gotten used to the certainty of Ahmed's swimming pool.

"I'm not convinced, Ben," Phelps said. "You were close. Even with a hood up, a person's face is partway visible. Body shape, posture, those things are clear."

"It was so fast, it was over before you could really—"

"Stop a minute. Do you want to be on the side of this person? To help them do this to Ahmed?"

"I think Ahmed's okay, though. He gets that these things happen."

Phelps sighed. "I'm sure Ahmed is putting on a good face. But put yourself in his position. What would it be like if that happened to you? In front of everyone there?"

Ben imagined all of Hawley House there watching him now, willing him to be careful, no matter what they hoped would happen to Ennis.

Ben inhaled. "He did mention that his father is thinking about withdrawing him."

Phelps turned a vacuum of focus on him. His eyes seemed to come even more to the front of his face, and he went very still. Ben wasn't ready for Phelps to need it this much.

"That's what I mean, Ben. This isn't just a prank."

Ben tried on what it would be like if he just said, "It was Ennis. His hood was up but you could still see the point of his nose, and everyone knows that's his sweatshirt, the dark mixed-gray one with the white border. It was the clipper that the wrestling guys use to buzz their hair. Ennis did it because of Ahmed walking out of newb boxing, and sort of because of his ostentation, and also because I kind of said that the upper-formers were letting him get out of line. Ahmed deserved it, in a lot of ways, but regardless, it was Ennis.

"And now I've been of service, I've made a tangible difference to the financial well-being of the school, because if you kick out Ennis then the sheik won't withdraw Ahmed, and the school will have the pool, and SJS will keep being the kind of school it wants to be. If I give you this, you will let me stay, and I'll win squash matches for the school, and I'll be an asset."

But how long would that credit last? And how would he negotiate it? Or would he just leave it unspoken, that you can't kick out the kid who made the swimming pool possible, who kept SJS in the running?

And how could he admit that his family needed the help, how could he be a tattle and a suck-up? Eventually, it would be known to all.

Underneath all this, at the nub, Ben knew that if his debt could be forgiven while he stayed anonymous, then he would tell right away. He had seen Ennis and he would give him away. Yes it would also strike a blow against Ennis's cruelty, but Ben knew he would trade that away too.

"Ben, you have to decide to be a leader now. You have to put the good of the school first." There was quiet.

"You didn't speak up after the hazing fight, and this happened. If you don't speak up now, who else will get hurt?"

"I wish I knew more."

"Okay." Phelps sighed, and the other two could tell that the sigh was partly theatrical. Phelps would be ready to hand this job to someone else when it was time. He sighed again, more privately now.

"Can I ask you something else?" Ben said.

Phelps's face rebloomed cautiously.

"I know ... I heard that my tuition hasn't been paid."

Markson's face paled and he kept very still.

"Ah," said Phelps, closing his eyes.

"And so I'm wondering—I just want to know where I stand."

"Ah," said Phelps. "Okay. Well—"

Ben wanted to apologize for making them all uncomfortable. "It's just, if I'm going to be asked to leave at some point, I want to know."

Phelps looked surprised. "Your parents haven't talked to you?"

"Well, some ..."

"Okay. Well, we typically don't like to bring students into discussions like this." Ben felt both encouraged and slightly disappointed that there were other students in his position. Phelps continued. "But you wouldn't be asked to leave. The school has been trying to contact your parents about the option of having you go on financial aid."

"Financial aid."

"Right. The school has a certain amount of money set aside for this."

Ben rested back against the structure of the chair. His parents had had this option the whole time? They'd left him up here with his dread for no reason? Ben wished he could open his anger without these adults looking at him. Then, almost against his will, the relief that he wouldn't have to leave St. James traveled through him.

And then, unexpectedly, came loss—not being able to just give up the St. James struggle, not being able to surrender and go to public school.

Public school. Wouldn't it be easier? The work less relentless? When classes and sports ended at public school he could just retreat home instead of encountering everyone in the dorm. Instead of his teachers handing back essays with all of his almost-correct sentences marked up, he'd be able to shock public school teachers with how well he could write. Everyone would admire his taste in music; he'd put on *Kind of Blue* in some social setting and everyone would close their eyes and nod at his sophistication. Public school girls would imagine Ben ruining formal clothes with someone's daughter on the beach in Nantucket; he would have lost one of his grandfather's cuff links in the sand. Public schools didn't have squash courts.

But, now, he could stay? He could drop the worry that maybe today the final letter would appear in his PO box. He could call his father and bring up whatever he wanted, asking how business was shaping up without needing a certain answer.

Ben thought of the times in the previous weeks when he had wanted to make some joke or some trailing observation but had swallowed it instead. Back home, he had been waiting to leave exactly that reserve behind by coming to St. James.

Now he could start thinking again about college, about the inevitable course that he realized his life had recently diverged from. That course was supposed to convey him to Princeton, and then beyond into some unquestioned rightness. This had once been so axiomatic as to be beneath notice, and he had invested only lightly in the life before St. James because of his faith in this course.

But then Ben remembered watching his father play backgammon against Russell. And Ben knew that Russell, in his role on the St. James board, saw every ledger, every asset, and every liability. He audited the Annual Report line by line. Ben didn't know which files were closed to him, if any. It was easy to picture him looking in at the names of the students on financial aid, making sure that the amount next to each name summed to the correct total. And he remembered from the Bath and Tennis: Russell had insisted that the piña coladas be marked down on his chit.

For Russell to discover that Ben's family couldn't pay, for Russell's smiling eyes to look at Ben's dad with that knowledge in them: that Harry had squandered exactly the gifts that Russell had caused to thrive so verdantly, this was out of the question. He felt some small closeness with his parents as they tried to avoid this shame together. Ben came to the end of this flood of feeling with a small whipping shudder.

"Who else knows about the tuition situation?"

"I'm sorry?" said Phelps.

"Does the Rector know? Does the board?"

"So far it's just the Bursar, Mr. Dennett, Mr. Markson"— Markson gave a subdued nod— "and me. But this isn't the end of the world. Your dad has contributed so much to this school. Things like this happen, Ben. We can be prepared for it."

Couldn't there be some middle way? Instead of the school putting him on financial aid, what if he just told about Ennis and they agreed to forget about tuition? Couldn't they simply know that he was of value and leave it at that? Why did everything have to be so official?

"If my family, my extended family, found out, it would—"

"We would keep it discreet, of course."

"I'll get in touch with my dad."

Phelps sighed once more, and Markson shifted, and Ben again wished he weren't making them so uncomfortable.

And then it was clear to them all that there was nothing left to say, and Markson and Ben went out into the hallway, and Markson put his hand on Ben's shoulder, and they didn't say anything as they walked into the stream of kids, each intent and concentrated: on the next time she would see that boy, the next time he would have a surprise quiz in chem class, the next time those upper-formers would be waiting back in his dorm, whether the next practice was the one that would move her down to JV.

★ ★ ★

At eight that morning, just like every Wednesday, Ahmed was down in the basement calling his father. It was five p.m. there, and every Wednesday the secretary put a forty-five-minute appointment on the sheik's calendar, even though he would never have forgotten to be there ready for the call.

Ahmed dialed the same long number, happy at least that no one would want to use the phone at this hour, and his father picked up—"Allo?"—as though he didn't know who it would be. Ahmed saw the boy his father imagined on the other end of the line, his hair neatly parted.

They talked for several minutes, Ahmed assuring him that

schoolwork was going well and his roommate was still very helpful. In just the same way, Abdul Rahman talked only about the things suitable for his son to hear. Very soon it would be Parents' Weekend, and both of them thrilled and worried with the idea of it.

They came to the end of their conversation. Ahmed wondered who in the dorm had ever heard him speaking Arabic. His father said, "work with good cheer."

As usual Ahmed waited for his father to hang up first. But this time the receiver scraped against the cradle and when the scraping stopped, the phone hadn't pressed the cut switch and Ahmed could still hear the connected phone line.

Ahmed stayed there with the receiver against his ear, feeling the humid basement air across his scalp, and now he faintly heard his father beginning to hum a tune. Ahmed listened to the quiet, absent, repetitive humming, and saw his father's fully carpeted office with the windows looking out toward the gulf, and the leather blotter across the wide lacquer desk, and he was there with his father in the mundane joy of straightening all his papers before going home, making sure everything was in good order. Ahmed remembered again that it was evening there, the light starting to turn thick, and as he listened to his father putter over these last few things, he closed his eyes to hold back everything he had left to do that day.

★ ★ ★

After soccer practice Ben came back to the room to discover that Ahmed had gone to the bookstore and bought a red Game hat with SJS and ST. JAMES SCHOOL across the front.

"You can't wear a St. James hat at school," Ben said.

"To cover my hair."

"It's ridiculous!" Ben was suddenly breathless, and he had to put effort into keeping his voice under control. "You can't advertise the place you are already."

"I don't understand."

Ben again felt in himself the teacher, the coach. "What if you were at home, just sitting on your couch, and you wore a hat that said 'Home' on it. Who are you even saying 'home' to? You're already home."

"That sounds nice. Why not do that?"

"You just can't."

Ahmed looked at the hat he had bought, now so much less than it had been a few minutes before.

"Perhaps I could wear that hat?" Ahmed looked to where Marlboro Racing hung on the post of Ben's lofted bed, and Ben followed his gaze.

"Which one?"

"The red one?" Ahmed pointed. "With the race car on it?" His r's fluttered at each end of "race car."

"The Marlboro hat?"

"Yes, that one."

Ben hesitated.

"You are often telling me that my clothes are too formal. I would look less formal in it. Of course it will still be yours."

Ben looked away from Ahmed. "I sewed a piece of webbing in the back so it would exactly fit me, so I don't think it would even fit you."

"Can I try? Maybe we are the same size."

Ahmed stepped over and reached for the hat, and Ben thought of knocking his arm away, but then he thought of the hair down in the trash can. This would be a kindness; Ahmed would remember this. Ben could have a steadfast heart.

Ahmed lifted the hat off the post and pulled it first over the back of his head and then down over his brow.

"It fits!" It fit him perfectly. Ahmed looked at Ben and his smile dimmed. "I shouldn't have it."

"No, it's fine. Wear it for a while. Maybe we'll get you a Red Sox hat eventually or something."

Ben decided to leave the room. He couldn't blame Ahmed for any of it.

"We'll go to the Dish for dinner?"

"I've got a couple things to take care of. I'll be over later."

And without explaining, he went to his closet, pulled out his big Prince racquet bag, and walked out. Down the steps, out the back door into the heatless air, toward the eternal Dragon and the courts behind. He half worried now that Rory would spot him and want to play.

The building was dark as he approached but in the light from the streetlamps you could still see the newness of the window frames and door handles. How could his father have gathered the money for this and now have none left? Ben pressed the thumb latch on the side entrance and wondered whose job it was to lock the hundreds of doors to all the campus's buildings at night and then unlock them again in the morning.

In the dark he walked through the lounge, waiting to hit his shin on something. At the doorway to the back annex he felt for the recessed switch plate, then flipped up all the switches. He turned off each light until just the farthest court, tucked against the emergency exit, was lit. His bag went under the wood-slat bench and he tied his shoes, then stepped onto the clean court and shut the door. It was so beautiful.

He slapped the dead ball up to the front wall. It lay down on the floor, and he scooped it up again and skipped closer to the wall and hit the ball high up so that it came back to him at shoulder height, and he took it out of the air and kept it on the front wall for three more volleys before tipping it with the frame and sending it spinning across the court.

He brought the edge of his racquet underneath the ball and flung it into the side wall, then volleyed it four more times, then let it bounce, and by this time it was coming up off the floor a little. Now he took his racquet back and instead of hitting at the ball, he just twisted his body and let his arm relax, and then the ball made a new sharp sound against the wall.

The worst thing about having no money was that it was coming at the wrong time. If he had already been at the school for two years—a couple girlfriends in his past, reliable crowds at his squash matches, a reputation for drinking now and then but nothing crazy, always the right comeback at the right time— the news that his family had no money could be glamorous. He would be facing real life while the rest of the school sailed around in complacency. Other kids would catch themselves worrying about exams or who to sit with at lunch and then they would remember that Ben had real things on his mind.

He would have had two years of skiing in Sun Valley and hanging on the beach on Martha's Vineyard, two years of mountain biking in the woods, two years of buying every third pizza, of letting someone else do the math when the check came. Cab to town? Bus to Boston? Tickets to Phish at the Garden? Gas when they got invited to grad parties? Vasque boots for a backpacking trip? All the things Teddy had done and talked about. A couple CDs every few weeks at Sonic Boom, packages of Maxell tapes from the bookstore. After that, suddenly having no money would be a trial to face down instead of an identity, or a barrier to forming any identity. Guys would say, "My parents took care of your ticket, man. It wouldn't be the same without you."

Then, with this foundation, when he decided to withdraw, he could depart on a cold morning. His friends would come out and shake his hand with some sort of strange envy, and the girls he had dated would come too, and Alice would be there and they would all watch the car pull away. They would wait for him to turn around and look between the horizontal filaments of the back glass, but he would keep looking straight ahead until the car was several minutes off campus.

But to be both out of money and obscure—there was no, absolutely no glamour in that. When the news of his family's emptiness got around—if enough people were even interested enough for it to get around—he imagined people saying, "Oh yeah, Weeks...Well, he was going to wash out anyway," or "Wasn't he supposed to be good at squash?" all while still thinking about that thing Lily Jarvis said at the toaster bar earlier.

Now the ball was warm enough to sit up off the back wall, and for several forehands Ben just coiled up his body and let it unwind, and the ball leapt to the front wall and traveled back flush against the side wall, perfect, and up off the back wall right to where the racquet face lashed it again.

Ben hit it crosscourt and began hitting backhands, and the sense of no-effort was even stronger on this side, with his hips turned almost entirely away from the front wall and his shoulders half a turn farther around and then the lean toward the ball and the arm and racquet unfurling, and the ball's weight on the racquet face confirming the mechanical rightness of every part of the movement, like testing the shape of a bell with a slim hammer.

Ben shifted farther up the court and hit a crosscourt volley that caromed front-wall then side-wall and arrived at his forehand, and he hit crosscourt again front-wall-side-wall and the ball arrived at his ready backhand.

It seemed to him now that his only task was to see the ball, and the rest of the valentine-shaped movement was taking care of itself. Sweetness passed all through his body. Again and again he hit it, losing any possibility of counting how many volleys it had been, and he almost wanted to close his eyes and see for how long the system could cohere.

Why couldn't all of squash be like what it feels like to hit alone? Why the moment during the match of trying to decide what to do with the ball? If only it didn't take so much money to create this place, this equipment, all the component parts of this experience. Without all that paraphernalia, it seemed that the ball, the racquet, the court, even the matter making up his arms and legs and torso, all of it had come together so that Perfectness could have a place to escape its usual hiding place.

Ben started to feel a little bored with volleys, and so he began hitting drop shots, trying to place the ball in the nick every time. He knew that this would get boring too, and that for the really good stuff he would have to wait, he would have to move through the boredom into the second and third and fourth periods of absorption. Not since the Um Club had Ben entered this kind of trance past past past past past past boredom. Ben felt a few moments of worry that he wasn't getting his work done, that he might miss dinner or even check-in if he kept going, but he couldn't bring himself to step off the court to look at the time, and so he kept hitting and kept hitting.

★ ★ ★

Price was there in the dim vestibule as Ben left the courts. The coach was clearly trying to create an effect by appearing this way, and Ben tried not to betray surprise.

"I heard."

Ben wished this could mean that Price had heard about hazing or Ahmed having his head shaved.

Price sighed, and to Ben it seemed that he was playacting his idea of a concerned person. "People get overextended."

Ben stayed quiet.

"You'd never be asked to leave. Your dad..." Price looked around at the room they stood in and held his hands out to all of it.

Ben shook his head. "It's the rest of the family knowing."

"Russell Weeks is the same—?"

"My uncle."

"Ah ha. Quite the i-dotter."

"And he and my dad..."

Price let there be silence between them.

"Don't blame your father too much. Sometimes people trying their best do things we couldn't have imagined. But you're fine here, Ben. You're part of the Tide. When I ask for money, it comes with exactly no questions attached to it. We can part the seas."

Ben suppressed a shudder.

"And think about it this way: this problem can feed you. It can help you go to the inside. All the kids from those other schools, they're just playing because it's something to do. For you, you're playing to survive, to cling to your home, to keep existing in the form you recognize. They don't stand a chance against that.

"Now go shower and get some sleep."

7. Landscaping's Edge

FALL ADVANCED INTO LATE OCTOBER. EVERY DAY WHEN THE school woke up the foliage had become even more intense, making clichés about fire and explosions seem meaningful again and then inadequate. The ground became cluttered with leaves. There was mist some mornings that reduced everything else to blacks and hunter greens. A single young maple in front of the chapel screamed calmly all day and into the electric lamplight at night.

The second tests that counted came and went, the first major papers. Fifth-formers sat in the college advisor's office, nodding as they were told to consider some schools other than the top few, and sixth-formers started second and third drafts of their application essays.

Ahmed joined the yearbook staff and found a study group of other international students. When Ben's absorption in classes or soccer fled he worried that his name was now on a list that would be seen by a few people, and then a few more. And then it was time for Parents' Weekend.

Ben's mom had called and said that Kenyon Family Weekend fell on the same date, and they thought Teddy needed them to go out there.

"Let's just say he could use the supervision," she said with a failed laugh. She explained that she wanted to let his dad go to Kenyon alone so she could come up to SJS, but Harry had hurt his hand and needed her to drive. Ben decided to believe her.

"Say hi to Dad for me," he said.

Helen covered the phone receiver with her palm and was saturated by her anger with Harry.

The St. James Parents' Weekend notice had sat on the pile of mail next to the kitchen phone for two and a half weeks. It was on the slightly heavier stock of magazine subscription cards and fundraising solicitations. Helen put the notice on top of the pile, knowing he would see it and hoping he would say something, but she knew he wouldn't bring it up. It had been hard enough for him to go up with Ben, wincing over the outstanding balance, half expecting some administrator to take him by the sleeve.

That Saturday, she finally went outside as he was raking the lawn. It seemed to her that the walls of their house might store their conversation and they wouldn't be able to escape it again.

His body still looked so right to her, long and properly braced against each stroke of the rake. Against her dread was the good smell of the leaves.

"Let's go up there. It's his first Parents' Weekend."

"But it's Teddy's, too."

He kept raking, its sound part of the wind's sound. "Harry, it's too late. We can't keep putting it off. Let's try to borrow some money, or just go on financial aid."

"But we're so close. The rezoning proposal is before the town board now, and they meet December first."

She remembered his reaction from the first two times, at the beginning of their marriage, that investments of his had gone beautifully. She had thought it was a kind of good taste and appealing lack of braggadocio that he had seemed a little surprised, happy in a sheepish way, unsure exactly what to do with the profit but putting what she guessed was a prudent amount away and then paying for a trip to Lake Como. She wondered more often recently whether his surprise had in fact been surprise. She had loved him for never seeming to have money on his mind.

Money had always dominated her family's mind, and her father's mood. Helen was the youngest of six. She knew very early that even the fact of six kids meant you weren't the right kind, and because she was the sixth it was vaguely her doing. Her father taught at Pritchard, a declining private day school near Gloucester, Massachusetts, where boys with good families but bad academics could go. As a teacher his pay was meager, and even after he was promoted to dean it was not quite enough. Later from her friends she learned to be glad that her father didn't drink, but at the time she had wished for some variation to the solemnity. Enrollment at Pritchard went down and the new headmaster brought in his own dean, and her father went back to being a teacher. In the morning her parents poured water over yesterday's tea bags.

Their mother taught piano lessons in the house, and all of the children went through the lessons as well. One shapeless weekend afternoon as Helen was trudging through "To a Wild Rose" on the upright, she started trying to figure out the jingle from the Alka-Seltzer commercial, and soon she had the little up-and-over tune. She heard Isaac and Anne laugh from the kitchen. The house breathed. Her father's footsteps came to the threshold behind her, and Helen decided to sing out "plop plop, fizz fizz, oh, what a relief it is" and she heard her father laugh too, and the pleasure of hearing his laugh traveled up and down her body.

She came to the end of the jingle, and even though she was a little tired of it, she started again. But her father said, "Let's come back to substance, Helen."

So then to meet Harry, who loved her exactly for this kind of playfulness. Harry had joked about practicing his handshake before she took him home, making it the world's firmest just for her. His giving smile had almost never failed to bring people over to him, but her father was as closed to Harry as he was to the Pritchard boys: letting them taste how it would feel if people didn't defer to their money.

As adults the siblings had dispersed, moving far away from that substance. Every so often she talked with her sister Anne, a nurse in Florida, and they laughed that, of all of them, Helen had stayed closest to home.

But even after she was free of her father's judgment, she still carried the vague wish that Harry's wealth *were* a more direct reward for something he had done himself. It would have pleased her if he had been an inventor who had created a thing everyone needed. When she thought of that it made her wince at her own naïveté.

Eventually Harry's first investing successes began to feel like failures when the companies he had cashed out of went on to multiply in size. He had made almost twenty percent on each deal, but what if he had held on? And so he began to hold for a little too long. But this impulse was tempered by his business partner, and they did more than well enough for what seemed like a long time. And then his partner left.

He finally had no choice but to tell her in the winter of Teddy's last year at SJS. But even then, after he had sold all the good stuff

147

to bail out what had been bought on leverage, after the businesses he had tried to salvage so people didn't lose their livelihoods went under anyway, after she answered the house phone and angry people asked for Mr. Harold Weeks—even then she couldn't fully disdain him, she couldn't just walk away in scorn, because she had gloriously let go of balancing her own checkbook six weeks into married life. Her father would have said she should never have put down her bone-familiar worry.

But Harry still needed his own family to be wrong. They had always said maybe he should just get into sales, make the most of his sheepdog smile. He needed to multiply his talents the way they were all able to.

There in the back field, none of that changed the horror she had considering Ben unprotected up in New Hampshire.

"So we go on financial aid," she said. "We have some uncomfortable Thanksgivings. The least we can do is endure some discomfort for his sake. He's up there thinking about it, and we're just leaving him to that."

"I know."

"I could leave the program, get a job."

"You're so close. Leaving now would be perverse."

She loved him for that. It felt so good to be serious about something for a change, to read every book in the footnotes of the papers she loved, to chase down gaps in her knowledge and obliterate them. To have discipline and rigor come naturally to her was now a fundamental joy in her life.

"If I tell St. James that I'm waiting to flip the land for a shopping center, they're going to put us on financial aid right away. I know how ridiculous it sounds. I know how ridiculous it *is*."

"Aid doesn't have to be forever. This deal pays off, we start paying again. We pay for the year we missed."

"But to my family, we'll always be on financial aid. They'll always pick up every check. They'll just be so happy they were right."

She wanted to shout at him that she didn't care about that, it didn't hold up against Ben's fear, but she knew it wouldn't get him to do what she wanted.

"You're a better father than Russell. You've been a wonderful husband to me. You're a good friend..."

He laughed. "To have them know I've left us so exposed."

It took her a moment to say it. "You have, though."

"But it's close, it's almost there. The rezoning is a technicality. There's already a ton of interest in the resale."

He turned to look at her. "Please talk to Ben. Please let him know that I'm close, that when this happens, SJS will be taken care of. You'll get an academic job, and I'll take the rest of this money and invest it. I'll build from there. My mistake until now has been investing in brick-and-mortar stuff, stuff where the roof leaks. Tech is frictionless."

"We can't let him keep suffering."

"We're almost there. We are."

"It's really December first?"

And so Helen exhaled there on the phone with Ben.

"I truly believe it's going to work out. Let me do the worrying, okay? Concentrate on stuff up there." She said they would try to come up before Thanksgiving.

I love you. I love you too.

Ahmed had talked about how excited his father was for Parents' Weekend, and, despite the buzz cut, he wanted his father to see the school. But then that Wednesday Ahmed got the news that there had been a collapse in negotiations that required his father at a last-minute session in London. He had said he would

149

try to fly in for the Sunday afternoon. Ahmed stopped tidying their room.

"Maybe others with parents not here could come to dinner with us," Ahmed said after they had both brushed their teeth.

"I'm going out with Hutch and Evan's parents," said Ben. He hadn't yet asked Hutch and Evan what they were doing. Ben managed to end up at dinner with the two of them most days after his soccer and their football practice, and a few nights a week they studied together in the library, but he had had to make up an excuse to get out of another trip to town with them. Two separate times Ben had seen Hutch and a few other guys heading into the woods, maybe to drink, maybe to smoke pot, maybe just to be somewhere faculty couldn't see.

"Okay. I will see who else there is. Or go to Boston."

Ben tried to hear whether Ahmed was angling for an invitation to his nonexistent dinner. But Ahmed just took his butter-yellow shirt from where it lay across the back of his desk chair and inserted the wide wooden hanger first into one shoulder, then the other, and hung it up in the closet exactly the way he did every night.

Then one morning the campus was full of unfamiliar adults. Many parents thought the grounds didn't look as lush as in years past. The chapel lawn—such a long expanse of grass that it seemed to be a portrait of the school's soul—had several prominent yellow patches. The black paint on a few of the streetlamps along Middle School Pond was flaking.

They couldn't know that Aston had made sure six sunken gullies in the red-brick pathways were fixed and the Math Building was finally repainted. Several panes in the chapel's stained-glass window depicting the rise of Lazarus had blown loose in a late-summer windstorm, and the school had brought in a specialist from

Wisconsin to repair it. Aston kept reminding everyone about the new squash courts: had they seen the old boiler out front that used to dramatically overheat the courts? And had they seen the raw patch of the pool building site? If everything went according to plan, the pool would be finished in eighteen months.

Ahmed and two other foreign students—Rolf Unger from yearbook and Hideo—banded together out of necessity, and Ahmed said he was going to take them to Lupo, an Italian restaurant. Ben thought it would be in Boston again. Then he saw Ahmed on the couch flipping through a glossy brochure filled with photos of planes from a company called Let's Jet.

"Where are you going?"

Ahmed said, "New York. It is not too far."

"You're going by yourself?"

"Mr. Rafsanjani is meeting us there."

"Who's that?"

"He works for our family."

Ben went with Hutch and Evan's parents to the Wagon Wheel in town, and Hutch's white-blond mother had too much to drink and said several times, "Well, your friend Ben is just the absolute cutest. I want to put him in my pocket! Another ice cream, just in a dish this time? He's about to disappear."

Hutch's father assessed the group. He said things like, "Have you thought that out to its end point?" or "Would you explain further?" and Hutch would grow quiet.

Back at the dorm after check-in, Ben went to Hideo's room and found him lying back on his bed with his eyes closed and all the lights on. He said Ahmed had refused wine because of *haraam* but insisted the other two have whatever the sommelier recommended, and Hideo had ordered a bottle of Barolo by himself. The chaperone had smiled and agreed.

Hideo had the chaperone's heavy business card on his desk.

S. Oliver Rafsanjani

Extension of the Hand of

Sheik Abdul Rahman bin-Mohammed

bin-Faisal Al-Khaled

+44-xxx-xx-xx-xx

+971-4xx-xxx-xxxx

"Ahmed insisted on ordering for us," Hideo said. "He read that the bluefin tuna at this restaurant was 'world-class,' and so he would not let us get anything but that."

Ben didn't say anything for a while. "Was it good, though?"

Hideo didn't answer right away. "It was so good."

The next day, the campus was newly empty.

★ ★ ★

On a beautiful day, JV soccer was beating St. George's 2–0, and Ben tried clumsily to take the ball from a clumsy forward with scalded red cheeks. Together they fractured what Ben would later learn was his fibula, the non-weight-bearing bone of his lower leg. Ben lay on his back looking up at the bright, placid sky, and the St. George's kid stood nearby with his hands on his hips as though trying to figure out how to start an uncooperative machine. The turf was cold through the back of Ben's jersey. He wasn't feeling much pain but knew he couldn't get up.

Mr. Falwell, the trainer, trundled onto the field with his orange plastic toolbox, and Ben looked at the common direction of all the hairs in his orange mustache and smelled his halitosis. He heard the chips of voices from the other fields and didn't resent those kids for continuing despite his emergency. He wondered what Alice was doing.

Ben hopped off the field with his arms over Mr. Falwell's and Greg Shelby's necks. Both teams and the small crowd applauded, and it felt good to be admired for bearing up well under pain.

Mr. Falwell wrapped Ben's leg in an air cast, and the team came up and patted him on the shoulder or neck and said he'd played tough. Ben stood on new crutches in the good-game-good-game line, and eventually the kid with the flushed cheeks came to him.

"Get well soon, all right?"

"Fuck you," Ben said quietly enough so that only the two of them could hear it.

Mr. Falwell drove Ben to the hospital, and after a two-hour wait they put him in a hard cast and discharged him. On the way back to campus, Mr. Falwell smiled.

"Well, at least you get the cart."

"The cart?"

"The golf cart."

"There's a golf cart?"

"Really? Sometimes I think kids get injured on purpose just to get the golf cart. A girl's father bought it a few years ago when she tore her ACL."

They drove to a shed behind the hockey rink. Mr. Falwell squinted at a tambourine-size ring of keys in the dark and tried three before he got the right one. Surrounded by shovels, extension cords, and a snowblower sat the golf cart, facing away from them as though in a bad mood. The key was in the ignition. Mr. Falwell sat, turned it on, and deftly backed it out of the shed as though he had spent a lot of time practicing by himself. Ben stood leaning on the crutches with his leg tucked up slightly, his hip flexor already starting to get tired. The cart was an ordinary little two-seater, just like the one his dad had let him drive the two times they had played golf with his squash buddies. Light grime filled the capillaries of the white vinyl seats, the hubs had some leaves and sand stuck to them, but otherwise the thing looked very good.

Mr. Falwell said, "You've driven one of these?" Ben nodded and they waved goodbye.

Now Ben cruised toward the Den with his cast glowing on and off in the passing streetlamps. People stopped and watched. Usually Ben would have been nervous to go to the Den alone and he always worried about spending money there, but now he didn't have a choice because he hadn't had dinner and the Dish was closed.

Before he got there he had three people on the cart with him: Diana Hayes, Tim DuPont, and Freddy Planchon, all sixth- or hard fifth-formers. Ben parked, clicked down the top of the brake pedal, and crutched in as the older kids held the door for him, and then he was answering questions about the game and whether it hurt and how long he was going to have the cast on. Hutch was there, without Evan, and Ben saw him trying to draw close to participate. Ben couldn't carry a tray and crutch at the same time, so people asked him what he wanted. When he offered money they waved it away.

The Den thrummed. Ben didn't have to determine the dynamics of the crowd. He just watched everyone slip along, moving from one end of the room to the other: guys wrenching the Street Fighter joysticks, boys timing when they went up to order food so they could stand behind pretty girls, staff behind the counter taking baskets out of the deep fryer and accepting money at the register seemingly without much resentment, as though these tasks were a decent way to spend time.

The sixth-formers sat on the fabric couches at the far end with their friends fanned around them, the big plate glass windows reflecting it all and enlarging the space. All the clusters of kids seemed to be part of some unthinking biological process, and Ben had his place as a chip of bone or a wad of cartilage, and he stayed still and let people come up to him, and he could answer every one of their questions and seem gracious for asking questions back.

He had told the St. George's kid to go fuck himself. He described the heat of the cast as it set. Some of Hutch's friends, a few of them girls, were laughing and he didn't have to guess when to laugh. Yeah, Ahmed was okay, and it seemed like Ennis was going to get away with it. He wished Alice were there but he was glad he wouldn't have to perform for her.

And then it was time for check-in, and Ben laughed at all the clamoring for rides, Hutch included, and he ended up taking three sixth-formers who basically made it not a choice. In the cool air, overtaking all the surprised walkers, Ben was suddenly struggling to keep his head up. It was a fantastic feeling, because he knew that tonight he could finally release himself from the effort of trying to go to sleep.

He would open the window so the room would get cool. He'd hop over to the bunk and haul himself up and fold the blankets back and lie down, feeling the strange weight take his leg as though it were being pulled underwater. He'd answer a few of Ahmed's questions. They wouldn't mention the slight victim's kinship they might have now, they'd just stop talking. Ahmed would get down to turn off the light. Ben would let sleep seep up into him like oil from the ground, and he'd sleep dark and well, at last.

★ ★ ★

Again he sat in the basement, now warm with the water pumping to all the clanking radiators. His heavy leg was stretched in front of him as he sat on the same chair and dialed the same number, hoping for his dad. They now had something else to talk about. It was his dad who picked up.

"Oh my god, kid, do you need us to come up?" His voice sounded okay.

"I'm all right. It's just a little harder to get around. They gave me a golf cart, though, which is cool."

"Nice!"

Ben paused. His dad wasn't going to keep talking.

"It's almost fun, though. Like, it's a hassle and it hurt, but it's sort of an event, you know? Like it's . . . people have been nice. It's not just the same routine." He wanted his dad to ask him what he meant.

"Got it."

Harry's distraction galloped through the phone to Ben. How could his father fail to relate to a broken leg's sense of occasion?

Their family had at one time seemed almost to fetishize the sense of occasion. When Ben's mom got her master's degree, they came home after the ceremony and all four of them packed into the kitchen pantry. Teddy slid the pocket door closed behind them. Ben's dad held a bottle of champagne, and they had to stand close enough together that Ben felt its condensation through his sleeve.

Ben got to pull the foil strip from around the cork. Teddy untwisted the wire cage. From the toolbox Mom had brought the plastic squeeze bottle of chalk, and she applied the funnel tip to the bare cork. Once it had a medium layer of blue chalk, she rubbed it lightly into the top of the cork with her thumb.

Ben's dad held the bottle for her, and she took hold of the cork, holding it still, and he began to turn the bottle slowly in a way that struck Ben now, as he recalled it, as sensual, almost obscene.

Ben braced himself but still wasn't prepared, and the cork thunked against the ceiling. His mom stepped up on the little stool and reached up and circled the new mark. In her easy tight letters she wrote "6/2/90—HTW MA."

Around it spread a constellation of older blue marks, circled and lettered for graduations, sports wins or graceful losses, the births of nieces and nephews, round-number birthdays.

But they hadn't gone into the pantry when Ben had gotten into St. James, he realized. Or when Teddy got into Kenyon.

His dad expressed his concern about the broken leg again, and said he'd have Mom make lemon squares and start a care package and send it up. She was at a thesis meeting.

"Are you okay up there?"

His father's voice needed him to say yes.

"Yeah," said Ben.

"I'll have Mom call you when she's back. I love you, kiddo."

★ ★ ★

Upper-formers were starting to remember Ben's name. Suddenly it was a little easier to be generous to Ahmed. They drove to Chapel together a few days a week, Ahmed always wearing Marlboro Racing, and Ben even let him drive once or twice. Now when Ben sat with Hutch and the rest at lunch, he caught more of the inside jokes. A lot of afternoons Ben would take people out to practice, then sit on the sidelines and watch the team do passing drills or throw-ins or Indian Line runs, but soon that was boring. He drove past the club soccer fields, and from far away Ahmed with his buzz cut looked almost tough.

But eventually Ben didn't go to practice at all, and two thirty to five thirty was a strange empty time. He knew he could probably find fifth- and sixth-formers smoking pot in their dorm rooms. Against his will he started longing to go to the courts and play.

Without all the kids, the campus was like an expanse of calm water. If he left St. James, would the water smooth over again as soon as his cab pulled away?

After lunch one Thursday, Hutch handed him a crutch and said overboldly, "I'm going to bag prac, man. Let's do something in the cart."

"Cool. Yeah, there's totally something black market about driving around when everyone else is at practice."

"Totally. Behind the library at two thirty?"

"Sweet."

Ben forced himself to delay until 2:35 before driving up, and Hutch was there waiting. They drove through a cold, hanging fog just shy of rain.

A lot of times Ben just drove out to the blinking traffic light at the edge of campus and back. By now he could tell where the school's hold on the landscape started to drift: the fields on each side of the road would begin to look half shorn instead of either rigorously cut or intentionally wild. There might be an empty soda can or a Lay's bag or a nip bottle of Jack Daniel's in the bracken.

"What do you want to do?" Ben asked.

"What do you usually do?"

"You know." Ben couldn't believe he hadn't prepared anything. He considered making up a wild lie—that he met up with a female kitchen staff worker way out in the woods to make out. The noise of the electric motor and the tires in the grit and the passing wind provided the barest cover against having nothing to say as they drove along.

They came down the path from the Dish, past the library, and in Ben's reverie of needing to think of something cool to do, he hadn't slowed down in preparation to take the corner toward the PO, which they had to pass to get out to the Two-Laner. They were almost past the turn when Ben realized he had to make it.

Hutch held on to the little black plastic armrest, and the back wheels lost traction and skidded through the end of the turn, then whipped back into line as they continued on their new trajectory.

"Whoaaaah," they both said.

And so they took that turn again. Even on the second turn Ben had improved, and then again, and each time Hutch laughed with a young, thrilling laugh. Soon it was time for Ben to drive Hutch back to Woodruff to get ready for Seated. As Ben went back by himself to Hawley he couldn't believe that Hutch hadn't once asked to take a turn driving. Ben would have told him no.

★ ★ ★

Ben's Chapel seat had been changed to the section just inside the main doorway so that he wouldn't have to crutch in as far, but it meant that he couldn't see Alice, who sat farther down. His cast had gotten wet in the shower—even though he had pulled a garbage bag over it and taped the bag to his skin—and now, as he sat there, wearing his North Face for the second day and looking up at the ceiling, the cast was starting to smell. Everyone else was coming in, chattering and settling themselves, and then Ben heard two separate whispers of "Ennis." He turned to the girls in the row behind him.

"What happened?"

"They busted Ennis for the Ahmed thing."

"How?"

159

"Apparently Dennett overheard him talking about it in the Dish hallway after Seated. Cooked."

A kind of caul came over Ben's vision. He imagined himself back in Phelps's office, knowing that it would all come out anyway, being able to use what he knew to his advantage.

He sat completely still in the building's splendor. Several kids were sleeping, their necks bent at unnatural angles, and he couldn't understand how anyone could get used to it in here.

Ennis's Disciplinary Committee meeting was that night, and the next morning in Chapel Aston announced his expulsion. By two p.m. that day his things were packed and he was gone.

"It's fucking bullshit, is what it is," said Hutch, sitting on his little stuffed chair, rocking forward and back minutely. "It's like, they should be *thanking* Ennis for setting Ahmed straight, for like keeping this place the way it's supposed to be. It's like the little blue book, like 'does your action benefit other kids?' How could they not see that?"

Evan was nodding emphatically. Ben just looked up to where the far wall met the ceiling. "I can't believe it," he said, happy that the other two couldn't know how much he meant it.

"You know what?" Hutch went on. "Fuck this place. Fuck their bullshit PR, their fucking pussy coddling. No one ever became great because things were easy for them." He crossed his legs and started picking at the place on the side of his Saucony running shoe where the fabric had started to fray.

"We should transfer," Evan said. "You know? This place sucks. My buddy Owen from home is at Milton and says it's breezy as fuck there. They're like half day students, so all of them have cars and you can do whatever you want."

Hutch could now fit his finger through the hole in the side of his shoe.

160

"You know, Teddy would never have let this stand," Hutch said to Ben.

"Yeah," Ben said noncommittally.

"He never would have let this go unanswered."

"It's totally true," said Evan.

"We should do something," said Hutch, "something, like . . . big."

"Yeah, like something that would make Aston think twice about being such a little bitch about shit like this."

The next morning Hutch organized twelve third-formers to stand up and walk out of Chapel. Later that day as Ben was coming into the Dish, Hutch was there in the common room and walked up as though he had been waiting alone for Ben to arrive.

"What the hell?" he said.

"What?"

"Why didn't you walk out?"

"Walk out? I'm on crutches."

"So? Think of how intense it would have been if you had walked out and everyone would have been like, 'Whoa, he even walked out on *crutches.*' And to have you, like the squash *guy,* walk out, that would *mean* something."

Ben in the warmth of this flattery didn't answer for a second. "All right, next time."

"No, this time," Hutch said, looking away. "No fucking maybe." And he turned and walked off down the arcade hallway.

In the Schoolhouse and at the Den, Ben didn't hear anyone talking about anything else.

"If newbs can do whatever they want, they'll never learn how to handle themselves."

"Ennis was everything right and badass about this school."

"Fucking administration just makes decisions for how it looks."

"His family hired this like admissions expert to work on his college applications with him. They curated his extracurrics and the guy edited his essays like four or five times. All that and then to get kicked out."

"They wouldn't've touched Ennis if Ahmed's dad didn't have a kerfrillion dollars."

A Confederate flag appeared briefly below the windows of the Chute before Dennett confiscated it.

Ahmed's life got considerably harder, and the fact that he was still almost bald didn't seem to win him much mercy. Twice his clean shirts went missing and ended up in the ditch along the site for the pool.

Hutch continued to organize. On the way to classes, people would draw up beside Ahmed and walk him off the path. Guys saved eggs and fish from the dining hall, left them in Tupperware containers, then opened them in the bottom of Ahmed's gym locker when he was in the shower.

Hutch talked at lunch about pulling some bigger prank—somehow getting the Rector's car into the chapel, putting bike locks through all the door handles of the Schoolhouse—something to bring the school to a halt, to let students get their hands around the school's windpipe.

Whereas before, Ahmed would stand in the Dish Common Room making conversation with everyone, now a group of girls would surround him with their backs to him, talking with a corresponding ring of guys, preventing him from leaving or speaking with anyone. Ben was amazed; no one had seemed to really like Ennis all that much. Faculty intervened as much as they could, but that almost made it worse.

"What are you doing in the room?" Hutch asked Ben.

"Dude, we've never been friends," Ben answered.

Ben watched Ahmed. His posture didn't change, but he had lost that air of frictionless unconcern. After Seated one Tuesday, Ben saw him run his finger over a name on one of the wooden plaques in the High Dining Room. Ben waited and then walked over to see the name: HENRY STANHOPE UNDERHILL.

That night Ben half turned around in his desk chair and asked, "Who is that?" Ahmed was on the couch. Ben didn't turn all the way around, as though Hutch could see him.

"Who?"

"Henry Underhill. I saw you find his name in the Dish."

"I thought I already told you about him."

"No."

"I hardly know where to start," said Ahmed. "Without him I would not be here."

"How do you mean?"

"Well, how did your parents send you here?"

"How?"

"How."

"Um, well, my dad went here, and my uncle. Our family actually . . . my great-great-grandfather was in the first class."

"Yes. When my father was a young man, he was a small trader, one of the first to bring cigarettes to Dubai."

Ahmed paused. He went on, describing how his father got to know the officials who ran the small port at the mouth of the town's river. The Emir of Dubai, Sheik Rashid bin Saeed Al-Maktoum, began planning a bigger port at the time, in the late 1970s, farther west at Jebel Ali.

Critics thought that the new port would be too big, a waste of money, but Ahmed's father disagreed, as he had become expert in the needs of Dubai's merchants.

Dubai hired Western architects and engineers, and among

them had been a man named Henry Underhill. He was an executive for one of the engineering companies and negotiated with
all of the interested parties.

As Ahmed told the story, he imagined his mother holding her
hands together in her lap, patiently hearing it again.

His father said that Underhill was easy, in control of himself. He
always had a joke, could understand what each side needed and
what difficulties each person faced. He negotiated without weak-
ness but did not tell lies. Ahmed told Ben that in Dubai, among
Emirati people, discussions and agreements tended to change often
and could make Western people frustrated, and so his father was
impressed by Mr. Underhill's simple, sustained calm.

Underhill knew about the world. He spoke French and German,
not very good Arabic but far better than that of the other Americans
in Dubai. His suits had been made for him in England. When the
first grand piano came into the country he could play it, and he
was able to obtain records, and ice, and books, and liquor, which
Ahmed's father didn't drink but still admired.

And then even though Ahmed had never met Underhill, he
described to Ben how he stood. Underhill had held himself leaning slightly forward, listening, and made it seem that you were
the only one worth hearing. When he didn't know something
he just said so, and he seemed at ease while he learned about that
thing.

Ahmed felt a new turn of embarrassment. He was glad that Ben
couldn't see his father's face as he talked so admiringly about this
other man. Ahmed wondered for the first time how Underhill had
seen his father.

Eventually Al-Khaled asked Underhill how he had become
the way he was, whether it was his family, the military, his
religious training, or perhaps contending with some illness or

disaster. Underhill at first denied that there was anything special about him, but after being pressed, he responded that, as much as anything else, he had been formed by his boarding school. Like Ben's, Underhill's family had come to St. James since the early classes.

At this time, Emirati children who went to study abroad almost always went to English universities, but this school was in America. Al-Khaled couldn't afford tutors for his older sons, but by the time Ahmed was born, he had made money from the cigarette imports and his portion of the shipping business. Cigarettes were very discouraged in Islam, so he sold off the tobacco importing and bought several mines, a construction business, and part of an oil refinery. Now he could afford what he wanted.

Underhill had left Dubai by this time, but Al-Khaled corresponded with him and with his help hired a tutor. Ahmed remembered his father looking into the room as he was studying for the foreign-school entrance exam with the tutor, Mr. Greenspan. Ahmed began to close his book to come for evening prayer, but his father, standing slightly angled away and with a look half proud, held up his hand and said in English, "Keep working. Tomorrow is exam." And the school for foreign students didn't have a call to prayer.

Even though few people in the Emirates sent their children abroad before university, Ahmed's father wasn't interested in what other people did. He wanted to be great, and he wanted his son to be great, to become a magnificent Emirati Leader.

Ahmed's father put it just like that, and so Ahmed relayed those words now to Ben. Ahmed wanted Ben to believe in this greatness the way his father believed in it.

Ahmed described how, because foreigners couldn't own property in Dubai, many Emiratis made their income by collecting rent and nothing else. They desired Rolexes and expensive cars, and this disgusted his father, who saw himself and his family as a way for the Emirates to be more, to achieve more, to take its place among great nations. Learning what Underhill knew could make this so.

"My father always repeated a warning to us that the emir, Al-Maktoum, would often say. 'My grandfather rode a camel, my father rode a camel, I drive a Mercedes, my son will drive a Mercedes, but his son may again ride a camel.' So it is important for me to learn the right things, to behave the right way."

Ahmed paused. This was different from how he had imagined telling Ben this story.

"But now it seems I am not liked. It seems I don't know how to be, here. Apparently I have done very much that is not right?" He looked to Ben. Ben paused for a second and then shook his head.

"No. It's just temporary. They give newbs a hard time all the time. It's part of fitting in here. It's just the process of becoming a part of the school."

Ben paused. Ahmed looked unconvinced.

"In a year you won't remember any of this."

Ahmed laughed. "I will remember."

"But it won't feel like a big deal. Really."

★ ★ ★

Everyone else walked out of the Dish into the long hallway toward those immense front doors, but Ben turned on his crutches and leaned back into the crossbar of the little side door. He wondered if Underhill had come out of this same doorway, maybe when the door itself was made of wood. Ben crutched through

166

the sandy parking lot toward the cart, planning to go back to the room and do some reading, but from behind him he heard the same door open and close, and when he turned he had the Alice-pang but it was actually Alice, in wind pants, running shoes, and that same blue sweatshirt. It took her a second to see it was him, but then she waved and easily caught up to him.

"Hey, Alice." He couldn't control his smile.

"Mr. Weeks. I haven't seen you since the leg. Fucking beat."

"Could be worse," Ben said. "What's shakin?"

"I'm going to run on a treadmill even though I live in a woodland paradise with many running trails. Because I'm a fan of irony."

"You're going to the gym?"

"I'm going to the gym."

They arrived at the golf cart.

"As you can tell, I don't have much reason to go to the gym, so I'll take this opportunity to drive you there."

"You will?"

"Why exert yourself before you take your run? That's not the American way." Ben wondered if this was how he would be without worry.

She nodded and climbed onto the passenger seat. As she situated herself, Ben took the opportunity to glance at her chest. The seams of her sports bra stood out even under her sweatshirt.

He stood his crutches in the loop of nylon webbing where a golf bag would go, and, holding the cart's roof struts, turned sideways and hopped behind the wheel. He found himself doing all of this with some faint added flair, as though she would be attracted to him for getting behind the wheel of the golf cart in some distinctive way. Again her smell came to him and every one of his movements became heavy with nonchalance. He turned the key and he wished that the starter made a roaring noise like a real car to break the sudden formality that he sensed she must be feeling too. He popped the parking brake off and they went whirring along. In the moving air her scent went away.

The cold passed over them and Alice hunched her shoulders together against it already in anticipation of the long coming winter. She looked at his heron wrists as he gripped the wheel.

"I've been chatting with your roommate," Alice said. "It was nice of you to let him wear that hat."

"Couldn't let him go around bald. And he wanted to wear an SJS hat."

"Good save."

Ben pulled out of the long Dish parking lot and onto the Straight Road. She sighed. "I just wish I could have told him everything that was waiting for him, you know?"

"Yeah."

"It's shitty of them. What did he do to get Ennis kicked out?"

"You don't think he deserved anything?"

"Is he actually a dick to anybody about money? And fucking Ennis and Fitz and Ian?" Ben scoured her tone as she said Ian's name. "Why should he kowtow to those shitheads?"

"That's how it works."

"But it shouldn't. And *Hutch*?" She almost spit the name. Ben was startled that she knew it. The previous day, Ben and Hutch had come back to the room together to find Ahmed there reading and listening to soft Duran Duran on his sound system, and Hutch had slipped *Fillmore '71* into Ben's tape deck and turned up "Not Fade Away" until Ahmed left.

"Everyone will leave him alone eventually," she went on. "But this place needs more Ahmed. It doesn't need Ahmed after everyone's finished with him."

"Aren't there girls you don't fuck with?"

"Ugh. I opt out of that shit."

"Really?"

"No, not really."

They turned the corner next to the PO.

Earlier that day Ben had come into the Middle Dining Hall and seen Ahmed sitting alone in the Marlboro Racing hat at a table toward the far glass doors. Ben had pretended not to see him, and went to sit instead with a few fourth-formers from the soccer team. He wanted to know whether Markson had asked Alice to read the *Companion* too, but he thought that would seem too goody two-shoes.

"It doesn't have to be this quiet," Alice said.

"I'm thinking of going off road to take the most direct route so we don't have to go through the continued agony of this conversation."

She laughed.

"You laugh, but if I got some gnarled tires on here, jacked it up on hydraulic suspension, I would terrorize this place."

"Consider me terrorized."

Ben paused. "I wonder if Ahmed has a crush on you," he said.

"What? Why?"

"You never know. You might want to start preparing to be royalty. Being the future sultaness has its privileges."

"I am not cut out to be royalty."

"No?"

"Too much waving. And his family is just rich, he's not royalty. And that's ridiculous."

"*Au contraire.*"

"Ben, even students at St. James should not say '*au contraire.*'"

"*Au contraire, mon frère.*"

"I ain't yer frikkin *frère*, bud."

169

"I don't know the French word for 'sister.' I'm taking Latin for some reason."

"I'm taking Spanish, as though I were going to some plain old high school at home."

"Hm."

"College-consultant-Dale told me he wished I were taking Japanese. 'Spanish doesn't stand out,' he says."

"Japanese seems cool."

"I agree. Japanese seems totally cool. And it's not like I adore Spanish. But now I'd rather kill myself than take Japanese. The Japanese language does not need me speaking it badly just so I can seem more interesting."

"Yeah, do I really have to want to make varsity soccer?"

Alice laughed. "Dude, ex*actly.*" Ben almost closed his eyes with pleasure. "Can't I just watch reruns of *The Cosby Show* for the rest of my life?"

They came up to the Two-Laner, and Ben wanted to take a right and drive out with her to somewhere he hadn't been before. To show her the mundane litter in the long grass, to find out what was in the white barn. Alice considered him as he turned away to look for coming cars. He didn't have the lacquer over him yet, but he seemed a little less like a nine-volt battery against the tongue.

Ben sped across the road and scritched to a stop in the sandy parking lot in front of the gym.

Alice turned to him and delivered a smile. He looked startled to be there with her; she felt reassured, and she wanted to give some of that reassurance back to him.

"Thanks, Ben."

It was all Ben could do not to lean over now and try to breathe her in, and not to look at her chest as she stepped down.

"Sure. Cover a spotlight with a stencil of a crutch and aim it at the night sky, and I'll come."

She laughed and waved and turned, and even though her butt wasn't anything in particular, he watched her walk away. He exhausted himself.

She turned back, and he managed to look up just in time. "Don't let them be mean to him." She didn't wait for him to react before she faced ahead again.

He considered the reality of actually trying to ask her out. He would almost prefer not to have more than this; just this could be exactly what he had been preparing for. Hawley was right on the other side of the Two-Laner, and he waited until the doors closed behind her to let up the brake again and pull away.

8. Basic Oxygen

THANKSGIVING APPROACHED. NOW GOING TO SEATED ALL THE well-off boys wore Gore-Tex jackets with the tails of their blue blazers sticking out the bottom. Ben got his cast off and went into a gray-plastic walking boot fastened with Velcro. Still Hutch talked about a way to get back at the school, but it had started to seem abstract. Worry about money sat constantly in Ben's chest, but after the weeks on crutches, he felt a leap there when Rory told him they were going to have another captain's practice. He went over to the courts, waiting to feel that unease with his father's overreach or with Price's bargain for him to earn his place at the school. But as he passed the Dragon he was just psyched to hit.

About a dozen kids were already sitting on the carpeted stadium steps, chatting quietly. Ahmed hadn't mentioned that he was planning to play squash, but there he was, in all-whites. Ben rode out his annoyance as Ahmed nodded briefly to him, but Ahmed continued talking to the two closest kids, and they seemed to be talking back. It was the most normal social interaction Ben had seen him have in weeks.

The captain was Colin McCaffrey, a sixth-former, a solid, athletic player whom Ben had seen play in the Under-17s and was positive he could beat. As soon as Colin came into the stadium area of the courts, with his short hard steps and his brown hair in front of his eyes, Ben could tell that he had been named captain because there wasn't really anyone else. Cole Quinlan, the sixth-former who would have been captain, had shattered his jaw and the floor of his eye's orbit in a grad-party car accident and likely wouldn't come back to school. Rory was clearly next, but he was still in fourth form. Colin seemed to have removed speaking from the room.

Price as head coach was expected not to attend a captain's practice, but Mr. Markson, who had been tapped as the team's strength-and-conditioning coach, came into the courts and said they were going to the weight room at the gym: nothing too crazy but just a quick intro. Markson wore boxy gray sweats, the elastic cuffs of the pants tight around his ankles. Everyone seemed a little relieved that Price wouldn't be coming.

As they walked over, the older guys said that Price had tried to get the team to lift, too, but the squash team in the weight room was never a directed affair. The players suspected that lifting weights would make their reactions slow, and there was also something sort of townie about lifting. Mostly the team had just talked and sat on the equipment so that when Price told them they were wasting time they could say they were taking their recovery between sets.

But Markson had a very particular circuit for them to work through: first leg press, then military press, then sit-ups, then pull-ups, then the rowing machine. Everyone started at one of the stations and rotated, so everyone was doing something specific, and Ben was surprised that Markson was right on top of them, not letting anyone dawdle or goof off. At the rowing station the three guys on side-by-side ergs would race to see who could get the most meters in four minutes. Even Colin looked relaxed, and Ben saw Ahmed laughing as he sat back into the padded chair of the leg press machine. Ben felt hopeful despite himself, but he waved off some of the exercises, saying his leg was still throbbing a bit.

Markson asked him if he just wanted to sit it out, but by moving, Ben was realizing how stir-crazy he'd felt over the previous weeks.

Another kid, not on the squash team, Jeff Snyder, was also in the weight room, by himself, with a bright yellow Walkman on and a rolled-up gym towel wrapped around the back of his neck and tucked into the collar of his sweatshirt. He was a small, night-eyed person, and Ben couldn't tell what the purpose of the towel was, but it gave Jeff the big-neck appearance of a bouncer or a bull, and there was something admirably non-St.-James-y about it.

Ben learned from the other guys that Jeff was the coxswain for the JV crew team, and he was trying to make varsity, and so he was ostentatiously at the gym alone in November because it was a point of pride for coxes, who on the day of the race are just cargo, to be in better shape than anyone else on the team. Their erg times had to be competitive, they had to run out to the Long Pond boat docks fast, and they always, always had to be able to do the most pull-ups.

Right now Jeff was working on the pegboard, which was a thick plywood panel mounted up on the weight room's back wall with a six-by-six grid of holes drilled into it and a numeral painted above each hole. To use the pegboard you held a pair of dowels like ice picks and stuck them into the holes to support your weight, and then by swinging from side to side to transfer weight off one hand, you removed that peg and reached it into another hole, then swung your weight in the other direction and moved the other peg, and in this way moved yourself around the grid.

There was a basket of dowels affixed to the wall, and taped next to it was a laminated sheet of different strings of numbers outlining routes of varying difficulties around the board. Football, wrestling, basketball, and crew spent a lot of time on the pegboard, and each team would have competitions, with two people spelling their names or swearing at each other numerically, or just traveling back and forth for minute after minute, trying to set a time up on the board that no one else could beat.

Jeff was having trouble. He had to stand up on a chair to comfortably reach the bottom row of holes, and although he was ascending relatively easily, he couldn't seem to come back down without missing a peg. Ben watched Jeff hang from one arm as he tried to fit the peg into a hole just above his eyes. Three, then four, then five times Jeff missed a hole and fell, always to his feet, but leaving a peg still up in the board. Ben walked closer, and Jeff finally sat down on the floor to the side of the board and leaned back against the wall. He kept his eyes closed and seemed to let his music submerge him, and Ben sensed that he was in the kind of exhaustion that brings a person past the categories of triumph or disappointment. Jeff's hair and face and neck looked like they had come out of a trough of sweat, but his clothes were fairly dry.

Jeff opened his eyes, looked at Ben, then pulled the gray tab of the yellow headset arm out of his ear. "What?"

"Oh, nothing, sorry. Just looking."

"Take it away, man."

Jeff held out the peg and Ben took it. It was soft with his sweat.

Ben looked up at the board. The wood around the rim of each hole had been worn down so each hole had a kind of funnel into it, and the ones on the bottom of the board were more worn than the ones at the top. Ben reached up on his tiptoes to fit the dowel in the first hole. He tried to elongate himself to get it in, and it fit, and the peg cantilevered snugly and he hoisted himself up. He swung back and forth gently and took hold of the other peg already up on the board with his left hand, then removed the right peg and it rose right up to the hole directly above, and he slotted it in there, and almost without his intention the other peg came out and rose up to the row of holes above that. Then he moved to his right by reaching over two holes and bringing his other peg over, and then back to his left.

"All right, but see if you can come down," Jeff said. Ben couldn't see him but knew the exact look on his face.

Ben looked at the hole near his right shoulder and placed a peg there. All his weight was hanging from his left hand, and he had to somehow place his weight onto his right hand to lift the left peg out, but his right arm was already curled up and didn't have much room to move. But he forced himself to lean over on his right even more and lifted out the left peg. Just as all his weight began to drop onto his right hand, almost definitely enough to break his grip, the other peg glided into a hole parallel to the right one and he was still up. He came down to the bottom of the board and whipped his body up to take the slightest amount of weight off his hands, then slipped both pegs out at the same time and dropped down and landed on his feet. There was just a slight twinge in his left leg through the boot but he felt steady.

He turned around expecting just to have Jeff glaring at him, but the whole squash team had come up to watch him in two sloppy rows, and a couple kids applauded with an inscrutable mixture of admiration and sarcasm. If only she were here to see him; if only the pegboard could be subtracted from his tuition. Mr. Markson clapped as well.

And behind them now stood seven members of the wrestling team, all with the same rolled-up towels wrapped around their necks and tucked into their sweatshirts. Almost all of them had crew cuts, and so it looked for a second like Ahmed was also on the wrestling team. To one side at the front of the group was Simon Paulson, one of Ennis's best friends and his replacement as wrestling team captain.

Ben suddenly got angry—why should he feel scared to attract the attention of someone like Simon even when he had done something well? He thought of the *Companion*. Why couldn't *this* be known to all? One of the other wrestlers whose name Ben didn't know strode up, took the pegs from Ben—his palms suddenly felt cold without them—and proceeded to hoist himself on two arms and then tried to use the same body whip to take both pegs out and move them to the higher row of holes. He missed and came back down, and in the process of crouching forward to take the impact of the fall, butted his head into the cinder block wall. He fell and then sprawled on his back with his hands over the right side of his forehead, but he was laughing.

"All right, squash," said Markson. "Let's finish one more station and then we're through."

Ben headed back to the military press stand that he and Rory had sort of been using, and Simon advanced and clapped him on the shoulder. He had Ennis's same build and buzz cut, but his face was flatter and his hair reddish brown.

"You're going to wrestle, Weeksy."

"What?"

"You're going to wrestle this winter."

"I'm playing squash."

"He's playing squash," said Rory, there at Ben's shoulder.

"You're going to wrestle," said Simon, not looking at Rory. "For real, it's happening. We need someone at one thirty-two."

"I weigh a hundred and forty pounds."

"You weigh a hundred and forty pounds *now*."

"I don't want to wrestle."

"You don't want to wrestle *now*."

"All right, kiddos," Markson said, standing in front of them, "one last effort and then you're free."

After the last circuit they pulled the weight plates off the barbells and leg press machine and haphazardly put them back on the A-frame racks. They filed out behind Markson.

When Markson was safely out of the room, one of the wrestlers yelled, "Fuckin lightweights!"

In the dry clear sun they walked back to do some drilling. The Dragon stood in front of the courts with stoic cheer.

Ben was overjoyed that he was in his rehab boot. There was no way that anyone could judge his performance seriously, but at the same time he could swat the ball and feel that same rightness coursing through him. He felt happy from the pegboard. He and Martin Bowles and Neil Gossamer were laughing as they came up to the courts again.

Colin the captain descended the stadium stairs, sat down on the bottom step, then started tying his shoes and prepping in some private, elaborate way, and the rest of the guys kept chattering. Martin and Neil were asking Ben whether he had any plans to play internationally; they had heard of a few guys training in England over summers. The attention felt good, and Ben said he had thought about it but still had more research to do on where would be the best place to go.

And then Manley Price came in through the double doors at the top of the stairs, smiling as though covering some recent mischief. Price wore the khakis, docksiders, and navy sweater that had all come to seem like part of his body.

Immediately everyone sat up straighter, and Rory seemed to vibrate with suppressed activity. Colin seemed to dim. Markson and Price shook hands, but they might as well have been from different species.

Rory almost pantomimed the act of looking around to see if everyone was present, even holding out his pointer and middle fingers and counting the assembled kids by twos. Price stepped to the side of the double doors and leaned against the wall, designating himself an observer but clearly relishing his influence on the room. Markson walked a little way in and sat on one of the top stadium steps. Rory nodded with satisfaction that they were all there.

Rory cleared his throat. "All right, should we start with boast-drop-drive?"

No one seemed to mind that the captain wasn't directing this, and everyone started shifting and taking up their stuff in a way that was like a collective nodding.

"Okay, cool," continued Rory. "Gary, why don't you, Josh, and Sam take Court One. Ben, you're cool to hit? All right, you, Neil, and Josiah—"

"Let's have Ben and Colin hit," Price said just loudly enough for everyone to hear. Rory went quiet, and Colin seemed to pull further into himself.

Ahmed looked at Ben. Even through his hope to fit in with the rest of the team, his wondering whether everyone was looking at his all-whites with appreciation or scorn, he saw a change in Ben. As soon as Price spoke, it seemed as though the particles of Ben's body cohered into a dense lattice.

Ben looked back at Price and Price nodded. Markson was looking down, folding and refolding a bandanna.

Ben came down the stadium steps with his racquet in his left hand and smiled to Colin in a way that he meant to be respectful.

Walking on court, he tested his weight on the leg. It felt okay. As he tossed the ball out and felt it spring to the front wall, he heard Colin come on court behind him, and the door latch clinked closed. Ben punted the cold ball over to where he sensed Colin had moved, and then turned around to walk farther back in the court and saw all the team there behind the glass wall. None of them were going anywhere for any drills. Price was still smiling and Markson was still looking down.

Colin hit a couple backhands to himself and then hit a cross-court to Ben, and soon the ball was warm and they turned to each other to decide what to do. Ben offered to feed Colin for straight drives, and for a couple minutes they did this. Then Colin turned to him and offered to feed him ("Your leg okay?") and Ben nodded, and with each rail Ben brought the ball closer and closer to the wall until Colin struggled to hit a clean shot.

And then with a sense of no choice, Colin asked if Ben wanted to play a few points. Ben did. Colin asked Ben up or down and Ben called "Up" and Colin spun his racquet and it was down. Ben moved to the backhand court to receive the ball. Colin hit a high looping serve, Ben put a return flush against the wall, and Colin barely scraped it out of the corner. Ben had already walked to the front of the court to await the ball, and he easily put it away. Ben served and Colin couldn't return it. They played four more points like this, Colin unable to get past one or two balls.

Ben kept himself from looking through the back glass. Suddenly the idea of Colin having a tantrum on court arose to him, and he pledged to himself that he would throw a couple points.

But he couldn't. He saw the ball rise off the front wall, and everything in him hit it crosscourt into the nick. He foresaw how insulting and shabby it would seem if he started serving balls out.

And then Colin anticipated Ben's serve and hit a good rail in return, and Ben gallop-hobbled to the back corner and hit a ball a few inches out from the wall, and Colin in turn volleyed a crosscourt drop shot. Ben saw it leave Colin's racquet; he knew exactly where it would arrive, how far away it was from where he stood at that moment, exactly how he would have to lunge to retrieve it, and he knew he should let it go, leave it to the fact that his leg was still recovering, that no one expected him to play full out. But then he was halfway across the court, taking full long strides as the ball caromed off the front wall. He set all his weight with sincere momentum on the boot heel as he reached for the ball.

From his shin an impulse leapt through him. Everyone in the gallery saw it. Ben tipped the ball off the frame of his racquet. He straightened up and tested his weight again and felt slightly sick, the pain now a duller thudding, and he held out his hand to Colin, who seemed to mirror his chalk face.

"I think it might be a little too soon."

Colin nodded.

"But it's going to be great to play for real when I'm back."

Colin looked at Ben's chest as they finished shaking hands, and Ben now let his eyes come up to all the faces behind the court, and all of them together were like churning water. Ahmed couldn't control a wince. Rory was in thrall. Everyone else was turning between disgust and bloodlust. Ben looked at Price again, who was placid.

Ben left the court. He looked back and saw the long black marks from the tread of the boot arcing all across the pristine floor.

★ ★ ★

The JV soccer season ended (Milton winning 1–0, leaving SJS at 5-5-1 and ineligible for the playoffs), the girls' varsity field hockey team went on to lose to Belmont Hill in the semifinals of the ISL championships, and then it was Thanksgiving. Hutch was going home to New York, Ahmed was going to London to meet his family.

"What should I tell them?" Ahmed said, palming his longer buzz cut.

"Everyone on the soccer team was doing it," said Ben.

Ahmed smiled. "When we get back, maybe people will forget a little of Ennis." They gave each other a short wave.

Ben kept hoping to run into Alice before he left, but instead he went by Hutch's room to say goodbye. "I heard Ahmed's playing squash!" said Hutch. "Dude, quit trying to like *be* St. James!" he laughed, and Ben shook his head. They clasped hands and exchanged a backslap hug.

Ben's mom met him at the Connecticut bus drop-off Sunday afternoon and he clunked down the steps in his heavy gray-plastic boot. The leg still throbbed off and on but it wasn't terrible. His slice of a face looked happy to see her, and they hugged tightly for what became longer than usual.

She smelled the unfamiliar school detergent from his clothes, and his torso was a little longer but still as thin. She felt retroactively even more protective of him, unsure how she could let him go back to school after break. Teddy was arriving the following day. When they got home, Harry was driving in at the same time, and he honked the horn and jumped out to hug Ben.

The house, his room, it was all exactly the same, but it seemed to him that he'd been away for a year. His parents realized they didn't have what they needed for dinner—steak and celery for stir-fry—and Ben's mom asked him and his dad to go to the supermarket.

Ben waited until they were driving back from the Waldbaum's to say it.

"Dad."

"Yeah?" he said, as though he had no idea. Ben came up to the edge, and pushed himself over. "I know about the tuition situation. My advisor told me." Ben outlined what they had discussed, but he didn't ask how this could have happened.

After he finished they were quiet. Ben saw weather traveling across his father's face.

"Hey," said Ben, "maybe we'll just say I didn't like it up there. It wasn't for me. We could say I wanted to be home, didn't like being so far away, and I could go to Leaford High. We could do it that way."

Ben's dad kept his eyes on the road. He cleared his throat to speak but wasn't able to start.

"Really," Ben continued, "the family wouldn't have to know, and maybe we could think about it again in a year or a couple years—"

"This thing on the West Coast," Harry suddenly began. "There's been a lot of buyer interest in this land, and the sale should happen before the end of the year. This is a good one. We'll be back on course." Harry checked Ben's eyes for an instant but it was an instant when he was looking forward. Ben wore the same fixated frown that Russell so often had.

Harry remembered looking into the study when he was eight or ten, seeing Russell in there with their father on a late-fall afternoon, the desk lamp on. The two of them sat leaning over the desk, and Russell lifted and turned the thin, gray page of what they were reading. Harry would learn later that it was the Value Line Investment Survey. With the light shining through you could see the print from the other side of the page.

After first glancing in at them, Harry sat to one side of the doorway with his back against the wall, and the sound of their voices carried out to him. He heard Russell's voice rising with a question, and their father's voice answered in a new tone, a tone that took this question seriously.

Later Harry found his brother reading the Value Line on his own, not ostentatiously on the living room couch but in his own room on his bed. Soon Russell had made his way through years of archived issues, writing out moot predictions for a certain stock and then checking its performance in the airless lines of the newspaper's tables.

After a few months their father brought Harry in for the same sessions, and Harry looked at the price-to-earnings ratios and the dividend yields and hoped he could match Russell's answers. He grasped the concepts, his father asked him questions, and he thought about it and gave responses that were eventually right, but he was ready to go when the sessions were over. He would leave a copy of the Value Line on his bedside table but it would sit there while he went through issues of *MAD* and *Sports Illustrated*, and *Treasure Island* and *Robinson Crusoe* and *White Fang*.

How quickly did the family start calling Russell "the Killer" and Harry "the Cloud"? What would they have called Harry if he had been the older brother? If Russell wrote sonnets or baked bread?

Sometimes Harry thought that if he had grown up with a different kind of family enterprise—biologists or artists—he would have gone a different way, but after college he went to Harvard Business School like his father and brother, and afterward took a job at Morgan Stanley as a kind of further education. If someone had asked him, he would have said it was challenging and interesting and most people couldn't say that about their work.

This was when he met Helen, at a party while visiting friends in Boston in the business school class behind his. He could feel his friends' curiosity about life in the real world, casting him as the young lion. If Helen noticed this, they still somehow ended up talking about books in the kitchen.

After they were married, while he was still working at Morgan Stanley, he and his friend Van from business school made a string of significant investments whose success seemed to be telling him something: he was only the Cloud because they called him that.

So he and Van left their jobs and went into business together. Harry spent more time with his young family. His office at home was different from his father's study—the desk and shelves and walls were white.

He and Van seemed to complement each other well: Harry enjoyed getting on the phone with analysts and the management of the companies they were researching, and Van relentlessly went through every contract, every earnings report, triple-checking the formulas in their models.

But without the bank salary, Harry needed investments to go well. That need wouldn't let up, it often kept him from sleeping, and Van, who could tolerate the uncertainty more easily, began to set aside time to talk Harry through his second-guessing. Harry couldn't let go of the times they had sold too soon or the times they had decided to pass on a good thing.

Then Van was recruited for the computer trading effort back at Morgan Stanley. Harry was happy for his friend. He began investing in real estate and mining and oil refining, assets he could see with his own eyes that Van had always vetoed as too hard to sell when the time came, and despite his anxiety Harry started borrowing to take advantage of a few opportunities too good to pass up. And then in 1990, when oil spiked and the economy went into recession, Harry was caught out. Russell meanwhile had timed the change perfectly.

Harry had to keep reminding himself that this was actually happening to him—every time the phone rang he expected good news but it was someone else he owed. And at the same time there was a sense of justice, that finally someone had put a finger straight into a gap in a wall that Harry had been trying to cover over since he was twelve years old at his father's desk.

Now in the car Ben was asking a question. He asked it again: "What exactly is the thing out there?"

Harry waited to straighten out of a turn before he answered.

"It's a series of retail areas."

"Retail areas?"

"Some land outside of San Bernardino, in Southern California, became available in an estate sale. It's not commercial land yet, but it's being rezoned soon. So there's a good opportunity to serve an existing demand for more retail."

"Like shopping plazas?"

Ben's dad didn't answer immediately. "There's a lot of demand."

Ben thought of the way his mother stiffened subtly when they had to go to Turner's Corner or Silver Way to rent videos or do the grocery shopping or find him a pair of pants. Always keeping part of herself elsewhere, always just getting through the shopping-center time, keeping her real self saved for the ocean and the dinner table. As though her contempt for these strips kept their family anchored into the correct order of things.

Ben remembered the friendly disdain he had felt for Ahmed's family getting their start in cigarettes. While Ahmed was telling him about it, he had felt swaddled in the rightness of his family: sailmaking and vulcanized rubber and public leadership. But now, provided the plan worked at all, his father would be remaking himself with strip malls.

Ben wanted to ask how long it would be until there was money coming in, but his dad was still talking.

"They've been really receptive out there. We'll be able to resell the land to a commercial developer. Okay? By New Year's we'll be set."

The next morning his dad picked Teddy up at the airport. As soon as Teddy came into the kitchen, Ben saw again how much he resembled their parents, fair like them; Ben's darker aspect apparently came from Helen's father. Teddy tested him with his familiar mischievous eyes, but his hug was sincere, as though he needed the contact. Ben could feel the slight padding he had gained.

"They beating the shit out of you up there?" He drew his leg back as though to kick Ben in the bad shin and laughed.

Ben looked at Teddy over the dinner table that night and thought about him walking to the squash courts filled with dread. He wanted to see Teddy's face if he said Price's name out loud. But he stayed quiet. Teddy mentioned Preston and Sammy from SJS and Will and Sean from home, and Ben wondered how he was keeping in touch with all of them.

On Tuesday, Ben thought about calling Tim or some of the other Um Club kids to hit, but after playing Colin he didn't feel like getting on court in the boot. So he studied for his exams and reread "Decision-Making," hoping to come up with some suggestions for improvement for Markson. They should change all the "boys" to "students." But that would be the first thing Markson would do. As he read back over his notes from bio, Ben found himself wondering where in their house the rolled-up architectural plans for the squash courts might be.

His mom came home from a meeting with her advisor. After she had taken a bath and was sitting in her robe with a glass of wine, reading *People* as a break from her dissertation, Ben asked her about what his dad had said in the car. She put the glass on the coffee table with the small fold-up wings.

"We've got to trust him, Ben."

Ben wanted to ask, "Do you trust him?" but he thought he wouldn't be able to tolerate her looking away.

"Okay. All right. You're right."

The next day she started to prepare the Thanksgiving meal. All of the thousands of kitchen tasks made Helen think of her mother, patiently teaching her how to stretch leftovers, how to salvage a spoiled apple and let down hems.

Helen had always been neat and presentable, and so she was allowed to help at Pritchard's school dances with the girls from Sawyer-Monclair. Helen would look at the girls so unlike her sisters as they passed in the half-light, their dresses with depths of tulle, their regular pearls and high heels and solid hanging curls. Their faces expected only bright things that Helen knew they would get.

One afternoon, her sister Anne caught the sleeve of her calico school dress on the front gate and opened a two-inch tear. Their mother held up the exhausted dress and then took Anne to Spencer's in town, where they bought a new one, a white muslin with small raised dots along the sleeves. Helen waited a week, and then with one leg of Orin's scissors worked a hole open at the front of her own school dress, and brought it to her mother in distress about catching it on the window latch. Her mother told her to sew it up again. After Helen was finished, her mother picked the stitches out, saying the repair had to be invisible. She made Helen redo it three more times.

Ben helped his mom make the Thanksgiving meal, watching her clean spinach and strip celery stalks off the bulb. Teddy had been out with friends from home until just before dawn and then slept until three, but he helped set the table for Thanksgiving dinner. They had a crisp-skinned turkey, no men came to roll up the carpets, and the only thing that could have possibly been a sign was the curling corner of the wallpaper in the hallway bathroom.

After two days the leftovers were finished, and so they ordered pizza. Ben and his mom drove to the little shopping plaza to pick it up. Just like San Bernardino but colder. They came out with the warm box into the hard early dusk, Ben pulling his boot along past the Supercuts and the Lemongrass Grill, and he saw a pocket of kids collected next to the McDonald's.

Ben had noticed them when he and his mom had walked from the car to the pizza place, but now coming back he looked more carefully. Immediately he discerned the leader. He wore a base-ball cap with a triangular logo Ben didn't recognize, and the cap's brim was completely flat. That flatness seemed not only incorrect, but a fuck you to the way Ben knew hat brims should look: like the narrow end of an egg, like the top half of a zero. The boy was bony, with light acne and ragged blond hair showing beneath the hat. He was dressed in a loose red-and-black-plaid shirt over black jeans torn at both knees and flat-soled black high-tops. All the other kids were wearing the same clothes, but everything was more right on him. A bright chain hung from his belt loop back to what must have been his wallet.

This blond kid leaned against the dirty McDonald's wall as though he couldn't have kept upright without it. He smiled under sleepy eyes and looked like he was slowly telling the story of what had made him so thrillingly exhausted.

Three girls sat shoulder to shoulder on a low concrete parking space stopper, their chins on their knees, shivering and waiting to laugh at things he said. Another boy leaned sideways against the same wall, listening to him. Two other guys were doing skateboard tricks nearby. One of them tried some kind of jump, the board clattered away, and before he picked it up, he glanced at the guy on the wall.

Ben looked at everyone orbiting around that one kid. So tired, so uninterested in going to St. James, so thoroughly unconcerned with making his action accord with God's will. In that kid's system, you wore your hat with a flat brim.

What if Ben went to their school? What if he had to learn their slang, make their jokes, learn what the stickers on their skateboards meant?

And what if he was part of their system for so long that something changed? What if eventually Ben became someone who believed in wearing his hat with a flat brim? Could he become someone who took in that flatness and saw it as correct? Before Ahmed had seen Marlboro Racing, what did he think hat brims should look like?

Ben climbed into the car with the spreading smell of the pizza, and suddenly so badly wanted to see his friend Tim. They could do something other than play squash. He saw Price's face smiling after setting Ben and Colin against each other like insects in a jar, and he wanted to be with someone again who didn't want anything from him, whom he didn't have to impress, who would be convinced that he was seeing the real Ben, who trusted Ben's history of worthwhileness.

But he had to go back the next day. Maybe he'd call over Christmas. He briefly thought about Nina, but that felt much too far gone.

Then it was time for his dad to drive him to the Connecticut bus. Ben's right calf was thinner than his left, almost straight from his ankle to his knee, but his leg didn't hurt anymore. He left the plastic boot at the bottom of his bedroom closet. He and Teddy hugged again, but this time they were both already preoccupied with going back.

9. The Actuator

Ben GINGERLY WALKED BACK TO HAWLEY WITH HIS BAGS. HE wanted to see Markson again. He wanted to dispute a few parts of the *Companion*. Even though he had just gotten off a bus full of other students, it seemed in the cold and the coming dusk that he was in private, that if he stopped on the path and started talking loudly to himself, no one would hear him. He wondered whether Alice was back yet.

He pulled open the back door to Hawley. The entryway light was out and he thought he should mention it to Dennett.

The door closed behind him and a shape moved from his right into his ribs and slammed him into the wall and he dropped his bags, and then he was on his back on the floor. There were three people there, one kneeling on each of his arms and one sitting on his legs. He was scared they would rebreak his healing leg, but both legs hurt just the same. The shape on his right arm unzipped Ben's jacket and Ben felt knuckle edges pressing into his sternum. Ben spasmed in the floor's grit and he pulled his arms and legs in as hard as he could and the kid on the right slipped slightly, and he managed to twist his right arm free for long enough to punch the person on his other arm weakly. Immediately that arm was back on the floor under two shins, and no matter how hard he pulled, he stayed pinned, and a breathless voice came up to his ear.

"This happens every day until you wrestle." Again the knuckles met his sternum, and with each syllable they dug in. "Every. Day."

They stood up off him, one of them punched open the door and they were all gone into the cold.

Ben turned on his side and lay there, pulling in air and trying to make his arms work. Eventually he could stand, and he made his way up the stairs and came into dark, empty room 24 and let the bags slide to the floor.

When Ahmed arrived, he shook Ben's hand tightly and said his parents hadn't minded his short hair when he told them that the soccer team all did it together.

★ ★ ★

Three days later Ben found Markson as he was leaving the Dish. They walked out together into the chastening dusk.

"Do you know anything else about the tuition situation?" Ben asked.

"Not a ton new. My understanding is that if they don't get a check before January first they'll move you to financial aid for the new year."

Without discussing it they started walking down from the Dish toward the library. Before he lost momentum, Ben said he thought he might want to quit squash.

"Okay," said Markson, much less surprised than Ben thought he would be. "How come?"

"Just, like, why does Ahmed have to play squash? Why can't he do something else?"

"Ahmed?"

"Yeah. He could choose any other sport, but he just has to be right on me all the time."

"Well, maybe he can't just play another sport."

"What do you mean can't?"

"For you, maybe for us, squash might be fun and interesting and what we played because we weren't on the hockey team," Markson said. "But for a lot of the world, you can get out of a bad neighborhood by being good at squash. My roommate in college was from Chennai, in India, and he was playing a different game than the other kids on the team. It's like basketball in LA or Baltimore. If you go to Mexico or Egypt or India or Pakistan, that's what the level of competition is like. Like survival. You get out by playing squash."

"I guess. But it's not like Ahmed has to lift himself out of poverty."

"Right, but also in those places it's the way for the recently successful to move to a higher social position. If you're a Pakistani family that's gotten rich by, I don't know, making and selling bricks, then how do you become respectable? How do you get to be around the people who've created 'society' there? British people. How do you gain prestige? You drill, and you get really good. It's fucked up and imperialistic, but it's how it is."

"I just need some distance."

"Really? That doesn't seem like enough of a reason. What else would you do in the winter?"

Ben had already agreed. The day before he had showed up to wrestling practice in squash shorts and a T-shirt and gone right into drills on the dense mats.

"I was thinking about wrestling."

"Wrestling! Huh."

For a moment Ben sensed how strange it was for an adult to be having a serious conversation about what sport a fourteen-year-old was going to play in the winter. They walked up on the footbridge across the meandering channel between Sluice Pond and Library Pond, and the sound of their footsteps traveled over the water and back.

"Why wrestling?"

There had been a few seconds toward the end of that first wrestling practice the day before, when Ben had landed flat on his back and was confused not to be able to pull air into his lungs. He tried and no air came in. He saw the spokes of light extending from each lamp fixture on the gym ceiling and the fans turning languidly through the light. He was utterly trapped in his experience, asphyxiating there with his mouth and nose clear, and so at that moment, nothing in the past or future troubled him at all. All his school dread, all his family worry, anything related to money, everything relented in the bare effort to get his diaphragm to stop spasming and draw in air. Followed by the crashing joy of then being able to breathe.

"It seems more direct or something. No racquet and ball and stuff in between. Just you and the other guy."

"I think it could be a great idea for you to wrestle."

"Really?" Ben had wanted Markson to object.

"Definitely." Markson turned to face him there at the end of the bridge, and they stopped. Someone walking by them wouldn't have been able to hear. "Listen, I respect Manley Price. I respect most of his methods. But what he did at that practice, making you play Colin like that, it was... I had some questions. I just think it wouldn't be bad for you to have a wider orbit from him."

"Okay."

Now Markson seemed to want to dispel the earlier seriousness. "Have you looked at the *Companion* at all? At 'Decision-Making'?"

"Yeah, a little." Ben laughed. "I need a peaceful and steadfast heart, that's for sure."

"Does it seem useful?"

"It seems good. But, I don't know . . ."

Markson nodded, waiting. His patience seemed sincere.

"It seems good if you're trying to decide something. But what if the person reading it doesn't have a decision to make? Doesn't get to make a decision?"

"Doesn't get to?"

Ben paused. "Like what to do when you can't change something that's happening?"

"Hm, yeah."

Ben waited for him to say something about deciding how to handle things you can't control.

But he said, "I know what you mean. That's not easy."

Ben almost pitied him.

They continued walking toward the library, now past the corner that Ben had skidded around in the cart, and along the pond with the chapel in front of them. It rang three Westminster quarters, and Markson half sang the last "bong, bong, bong, bonngggg." Up the rise was Calder House, where Markson was the junior faculty member, and eventually Ben slowed down to let Markson go in.

"Don't worry about squash, Ben. Life is long."

★ ★ ★

"I don't want you to wrestle," said Ahmed.

"What?"

"Underhill played squash."

196

"Dude, I don't give a shit what Underhill did!"

"But he brought players to Dubai! The first *real* players. From England, and Australia."

"I'm not telling you that you can't play, Ahmed. I just don't want to play."

"But that is not the way it is supposed to go."

"There is no 'way it's supposed to go.' This is just how it's going."

Ben had officially changed sports with the Athletic Office. He had called home and told his dad. His dad didn't blow up, but instead just said, "I think it would be a shame, but you have to make your own choices." Ben couldn't decide whether this was an unforgivable abdication of limits-setting or exactly what a good parent was supposed to do.

And then, inevitably, Price found him in the hallway of the Schoolhouse. He gripped the shoulder strap of Ben's backpack and pulled him with surprising ease into an empty classroom.

"Sit," said Price.

Ben stayed standing but let his book bag drop to the floor and leaned carefully against a chalkboard.

"Squash lets you out," Price said. "Don't you feel that? Isn't it a relief?"

Ben stayed quiet, but he had remembered that feeling of going down the stadium steps toward the court, as though all his impediments had forgotten him. He could feel Price pressing him to make eye contact, but Ben kept looking at the end of the closest chair leg, where it met the floor. "I just need time away."

"Is it about your dad? About the courts?"

Ben shrugged. He wanted to convey how simple wrestling seemed.

"All that stuff about your dad, about money, it's all incidental.

It's all just tissue paper getting between you and what comes out when you play."

Ben shrugged again.

"I asked you before whether you could kill. That sounds frightening, but 'killing' is just another way of saying 'getting to the last, indivisible grain of experience and acting there.' Instead of deferring, instead of postponing, saying 'maybe next time, maybe I'll do what I need to do in the next struggle,' you stay in that moment and do what you have to do. If you avoid that, if you avoid learning how to kill like that, you may as well already be dead."

"But that's the reason I want to do something else." Still Ben kept his eyes to himself. "Something where there's no history. I've been waiting for so long to get to school, but so much has gone wrong that I still feel like I'm not here."

"Ben," Price said. "Ben." Now he looked into those eyes.

"History, the money stuff, that isn't why you're hiding. You would have looked for another reason. You'll always find a reason to stay hidden unless you decide you don't want to be hidden anymore. You can't wait for things to be ideal."

Ben stayed quiet.

"You only have a few chances in life to be great. And it's something you learn. If you step away from this now...Why would you want to practice avoiding greatness?"

Ben picked up his backpack and moved toward the door. Price didn't stop him.

"You don't want me at the courts if I don't want to be there. You've chased other kids away." Ben looked full into Price's startled face. He walked back into the hallway.

★ ★ ★

And then, almost blessedly, every wrestling practice was a humiliation, a confusion of limbs and a string of unknowable forces that left him on his back unable to move again and again and again and again. Of course Ben was frustrated, but there was also a relief that no one really cared how he did; no one could expect him to be good. The other newbs on the team—Dave, Eben, Anoop, and Matt—tried to help him along but had their own struggles to worry about. Ben flung himself into every practice. He dove after exhaustion, both absorbed in and detached from his effort. Simon started hassling him about his weight; he was no good to the team if he couldn't make weight. Coach Weber worked one-on-one with him. Ben could sense that he missed having Ennis on the team.

Ahmed turned out to be upsettingly decent at squash. He was calm and diligent, hitting ball after ball against the wall of Court 12 after practice, never expecting too much from himself. Even though he was a little heavy, he had a good sense of where the ball was going to be, and he was very flexible and able to take longish strides, and so, to the despair of the players around him, he started beating guys with ambitions of playing varsity. When he lost a point he just moved on to the next one, always just making sure he got the ball back and reasonably close to the wall, and sooner or later his opponent would mishit the ball or try too complex a shot and hit the tin. Eventually his opponent would lose himself in a rage and hardly be able to see. People began to fear playing Ahmed, not because he himself was fearsome, but because the prospect of losing to him was so humiliating. They would freeze up and Ahmed would win.

Every time Ben passed the Dragon now he seemed to see it anew. It wasn't aggressive or abusive or mean. It just seemed to see underneath Ben's new wrestling persona. And maybe so did everyone else: Hutch and Evan, Alice, Markson, everyone.

Ben considered all the time he had put into squash, all the ad hoc afternoons he had just stayed at the Um Club hitting out of inertia, all the time other people had invested in him so that he could be excellent at this thing. Human beings are so often ridiculous, petty, confused, bored, scattered, ugly, wasteful, a detriment. Through a combination of luck and dedication, Ben had been able, in this one limited way, to defy all that, to be directed and efficient. He could access and create beauty without any of the embarrassing attention-seeking that other kinds of beauty required. He had adapted to the task; the task itself had shaped him so that his own will didn't botch the job.

The Dragon—this other thing supremely shaped by the simple task of generating heat—stood there stating its own past purpose, constantly reminding Ben of the potential he was shirking.

On any given day Ben would become distracted—absorbed in a class, studying for pre-Christmas exams, waiting to see Alice in the halls, talking about other girls with Hutch—but before Seated he would start heading back to Hawley. Then, just as he turned toward the quad, he knew the Dragon would be there standing in the cold.

And behind it, the building that his father had lavished so much money on. Lavished his effort by drawing money from other people in order to build it. The Dragon was nothing but itself, an ultimately useful and dependable object, now set out on a block with its use ablated. But the courts had been built on leverage, a whopping overextension, and they still hadn't peeled off the stickers from the Andersen windows.

★ ★ ★

The Thursday before the first meet, the wrestling upper-formers brought together the wrestling newbs, the wets. Every year as initiation they had to pull a prank, and the other wets had been thinking about it all year. Every suggestion was ruled lame. Until Ben said, "What about the Dragon?"

Everyone's eyes went wide.

"Totally," said Simon. "Totally."

Ben thought, *TP it?*

"We could spray-paint it," said Matt. "Like, write graffiti on it."

"Whoa," said Simon. "Whoa, that would be so intense."

"Wait, spray-paint it?" said Ben.

"You're doing it, Weeksy," said Simon. "You're the one who has to come up with what it's going to say."

The next night Ben sat alone on the bottom step of the Hawley stairwell near the back door. He hadn't eaten lunch or dinner, and he had spent all day spitting into a cup to get to 132. Now that he was here on the steps, studying earlier that night for his geometry exam seemed like a luxury. All the wets were supposed to congregate behind the courts at one a.m., then do the tag and disperse. With luck it would not be known to all. It was 12:53.

Ben was sure that security's Land Rover would materialize around the corner and skid to a stop as soon as the Hawley door closed behind him. More than anything, Ben didn't want to be the only wet to get caught, the only one so clueless and lame. He didn't want to have Snake Eyes turn him around and put his hands on the hood like a perp on TV. Or to sit in the passenger seat of the Land Rover, all the other wets hidden carefully nearby, seeing his pallor in the reading lights of the car as Snake Eyes wrote up his report. Then the school would solve everything by just kicking him out. Ben wanted to stay inside, to lie in bed and look up at his glow-in-the-dark crumbs.

It was time. He put his face up to the cold window panel. He didn't see anyone. Slowly he pressed down the crossbar. The latch retracted, no alarm bell went off, the door swung out and the cold air came freely into the entryway.

Ben put his head through the opening and looked outside while keeping his feet on the inside tile. Would that be considered cruising? Up by the courts he saw a dark shape pass under a lamp. Even in that quarter of a second he registered the shape as Matt. They were all going to be there without him. He had to go. Through curtains of dread he stepped all the way out the door, and then remembered that it would lock behind him. He stood there holding the door open, second after second, looking for something to prop it with. All he had in his pocket was a Bic Cristal pen, so he held it down at the bottom of the frame and let the weight of the door gently come against it. Spending so much time on the bright stoop was going to get him caught.

He jogged down the steps and then back against the wall of Hawley, out of the light. Now he felt safer. He could hear wind passing through the bare trees. The crickets or toads were long gone, and so other than the wind he couldn't hear anything, and he knew that the motor of the Land Rover would clearly give itself away. If it came by he would just get over to the bushes along each building and lie down, and there would be no way for Snake Eyes to see him.

And then, with an almost audible rushing, he felt his awareness cover the campus, gathering around the PO and the Schoolhouse, spreading across the playing fields and against the chapel, from the hedges surrounding the school entrance to the long road to the crew boathouse. He could be anywhere. And if they caught him, good. They couldn't put him on financial aid; he wouldn't have to worry about Russell and the rest of the family; feeling like prey would be finished. He would see Alice one last time. He would have a reason to go see her, and he would finally have nothing to hide from her.

He jogged slowly from the side of Hawley to the side of Smith House, the same design as Hawley but oriented east-west instead of north-south. He stood under a darkened window. Not more than five feet away was some safe, sleeping girl. Across the back grass was Paige House, all dark, and somewhere inside she was sleeping.

The next leg, from Smith to the woods behind the courts, was the riskiest. It would take him under two streetlamps, past the Dragon, and then into the darkness against the building. He thought he could hear wets back there, but he couldn't be sure. Now, frustratingly, he was scared of getting caught again. He listened for the Land Rover but didn't hear anything, and so he jogged across the lane, through the light. His feet scratched loudly on the blacktop and then were quieter on the dirt of the path to the Dish. Ben ducked off the path and was safe.

Behind the courts were Eben, Matt, and Dave. Their faces were scared and smiling. They didn't say anything. Only Anoop was missing. The purple backpack with the spray cans was there for them, just as Simon had said it would be. Matt unzipped the bag slowly, quietly, and they saw three cans of white paint and three of red, the school colors. Ben still had no idea what they were supposed to write.

They all heard huge stomping footsteps, and Anoop came sprinting up. With wild, terrified eyes he turned and sat in the fallen leaves with his back to the wall. He closed his eyes and his chest leapt as he tried to catch his breath. Eben whispered, "Don't run so hard. It's more important to stay quiet and alert than to go fast. Did Snake Eyes see you?"

Anoop shook his head.

"Sure?"

Anoop nodded.

There was no leader among them, so Eben said, "All right, what are we going to write?"

"Squash sucks?" said Anoop.

"That's lame, Anoop," said Eben.

After a moment, Ben said, "Squash is for the weak."

"Yeah." Matt nodded. "Yeah, I like it."

"Squash is for the weak," said Eben. "Okay, fine."

"All right," said Ben, "Dave, Matt, and I will hit the Dragon. Anoop, you go to the other end of the courts and watch for the Land Rover, and Eben, you go behind that hedge and watch for Snake Eyes the other way. Can you guys whistle?"

Anoop nodded.

"I want to tag it, though," said Eben.

"Fine. Dave, do you mind being lookout for Eben?"

"Sure."

"Okay, cool. Everyone ready?"

They nodded.

Just as they were all leaning forward to start jogging out, Eben said, "Should we wait for Snake Eyes to pass once? Then we'll know he won't be back for a while."

"But we have no idea how long that could be," said Ben, even though it wasn't a bad idea. "Dave, Anoop, get set up." The two of them spread out.

"Where do we go if Snake Eyes comes?" asked Matt.

"The other direction," said Eben. "Ready?" They went.

★ ★ ★

Ben crouched with one hand on the cold rusty side of the furnace. He took the cap off the white and it became immediately clear what he needed to paint. It arrived in him joyfully and entirely on its own. "Decision-Making" had nothing to say about that moment of choicelessness. Ben saw Price's smiling eyes, and the ball bearing clacked in the can horrendously loud. Ben started making letters before he could stop himself. He outlined several large amoeba shapes on the side facing the road. His fingers started hurting in the cold and he stopped to whack them against his thigh. He filled in the shapes with back-and-forth strokes. The paint stayed wet in the cold and pulled together into rivulets down the surface.

"THE COW"

SJS SQUASH

SUCKS

Ben took two steps back, off the platform, then crouched down and sprayed a cross through the plaque on the stone block. He squeezed his jaw shut with the savor of it.

He heard Matt spraying the other side. He looked for Anoop. They made eye contact across the road—everything okay—and he looked for Dave but couldn't see him.

"Let's go," Ben said hoarsely. He suddenly had the feeling that Eben had sprayed swastikas on the ends of the Dragon, but when he checked he just saw SQUASH IS FOR THE WEAK.

"Go," Ben said to Matt and Eben, and they ran ahead of him back to the hiding place.

Ben's index finger was white. He tried to wipe the paint off on the leaves, but white remained down in the grooves of his fingerprints. He'd need paint thinner if he wanted it out tonight, and he knew he wouldn't be able to find paint thinner. He wanted to sand the skin itself off, or peel it off with a razor blade. Anoop came back, and finally so did Dave.

Anoop still looked terrified.

" 'The Cow,' " said Eben, laughing. " 'The Cow,' man, that was nice."

"Did you see the truck?" Ben asked Anoop.

Anoop shook his head. As soon as he caught his breath, he waved shortly and jogged away down the Dish path toward Woodruff.

Once Anoop was gone they all wanted to be gone. But far away they heard the engine of the Land Rover, and they all went flat on the leaves as the sound came nearer.

Soon it came adjacent to them, just through the low evergreen bushes, and they heard it stop. The door opened. Ben had his eyes closed and his cheek against the frost. Footfalls in the sand over the blacktop, then quieter over the dead grass. Ben had never seen Snake Eyes—almost no one ever had without getting busted—but now he imagined a man in a black Kevlar helmet bringing the pad of his thumb up to the paint on the Dragon's side and pulling away quickly at its freshness, then looking carefully around.

Along with the others Ben tried to soak himself into the leaf-smelling ground. The engine continued to idle. Its fan came on, continued for several seconds, maybe a minute, then turned off. More footfalls against the blacktop, then the door to the Land Rover opened and thunked closed, and slowly the truck drove away.

Almost too soon there was no engine noise left. The wets lifted their heads and looked at each other, and Matt whispered, "He could be set up waiting right down the road." They all nodded.

And so even though Hawley was just across the street, close enough to send back an echo if they shouted, Ben crept out of the little clearing with the rest of them the opposite way along the wooded Dish path. One by one each of them came to his dorm, and soon Ben was by himself, moving past the Dish, past the looming chapel, across the road to the Schoolhouse, down the hill and up again into the quad approaching Hawley from the other side.

The entire way Ben kept his head moving and eyes wide, and as he came up to Hawley, pressed against its south wall, and then around to the back entrance, he tried not to glance at the Dragon.

But in his peripheral vision he saw the crude white shapes on its side. He had to look. As soon as Alice went outside the next day, she would see it. And still, the Dragon itself seemed to take on even more dignity, like a solemn servant wearing a cone-hat at a birthday party.

Ben came closer to the back entrance and saw the pen still in place and the sliver of light along the edge of the door. He almost couldn't believe that Snake Eyes had missed it. He was nearly safe, just ten or eleven more steps. And then he let his feet slow. He straightened up, stopped looking for the Land Rover, and let his eyes close. As he slipped through the door, he had a moment of wishing he were still out there.

Ben went upstairs and got in bed without taking his clothes off. He shut his eyes tight and burrowed down under the covers, greedy for hiddenness.

★ ★ ★

"We're pretty sure it's basketball, Coach."

Coach Weber had found Simon the next day and had asked him to round up the rest of the team for an emergency meeting in the Trophy Room before their match at four against St. Mark's. It was a Saturday and so there was no Chapel for two days, but already everybody knew about the tag. When Ben woke up, his fingerprint still defined in paint, he knew there would be a crowd of kids around the Dragon, and when he looked out the window, there they were. It was as though he had created them with his mind.

Hutch had found Ben at breakfast and hugged him and said, "Yes, exactly. This was exactly it. So fucking sweet."

"Simon," said Coach Weber with a smile, "you're lying straight to my face. You are apparently laboring under the misconception that I am an idiot, and you have decided, on the basis of that misconception, to look at me, your coach, who knows you and has seen every one of your weaknesses on full display, and lie. How does it feel to lie to your coach?"

"I'm not lying, Coach. It was the basketball guys. They want to take our spot as most badass winter sport, and so they punked squash. It's kind of bullshit, actually."

"Simon, listen. Here's how it's going to go. You're going to say you got carried away. You're going to say that you didn't realize the ramifications of vandalizing school property, especially the school's most recent and very public facilities upgrade. We're going to go together to Phelps, and then for three straight practices, the wrestling team is going to work on removing that graffiti from the boiler."

Weber couldn't bring himself to call it "the Dragon."

"We would totally say if it was us, Coach," said Simon, and all the other wrestlers nodded. "It really wasn't us."

Weber was quiet for a few seconds. Ben wondered if he would bring up "Decision-Making." "They're going to ask me," Weber said. "The AD is going to ask me, and Phelps is going to ask me, 'Did wrestling do it?' If I say no, and you're lying to me, then I'm going to be lying too. Are you ready for me to lie on your behalf?"

Ben raised his hand and then realized how stupid that was. "We're really not lying, Coach. It really was basketball this time."

Simon and Weber looked at him. It was as though both of them had agreed beforehand to have the same expression of anger and surprise.

"No one fuckin asked you, Weeksy." Simon seemed to be trying to bury Ben with his gaze. Ben looked away and Simon looked back to Weber.

"I'm going to give you until tomorrow morning to think this over," Weber said. "Then you, Simon, are going to come to my house and we'll decide what to do. Now let's get our heads together for St. Mark's."

★ ★ ★

An hour and a half later Ben stood in the dark locker room passage, behind the wooden double doors that led out into the public hallway, leaning against the cinder block wall with his eyes closed. He had made weight, then eaten three PowerBars and drunk two Nalgenes of water. Until he stepped onto the scale, the match had seemed abstract, something that would exist always in the future. But once he weighed what he needed to weigh, then it had to happen. He had hung his clothes in his locker and pulled on the singlet, and now with a half hour to go he waited in the hallway, riding out the dread that pressed his body in long, slow squeezes. He had felt this before—for big tests and important squash matches—but nothing close to this level. He wanted the match to happen now so he could finally confront it and not have to wait like this anymore, but he also wanted to stop time so that he would never be out there on that mat, about to end up on his back humiliated in front of his team and his friends, such as they were.

Above the locker room's unkillable scent of mildew, sweat, and bleach hung the smell of two stories of old open space. The locker room had high ceilings for no good reason that Ben could think of, and kids regularly lobbed sopping socks or half-eaten apples or wet soap across the expanse. The lockers were arranged back to back in freestanding rows with aisles in between like a supermarket.

Something about his anxiety now felt good, epic, as though finally in this fight he had something admirable to fear. And still, tenacious little worries wriggled free. As Ben walked toward the gym, he had seen a bored maintenance worker gently passing a power grinder over the side of the Dragon and another on hands and knees scrubbing at the plaque with a wire brush.

Back in the room Ahmed had been quiet with anger. "I would never imagine such disrespect." He was wearing Marlboro Racing as he said this, and Ben could hardly look at him. "When so much is given here, to spoil it like that is just... Who would do that? Do you know who it was?"

"It's just a prank."

"It is not. It rejects the gifts that the school offers."

"This school is not a gift, Ahmed. Nothing about it just arises because it's right and good."

Ahmed gave him a startled look.

This was the first time Ben was wearing a wrestling singlet in public: its tightness was unsettling, its lack of division between top and bottom, the straps like an undershirt, its fit at the crotch that might reveal that he didn't have enough there, its blatant bid to be the center of attention. But being in a tight singlet did also sort of turn him on.

His headgear dangled from his hand. Anyone looking at Ben leaning on the wall would have thought he was dozing. If he got kicked out and went to public school, would he have to wrestle because there would be no squash team?

Ben lifted his head off the wall and returned. From the hallway came the sound of double doors banging open, and several rowdy voices: someone had won his match. Ben had to go back now, he knew his slot was coming up and Coach Weber was starting to worry. He stood off the wall. In his singlet he walked into the hallway and toward the arena.

Ben's opponent had bangs that he brushed out of his eyes as he went into his crouch. The referee dropped his hand and they came together. By the end of the first thirty seconds, Ben's throat had the same hardness and smoothness as the wood inside a sauna.

10. The K-Point

AFTER MONDAY PRACTICE AND BEFORE SEATED MEAL, AHMED came back to the room carrying a large cardboard box with many complicated postage and customs seals. He set it on the couch and went to the bathroom for his long shower. Ben stared at the package impatiently. He was still sore from the meet, a loss that everyone seemed to consider admirable. Matt had also lost, but the team overall had won. That same day squash had lost to Andover, with Ahmed winning at the JV team's number two spot. Ben hadn't looked at the printout of Andover's squash lineup—he knew he had probably beaten most of them in Juniors.

Ahmed returned to the room in his robe, his hair now long enough to hang on to water from the shower, and laid two ties out across his desk—purple-and-gold stripe vs. purple-and-green paisley. Before deciding, he cut the tape on the box with the edge of his plastic ruler. He lifted out a shearling coat down to mid-thigh with white fur lining and three-inch-long horn fasteners that fit through leather thong loops.

"Absolutely not, Ahmed."

"What?"

"There's no way you can wear that here. You're going to get crucified in that coat, man."

"No, this is an excellent coat." Ahmed opened the fold-over card that had also been in the box. "My father sent it from Spain."

"You really can't."

Ahmed looked like he couldn't bear Ben's disapproving of it. "It is an excellent coat," he insisted.

They took a cab to the Mountain Man in the shopping strip fifteen minutes away.

"Trust me, one like mine is going to serve you a lot better in the snow." Ben showed Ahmed how the sleeves on the North Face were cut so that when you lifted your arms above your head, the waistline of the jacket didn't lift up.

"But my coat is so long that when you lift your arms it comes up only a little bit."

Ben explained how Gore-Tex worked, how it let moisture escape but didn't allow rain or snow in.

"But this is so thin, it will not be warm," said Ahmed, pinching the sleeve of the jacket on the hanger.

Ben explained layering, how Ahmed could get a down underlayer and a fleece underlayer for different temperatures.

"But then I would need to have three coats instead of just one."

Ahmed could get a dozen of them and not even notice, but Ben stayed quiet. Ahmed instead bought a dozen break-open hand-warmer packets before they left.

★ ★ ★

213

The next night, after his bio test, Ben called home to make sure his dad was going to be able to send a check before the end of the year. His dad said things were still looking really good, but the municipality had postponed the rezoning hearing to March first. His voice sounded as variable as a young boy's. Ben understood that this was simply outside his father's control. *So, okay,* Ben thought, if the school made the call before the end of the year, somehow he would figure out school at home.

That night Ben woke up feeling close in the radiator heat. He went to the window and saw that it was snowing, snowing so heavily that he seemed to be looking through the windshield in a car wash. He pushed the window open and snowflakes came into his field of vision to assert their individuality for an instant before mixing back into the purple-gray.

Ben left the window cracked to cool down the room, and when he woke up there was a four-inch snowdrift on the windowsill. He looked out and the landscape was completely smoothed out. The squash courts looked like they were made of white Nerf. The Dragon carried a hump of snow, and its freshly shiny surface didn't seem as naked.

Without any of its details, the school seemed momentarily a much easier place to live. The day before, Ben had passed shoulder to shoulder with Manley Price, whose gaze remained fixed a hundred yards beyond him. When he was forced to withdraw, none of it would matter.

He turned back to see Ahmed getting up with his usual closed eyes and creased face, and he was so excited that Ahmed was going to see snow for the first time. Ahmed stood up in his crimson boxers and went for his shower caddy to go to the bathroom, the whole time having no idea what it looked like outside.

"Hey, Ahmed, come look at this."

"Look at what?"

"Look out the window."

Ahmed walked over. His face was even better than Ben had expected.

"It covers everything!"

They hauled on their winter gear with an exaggerated sense of adventure, and Ben didn't even mind Ahmed's ridiculous coat or the gigantic Russian rabbit-fur earflap hat his father had also sent. At least he had a good pair of Sorel boots with nubbly black tread on the sole.

When they walked outside, at least two dozen kids were on the quad entirely losing their minds. Ben and Ahmed tromped toward the chapel, Ahmed picking up wedges of powdery snow between his stiff-mittened hands and lofting them into the air. The road was plowed enough to let one car through, but the walking path along it still only had a couple sets of partly snowed-in leg holes. Ben hauled Ahmed forward by the arm when he foundered.

They crossed the main road and there was the chapel lawn, a pristine mini-Sahara. Ahmed charged into the snow, churning it up behind him. Ben charged along beside him, and when they got to the chapel door, they saw the best sight that could have greeted fourteen-year-old eyes, a sign on laminated Rectory stationery with two words in black permanent marker: BLIZZARD HOLIDAY.

No Latin exam. No wrestling.

"Duh, everyone knows already," said Fitzy when they got back to Hawley to tell everyone.

And then they had to figure out what to do. Hutch and Evan had talked to Ross Callard and Rich Debrett—two very hard fifth-formers in Hutch's dorm—who were going out to the Ski

Jump with some people to go sledding. Hutch said Ben had to be ready, because it was at least a twenty-minute walk and people didn't want newbs slowing them down.

In the Hawley common room, Leon and Hideo had *Alien* and *Aliens* on VHS.

"You should see these movies. They're great," Ben said to Ahmed.

"There will always be time for movies. Only today is my first day of snow," said Ahmed.

"You're sure you can make it out there?"

"Yes, I am sure."

"But you don't necessarily know how cold it can get."

"Well, I will find it out."

They met up with Hutch, Evan, Callard, and Debrett at the PO. Everyone seemed not to see Ahmed. Hutch and Evan both had Patagonia jackets, Callard had a North Face like Ben's, and Debrett had a Marmot. Hutch and Evan each had a flying saucer, and Ben wondered when they had gotten them. They passed the chapel, entered the white woods, and tromped around the pond.

The water was half frozen in long snowy peninsulas. They walked over the Sluice Bridge and way farther out into the woods than Ben had ever been. Snow sat in impossible vertical drifts on the tree branches around them, right down to shavings held on the edge of every wire-thin twig.

The group made a right turn at a spot that seemed arbitrary to Ben, and then suddenly they were at the foot of a hill that rose at least thirty yards with a straight, landing-strip-wide track down the middle: the abandoned ski-team hill. This was something Ben had never heard about from Teddy. A whoop went up from the expedition. Ben realized he hadn't eaten any breakfast, and he was lighter than he had been a month ago. There were about a half dozen people already there—some guys from Astor House and a couple others Ben didn't know. People had brought out dining hall trays, either solid matte-orange plastic ones with a slight tread on the upward-facing side or gray spun plastic that was harder, glossier, and better for sledding.

At first the snow was too deep to slide over. Kids were sort of leaping out over the slope to try to get on top of the snow to build momentum, but they'd inevitably dig down into it. Everyone tramped up the side of the course, and some of the Astor kids yelled at Evan that he was too far in the middle and chopping up the snow bed. But eventually the course was flattened down enough, and four Astor kids sat on their trays at the top, scootched forward at the same time, and verged over the point of no return, two of them rotating so that they ended up sliding down the last half of the slope backward. The runs got faster and faster. Two guys showed up with a full three-person toboggan, and they ended up ten feet past the farthest mark, buried to their shoulders.

Hutch and Evan went down together, and then Ben dove with a tray under his chest, the first one to go headfirst. Halfway down, the front corner of the tray caught and lifted Ben off the course and he tried to tuck his body together so he would roll, but he landed hard on his back, the sky absolutely gray with so little depth that it could have been hanging a foot above his face. He stood up to a huge mocking cheer with an edge of sincerity, and he raised his arms above his head. When he got back up to the top he saw Ahmed letting someone else go ahead of him.

"How are you doing, Ahmed?"

"Good. I have on long underwear top and bottom."

"You going to take a go?"

Out of the woods came a group of girls, the Paige girls, it looked like.

"Yes," and Ahmed went to the edge of the slope like a harried shopper emerging from a department store. He sat down on Hutch's flying saucer and paddled himself forward. He disappeared, and Ben ran up to the side of the pitch to see him, his earflap hat almost like antlers, his giant boots lifted, jacket gathered tight around his legs, going down so fast that it looked slow. He came to the bottom and lay back for several seconds as though beautifully dead.

The Paige girls hiked to the top of the slope, and Ben saw Alice's light blue snowflake hat. She was wearing a long L.L.Bean insulated parka.

"Ladies," said Hutch.

"Newbs," said Hillary Lynch. Hutch laughed. "We're working into the rotation, my friends," she said. Two pairs of girls went, laughing hysterically, neither of them making it all the way to the bottom and putting footprints in the course on their way back up, but no one said anything. Ben didn't want to make a big thing out of saying hi to Alice as they all stood there waiting to go, but he checked her face quickly a couple times so if she turned to him at the same moment it might look like a chance thing.

"Hello, Alice," said Ahmed.

"That is an amazing hat, Ahmed," Alice replied. "That is an Ahmed hat."

"Thank you."

"Hey, Benny boy."

What did he have to lose? "Hi, Alice. Nice and warm, I trust?"

"I'm gonna have to trek up this hill a few times to get warm."

Almost before he heard it, Ben knew that a comment was coming from behind him. Barely audibly, Nick Sprague said, "She'll have plenty of padding if she goes down headfirst."

Hutch murmured, "They'll tear up the course. It's not made to handle that kind of cargo."

They both laughed quietly. Ben couldn't tell whether Alice had heard it. Her hunch seemed the same as always.

Alice went down with Katrina Nemadova and the rotation kept going. Ben started to feel light-headed from hunger, and twice his body was taken by shivering.

Between runs people were talking about the Dragon. The maintenance staff had ground down the entire outside surface so that not only was its graffiti gone, but its metal shone with dense zigzags in the cold sun. Everyone knew it had been wrestling, but the team had refused to say anything, and so after Aston had made a statement in Chapel excoriating the vandalism, there was now just a mute standoff between the kids on the team and the administration. No one there seemed to realize that Ben was on the wrestling team, so they weren't looking at him full of suspicion, but the rest of the kids on the squash team now refused to acknowledge him. People said that SJS might just ask Simon not to come back for Spring Term, and that when you weren't asked back, the letter came over Christmas break. Ben had taken six runs by now and wanted to go eat something.

But then Tommy Landon, a small but funny and very hard fifth-former in Gordon House, came over to Hutch and Evan. His gaze fell on Ben and Ahmed as well. He was the kind of upper-former who loved to take up certain newbs. He said, "You boys have interest in getting baked?"

"Baked?" said Ahmed loudly, and Tommy laughed and shushed him. Tommy had tar-black hair and big, almost Slavic cheekbones, and there was always some squint in his eyes. Ben had been just about to suggest getting toast and coffee in the Dish. But you were not asked to do drugs with Tommy Landon every day. Ben thought he could see Ahmed waiting for Tommy to look at the whole array of them and then ask him specifically not to come.

Ben took another run, then hiked back up with the saucer over his shoulder. Hutch and Evan were still talking with Tommy and they looked over at him. They clearly wanted Ben to nod, so he nodded.

Ben wanted to stay and talk to Alice. He realized he hadn't seen her with Ian in forever, and he felt a rise in his chest. He wanted to be cool and witty with her friends; to maybe sled down at the same time, and to crash at the end and be entangled with her. He wanted to walk her back to the dining hall and make himself a half-coffee-half-hot-chocolate and then make one for her and have her think it was the best thing she couldn't believe she hadn't tried. That might be her last impression of him.

Instead, he followed the rest of the guys along a path at the top of the jump, and then back farther into an untracked patch of snow under a stand of trees. He couldn't believe they had brought Ahmed with them. It seemed to be enough for Hutch that Tommy had selected Ahmed. Ahmed showed no recognition that they were doing anything wrong. As a Muslim, wasn't this way against the rules for him? But maybe that was just drinking?

The pipe was cheap rainbow-colored metal. Tommy had a little baggie and he packed the pipe, and with the flame over the bowl he sucked at the mouthpiece the way Ben pictured people trying to get venom out of a snakebite. Tommy coughed once as he tried to hold it in his lungs, and then it went to Hutch, who coughed too. Ahmed was next and he tried the lighter a few times but couldn't get the flame to catch, and when Tommy did it for him he gave an appreciative eyebrow raise as he took in the smoke. Ahmed didn't cough at all as he held the smoke in, and then he let it out in a long stream.

The pipe came to Ben, and he considered holding it to his lips without inhaling, but he knew the flame wouldn't pull down convincingly, and once he was doing it he couldn't do it for a shorter time than the others had done. The urge to cough came up but then subsided as he exhaled the smoke smoothly. It went to Evan, then back to Tommy and eventually back around to Ben again.

And then the rush of the trees seemed to squeak in Ben's ears. And someone said that sledding is going to be sledding. And everyone laughed, and Ben wanted to say, what do you mean it's going to be sledding, what else would it be? But he couldn't keep track of what that person should have said instead, and so protesting seemed stupid, and then someone asked him a question but he had been thinking about the sledding thing so he said, "What?" and Hutch laughed and asked the question again, and Ben said, "Sure," but wasn't sure what it was an answer to. His throat felt as dry as the wrestling match sauna. He should have known what it was an answer to.

There was Ahmed on his back now, waving his arms and legs. Someone said he was making a snow angel, and they worked around to the fact that Ahmed didn't know it was called a snow angel, he had just been waving his arms and legs. But Tommy pulled him up and he turned around and looked down at the pattern.

"Oh! It looks like a person with wide arms and legs!" And everyone including Ben couldn't stop laughing, but Ben felt like the outside of him was laughing and the inside was wondering how to stop laughing. Laughing the right way was supposed to be St. James.

"See?" Tommy said to someone. "I told you Ahmed would be amazing."

They decided to go to the dining hall. Ben knew he should just follow the tracks of everyone else, but he thought that getting

221

to the dining hall was the other way around the pond, and turning in that direction and looking out in front of him at the untracked snow, he was convinced that he was lost in the snow.

He felt a glove against his arm and it was Ahmed, passing him a hand-warmer packet. Ben broke it open and nothing happened. And then it became a lion-yellow summer against his skin.

Everyone was around Ben again, and he just put his head down and followed the boots of the kid ahead of him—he didn't even want to know who it was—and read

Bean Boots
By L.L.Bean®

on each heel until they got to the dining hall, and he took the door that was being held for him and went inside and tried to gather his senses together to make toast, his last toast. He wished and hoped that Alice wasn't here to see him like this. The structure of the toast broke so delightfully in his mouth; the butter and the honey were together but also separate.

When they came back to their room and it was time to sleep, Ahmed said, "I am tired in the best way." Ben was quiet for a little while, feeling the sheets against his skin. "How much would it have rained if it had rained instead of snowed?"

★ ★ ★

They woke up the next morning, and after Ahmed came back from the shower, he said, "Maybe we could have one of your posters framed and hang it here on the wall instead of the picture of the chapel."

This moved Ben to a degree that embarrassed him.

"I don't think we need to, Ahmed."

"No, really. I think that something other than these photographs would be positive change."

"It doesn't matter."

"I insist."

"Ahmed, you're going to have the room to yourself soon, anyway."

"What do you mean?"

"I'm not going to come back next semester."

Ahmed looked like someone had sprayed water in his face. "I don't understand. Are you not liking it so much? We can put up more of your things on the wall, or if you would like to have your bed on the ground again..."

"No, it's not any of that." He paused. "My tuition hasn't been coming in." This didn't feel as hard to Ben as he'd imagined.

"But that cannot be the case."

"It is the case, though, Ahmed. So they're not going to ask me back next semester."

"But I need to become poised like you. We are so behind on that." Even as he said it, Ahmed heard that he was trying to convince himself of an old possibility. "The school can't help you pay?"

"It's not easy like that."

"Oh."

Ben knew he should just leave it here.

"You are supposed to stay."

"Well, it's going to go a different way."

"I don't want it."

All Ben could do was shrug. He left for the Dish to get an omelet.

He walked toward the PO and found that all the paths were already shoveled and salted and the edges of the snow along the road were turning brown. He turned along Sluice Pond, and the crystals of snow puffed off the countless moving branches in the cold sun. He knew exactly what all this austere loveliness was supposed to do to him, exactly what it was supposed to have shaped him into.

That night Ahmed said he'd had an idea. His father had agreed. Ben refused, said he couldn't accept it, and then slowly let himself be persuaded.

Ahmed said, "This is how the *Companion* would say to act. This is to the benefit of another person."

But it could not be known to all. They agreed that the money should go from Ahmed's father's account to Ben's checking account, then from that account to the school so that no one would know its source. The next day they spoke account and routing numbers into the phone in the basement, and then it was done.

★ ★ ★

After three days of exams they were up early, Ben for the Connecticut bus home, Ahmed for the black car idling next to Hawley that would take him to the airport.

Ahmed had everything neatly packed as Ben finished stuffing laundry into his duffel bag. Ben felt Ahmed's eyes on him.

"Please think about coming back to squash."

Was Ahmed already trying to pressure him with their arrangement?

"Price won't even look at me," Ben said.

"Please think about it."

The days at home passed slowly. Teddy had been invited to ski in Aspen by one of his Kenyon friends, and Ben wondered how he was paying for his plane ticket and lift ticket. It occurred to him that Teddy could be dealing drugs at college.

They bought an Advent calendar. Ben had always loved to open each cardboard door.

It snowed heavily on the night of the twentieth, and the next day, in a fit of relief from cabin fever, Ben and Harry began clearing the long driveway. They had a snowblower but they left it in the garage in favor of the big shovels, and they felt the weight of the snow in their arms and backs.

After half an hour or so, they stopped in the sun. They stood their shovels straight, laid their forearms over the handles, and turned their faces into the warmth.

"I just wanted to say, I talked to them," Ben said easily. His father kept his eyes closed for a few seconds. "They agreed to put me on temporary aid."

Harry looked at him, not as surprised as Ben would have expected. "I just need until the spring," he said.

"I made them promise not to keep records of it. They're making sure not to let the board or anyone know."

"But it's close—"

"It's okay, Dad. When we get there we can talk to them about transitioning off."

They started digging again, and finished in quiet. His dad could discover his lie with a three-minute phone call.

Two careful days later, he finally called Tim's house, relieved when Tim's mom answered the phone and he could leave a message.

Tim left a return message that sure it would be great to meet at the HMV on Route 44—maybe they could do one o'clock the following day. When he read the message, Ben was taken over by it. With Tim he could leap out into the uncertainty of a joke and not worry if it wasn't quite right, and so maybe a great joke would happen. He wished he could drive so his mother wouldn't have to be anywhere around them, but she said she was happy to take a break from dissertation stuff, to sit at the little tea place and read her novel.

Tim saw Ben first, standing up out of his mom's car and squinting into the bright overcast sky. You could still so clearly discern the bones under the skin of Ben's face, but he looked different, too. His matte-black hair had grown out; it followed fewer rules now. Tim wouldn't have thought Ben could get thinner, but he was, and still more tempered; a childish softness had left him.

Before he could help it, Tim felt a shiver of aversion. Why was it so hard to bear up under being with Ben sometimes?

Ben said goodbye to his mom and she waved to him as though they had a fun shared secret. There Tim was, a new cowrie-shell necklace visible at his throat behind his unzipped fleece. His molasses-colored hair was a lot longer, and there was a much-encouraged start of a beard under his chin and over his upper lip.

They ordered what they thought was the right thing at a coffee place. Tim said he was playing in a band at Sussex, the private day school he was going to, that they had performed a couple times at dances. Ben said cool, and imagined Tim feeling a preshow anxiety like Ben had felt in the hallway before the wrestling match. He wanted to say something to establish between them the shared stage fright, the sensation of pushing yourself over the precipice into some act.

Tim said, "I got to school and the first day I saw this flyer in the hall that said, 'Guitar player needed. Zeppelin, Stones, Bowie, Hendrix, Allmans. No Dead. No fucking Phish.' Except the 'u' and 'c' in 'fucking' were a number sign and asterisk. And I was like, *exactly*. These guys, they'd been playing together for two years and their guitar player graduated. But I could hang, and just before Christmas we had this semester-end concert. My ears are still ringing."

Tim asked how St. James was, and they both heard the slight unkindness in his tone.

"It's good. There's a ton of work, and I'm still like figuring out the whole place. But it's amazing. I quit squash, though."

Tim put down his paper cup. "No."

"Too much pressure."

Tim felt a rise of affection and forgiveness for his friend. "Are you sure, though? I mean, I remember you playing the semis against Addison Garner"—they both laughed about Addison's long bangs—"and just seeing you playing a whole different game from him. It would be too bad if you didn't..." Tim could see Ben was flattered but put off, and he didn't know which part of what he was saying was having which effect.

They pretended to be adults and kept sitting in the front window of the coffee shop, watching people walking from their cars to the other stores in the strip. Tim wasn't bringing up going to HMV, and Ben let it go; he didn't want to worry about spending money on CDs. They should have gone sledding. Ben didn't think he was good enough at piano anymore to jam with Tim, and squash was off the table, so what else did they have? What was their friendship other than methods of passing time in the same place? Along with everything else, they both felt relief when it was time to go.

Christmas Eve approached. They bought a tree and hung ornaments on it, but no presents went underneath. On Christmas morning Ben got two Tintin books and a travel backgammon set. His parents said they had already exchanged presents.

The night before Ben was going back, he and his dad went to the movies, but Helen didn't want to see *Dumb and Dumber* and so she let them go and started reading her book.

When she was sure they were well gone she went up to Ben's room and saw his closed-up duffel. She held a packet of lemon squares wrapped in two layers of Saran wrap and a layer of tinfoil, and she paused there for a few moments in the darkness of the room. The duffel was somehow like his face when she had dropped him off to meet Tim, busy with not-knowing her, and she felt the anticipation of missing him and wanting him to come home again. She went to one knee over the duffel and unzipped it partway, starting to slip the lemon squares inside, and then she saw a gleam. She looked closer: their three-quarters-full bottle of Old Grand-Dad.

She smiled in the darkness, absorbing this lie. He was smart. She would bet they'd had that bottle for a dozen years. How could she let him go up there again without any assets? She pulled the zipper closed, stood up, and turned her back on the duffel, and when they got home that night she handed Ben the lemon squares packet directly and said she hoped he liked them and hugged him around his uncushioned rib cage and went upstairs to bed with her throat tight.

11. The Light of Setting Suns

THE FIRST EVENING BACK, WRESTLING HAD A THREE-HOUR practice. Simon was there and trying to act as though nothing was different. Ben was relieved that he hadn't been kicked out for a thing that Ben was partially responsible for. They did all the same drills and everyone said the same things, but Weber had lost faith in them after the Dragon, and making eye contact still seemed too hard to manage.

Ben was amazed at how glad he was to see Ahmed again back in the room. His hair was neatly trimmed and parted, and it was shocking that it looked intentional again. For a short moment each of them looked hard at the other one to see if their arrangement was there behind the eyes. Instead of hugging they traded a handshake and then Ahmed asked him how his break had been. There was something more careful about Ahmed; his smile was more subdued and his voice quieter. Ben saw this new quiet even when Ahmed was turned away, occupied with his shoe trees or three-ring binder.

Ben imagined the conversation Ahmed had had with his father;

maybe it hadn't even come up between them after that first arrangement. Or maybe it had blown apart how they imagined the Underhills of the world to be. Would Underhill ever let himself be so vulnerable? Or could Underhills always expect this kind of service from those around them?

Ben expected to feel relieved as he walked around campus. Money was settled and he could finally get back to the things he should have been attending to the whole time: girls, excelling, the right path. But at dinner the first night the group around Hutch seemed suddenly cemented with Ben outside: disposable camera pictures had come back of them getting wet in Kyle's room a week before break, and all of them had several nicknames for the others, each a differing degree of insult. But they just called Ben "Ben" or "Weeksy."

There in the dining hall he sat with them and laughed, and wondered when they would find out that Ahmed was paying his way. He remembered the whiskey he had brought back, and wished he could put it right out on the dining hall table. Hutch looked at Ben and said, "I spent all break hoping Ahmed's dad would withdraw him. Fuck."

The next morning as all the students streamed out of Chapel through the grit on the path, someone arrived at Ben's shoulder. In the sun off the snow after the chapel's darkness, Ben had to stare for a moment before he realized that it was Markson, who was now leaning into him gently and then away.

"I know I should probably keep my mouth shut, but I had to check with the Bursar." He smiled. "You must be so relieved! What did your parents say?"

"Apparently a deal came through," Ben said, and smiled as well. After a moment Markson raised his eyebrows to invite him to continue, but Ben just said, "How was your break?"

"Ah, good," said Markson, the light in his face turning inward. "I was in New York."

Ben was relieved for this something-else to talk about. "Is that where you're from?"

"No, I'm—I'm actually seeing someone there."

Ben looked again: this was what new love looked like in Markson's face.

"So, ah, we obviously, we don't get a ton of time to see each other, so it was great. It was great to have some time there."

"That's great," said Ben, and they smiled.

"I'm happy the tuition thing worked out. I was worried for you."

Ben forced a smile, but there were no other words he could bring to his mouth.

After another minute of quiet they waved and parted ways— Markson to the Schoolhouse and Ben to the Math Building.

Ben saw Rory coming down the adjacent path, and expected him to walk right past as usual, but he came right for Ben with defiance in his face.

"We got someone else."

"What?"

"Price recruited someone new, a British kid, Gray Dalton. You were good for here, dude, but this kid is good in *England*."

Rory seemed to expect him to crumble at hearing this, but instead Ben shrugged. "I'm not playing squash. I don't care, man."

"Bullshit. I know you. When you see him play it's going to kill you."

"I guess I just won't watch him play, then."

As he walked away, Ben tried to sense the whole campus again to see if he could feel this other player, and then he caught himself.

★ ★ ★

Ahmed still wore the Marlboro Racing hat whenever he wasn't wearing the Russian earflap hat, and Ben resigned himself to the idea that Marlboro Racing was now lost. To the benefit of other boys, etc., etc.

The January days surrendered early, and streetlamps softened the landscape. A check arrived from his dad for sixty dollars, with a note that just said, *Pizza*. Ben kept going to wrestling practice, even won an away match against another absolute beginner from Deerfield, but several nights a week he had the urge to go to the squash courts to take a break from working. Then he remembered the new kid, and Price. He hadn't seen either of them around campus, but then on Wednesday there was a home match scheduled against Milton on the new courts, and as Ben walked past the courts to the gym, he saw people's sweaters pressed against the glass of the doors at the top of the gallery, and heard the noise of the cheering even as he kept walking. Squash ended up beating Milton 6–3, and Gray was the lead story on the front page of the *Colony,* the SJS paper. He had lost only three points during the entire match, and the paper had a quote from the Milton number one: "That was awful."

Ben wondered whether he could just stop showing up to wrestling without anyone missing him. Ahmed stayed toward the top of the pack on the JV squash team and kept winning matches against kids from other schools. In the Dish the kids moved with the thrum of a healthy hive, and in classes Ben sat back and let the conversation wash around him. He let himself get used to his spot toward the outside of Hutch's circle. He saw Alice in the halls a few times, and they stopped and talked and Ben managed to wrap up the conversation without making a fool of himself.

One time she said, "Hey, there's this thing: I've been doing a photo project for a little while. Like I started it toward the end of last year."

Ben nodded.

"Would you ever come sit for me?"

"It's like portraits?" For an instant Ben thought she was asking him to help her set up the equipment.

"Yeah. *Portraits* sounds so ritzy, but yeah, I've been taking pictures of people. Think about it."

"Sure, I will," he said, meaning he was agreeing to sit for a photo, but he heard that it meant he would agree to think about it. He began to think he should go to her room to visit her.

In the common room after Seated, Hutch teased the girls he knew, and they rolled their eyes but laughed, and the boys with him wanted the same response but were too timid to say anything potentially disagreeable to the girls, and so they seemed to go up on tiptoes with the effort to get closer, to take part, like young dogs preparing to put their feet up on a new person's shirt. Ben tried to hold himself back from doing the same thing but he knew he was only partially successful.

Ben finally saw Gray across the common room; it had to be him. He was tall, like a long brushstroke, with close-cut black curly hair and a maybe-I'm-putting-you-on smile. Gray had several people around him, maybe excited about an English accent, but Ben didn't need to care.

Hutch kept talking about Ahmed. "St. James is in decline. The administration is trying to, like, mass-market the school, make sure it's safe for new money to send their kids here for the stamp of approval."

Ben stayed quiet, hoping it would just dissolve away, but then Evan squinted and said, "Yeah, but what can we do? I mean, if the upper-formers are willing to have things go to shit, how can we do anything about it?"

"Desperate times, man. We have to lead the charge. We have

233

to make it clear that not only can't you act that way, but the rest of the school in good conscience can't let it stand. Once we remind upper-formers how it's supposed to work, they'll take up the flag."

"All right," said Evan. "So what are we going to do?"

Hutch turned to Ben. "What do you think, man? What would work on him?"

Ben wished he could close his eyes and have them forget he was there. "He already feels really bad about it. He told me he wished nothing had happened to Ennis. Yes, it sucks, but it's on the administration."

"But see, that's especially not good enough. Even if the administration doesn't understand, everyone else has to understand that if you cross authority, you'll regret it. That's our responsibility to maintain. My dad would be appalled if he knew shit like this was going on. And people just forgetting so quickly."

And most people did in fact seem to have forgotten what the problem with Ahmed was supposed to be, and more than a few started to think of him as a funny curiosity. But a core number of guys still turned their shoulders from him when they passed him on the path. Ahmed seemed to be reaching for his old buoyancy, and he joined the robotics team.

In their room, imagining Hutch just outside in the hallway, Ben again started to give Ahmed a little more guidance. Maybe cuff links weren't always the best idea. Maybe it was time to replace the Coach leather satchel with a JanSport zip-up backpack. Before, Ben would just wince as Ahmed stood in front of the hot lunch options for a minute and a half, inquiring politely whether each one contained any pork while the server and the students in line behind him seethed, but now he tried to take Ahmed aside and explain why people might object. He began to sit with

Ahmed at lunch if he could be reasonably sure they wouldn't be seen, working bits of slang into the conversation.

In his head Ben began to think of general wisdom he would want to write down for Ahmed if he ever had the chance, his own version of the *Companion*. It would be a good idea for Ahmed to visit Nantucket, Martha's Vineyard, an apartment on Park Avenue. The apartment of someone who disdains Park Avenue. A concert of sixties and seventies rock or bluegrass. Eventually he should branch out from squash and learn or at least try tennis, sailing, canoeing, cross-country skiing, downhill skiing, jogging, fly-fishing, hiking. Hiking was good and didn't demand much practice. It was important not to complain while doing any of these things, but Ahmed hadn't ever seemed to be much of a complainer. And anytime you were in any kind of contest with anyone, you had to laugh off any defeat or victory no matter how important it actually was for you. This could work, Ahmed could get this.

And then, about ten days into school, Ben saw Ahmed and Tommy Landon together again, leaning against the wood paneling in the Schoolhouse hall. Instantly Ben could tell that they were talking about getting high. Ahmed almost always stood with his chest out, but now the two of them hunched conspiratorially.

Tommy looked up and scanned the hallway, and then Ahmed looked up and scanned the hallway in exactly the same way. Ben moved his gaze to the dull brass doorknob on the closest classroom. Tommy and Ahmed straightened up and began walking away together, turning left down the short flight of stairs to the south exit.

That night back in the room, while Ben stared at his first trigonometry problem set and Ahmed tried to read "Tintern Abbey," Ben looked up and said, "So I saw you hanging out with Tommy Landon today." Ahmed gave him a look that Ben wouldn't have thought him capable of a month before.

"I can be with whomever I want."

"I didn't say you couldn't. What's he like? What do you guys do?"

"We see each other. What do you and I do?"

"We live together, Ahmed."

"Well, Tommy and I go to the same school. So we are together at some times."

"All right."

Over the next several days it got colder and colder, and Ben saw less and less of Ahmed. Every night Ahmed came into the room late, after Ben was lying in the dark looking into the phosphorescence, and he began sleeping until the absolute last minute before getting up for Chapel or class. Then he began sleeping through Chapel, and then Ben would see him with Tommy and Tommy's friends near the power plant when he definitely had class scheduled.

Before Christmas, Ahmed had asked Ben for some of his music to listen to, and Ben had made him a long, careless tape of the Allmans, Stones, *Kind of Blue,* and some Blues Traveler as a required nod to music from their own decade. Ahmed hadn't mentioned it since then, and now that Ahmed was pulling closer to Tommy, Ben intensely wished he had taken it more seriously.

"Hey, Ahmed, did you listen to that tape I gave you?"

Ahmed took his robe from the hook on the back of the door without looking around.

"Yes, it was very good."

"What did you like the best?" Ben heard his voice from outside himself, and for the first time he had the feeling adults have when trying to relate to children.

"I liked the first song."

"The Hendrix?"

"Yes. That was very good."

"Cool, I'm glad you liked it. Let me know if you ever want more."

Ahmed turned to look at him and smiled. "Yes, I will."

"I've got tons of stuff I could give you."

"Yes, definitely."

Ben started asking Ahmed if he wanted to go to the movies the Film Society screened on Friday nights, or to the Den to play Street Fighter on the old arcade coin-op, or to study not at Kuyper Library but in the smaller, less hectic stacks of the Art Library. Ahmed agreed to go to the Den and to study a few times, but most of the time he had something else to do. Even as he started to miss Chapel and a class here and there, he still came to squash practice every day.

When he saw Ahmed and Tommy together, Ben kept expecting Tommy to wear a mocking expression, like the grin of a child teasing a dog, but it wasn't there. Tommy and his friends looked like they had been given some new kind of kite. And, impossibly, the Marlboro Racing hat was starting to look cool again.

To applause, Ben brought the Snapple bottles of Old Grand-Dad over to Hutch's room for crank time on a Tuesday, and he had a careful two shots.

"Tommy's making such a huge mistake," Hutch seethed. "He thinks he can bring Ahmed up, but it's just capitulating. I bet Ahmed's paying for all their shit. I bet that's the only reason they keep him around, just using him for his money."

At Seated, Ben kept putting his hand in front of his mouth to contain any smell, and everything was more glowing.

When Ahmed came into the room early on a Thursday night— 8:07 p.m.—relief washed through Ben; he hardly ever saw Ahmed before eleven anymore. Ahmed placed his backpack on his desk. Ben suddenly felt sorry he had suggested that Ahmed switch away from the satchel. This maroon backpack with the black padded shoulder straps seemed so bland.

"Ben? You enjoy writing papers?"

"I don't think anyone enjoys it. I don't mind it, I guess."

"I do not like it at all."

Ben laughed. "No?"

"No. Mr. Twombley keeps telling me I am getting closer, but I do not really know what I am trying to get closer to." Ahmed stopped and was quiet for several seconds.

Ben started, "Do you—" and then thought about whether this would make him an employee, but Ahmed's face brightened to a near-satire of someone seizing on new hope. Ben began again. "Would you ever want me to . . . look at something sometime?"

"That would be very good. I would like that."

"All right. When's your next paper due?"

"Two weeks."

"What's it about?"

★ ★ ★

Leon knocked on Ben's door and said he had a call down in the basement.

Ben heard Teddy's voice and had so expected his mother's voice that it was as though he were actually hearing her voice when his brother said, "You're quitting squash?"

"Yeah, I quit before Christmas."

"That's what Mom said."

"Yeah."

"Is Price pissed?"

"I think so, but they got this new player, this English kid who's amazing, so I don't think he really cares."

"Oh," Teddy said, and stayed quiet. Ben wondered if that was it and he had already ended the call.

"Do you miss SJS?" Ben asked.

"Miss it?"

"Yeah."

"What's SJS?"

Ben laughed. "Shut up."

"I got to go," Teddy said, and hung up.

★ ★ ★

Two days later, Ben skipped wrestling and walked to the courts; the squash team had an away match. For forty minutes he lost himself in the ease of his body.

But when he turned to leave the courts, Price was there, smiling. He looked as stiff and upright as a wooden stepladder folded together.

"See?" Price said. "It's not up to you."

"Aren't you at Brooks today?"

"You even know the schedule."

Ben didn't say anything for a while, staying very still. Finally he said, "You said you don't want me on the team if I don't want to be there."

"But you do. Look at you."

"You've got the Brit now."

"Gray can take care of himself."

Ben felt like anything he could say would make him more vulnerable, so he stayed quiet and went to slip his racquet into his bag.

"The Dragon doesn't matter. Vandalizing the Dragon can't pry you away from this." Price laughed. "The Dragon has nothing to do with squash. Even you and me, this building, none of it has anything to do, really, with squash. So you got a little rebellion out of your system. Now your tuition stuff is settled, so we're back at the beginning. We can start again."

"Why do you want me to do this? Why do you care?"

"I care, but not that much, not really. If you don't play, there'll be other kids after you. Always another year. This season is already over in a couple months. Pfft, like that. When I don't see you, I don't think about you. But *you* care. I'm here because, for you, if you don't let this through you, it'll run you over. Or you'll have to cut out that part of yourself, and you're empty.

"It's worse to stay away and be empty than it is to come back and lose. Gray is very good. He's better than you, but that's not enough to keep you away."

"I'm getting what I need from wrestling."

"No, you're no good at wrestling, so you can let yourself just 'do your best.' You can blame giving way on just not being very good. You have to play squash because in squash, you're good enough to know exactly when you're giving way."

Ben's eyes began to unfocus with tears. "Please leave me alone," he said.

"It's not me," Price said softly.

And he waved in a small way and turned to leave, coughing as though armoring himself for the outside cold before pushing through the emergency exit.

★ ★ ★

That night Ben came back to the room after dinner, expecting Ahmed to be frowning at his computer screen, working on the Twombley paper. But instead he was sitting on the couch with his head all the way back on the leather headrest, his eyes open and glassy. Ben put down his bag and turned to Ahmed, who didn't move. "Are you baked?" Ben asked.

"No." He laughed.

"Ahmed, why are you doing this?"

He didn't answer for several seconds. "Doing what?"

Ben wanted to say, *The school expects that a boy will never use intoxicants of any kind.*

"Hanging out with Tommy."

"Who else treated me well after Ennis was expelled?"

Ben didn't answer right away. "You've had other friends."

Ahmed laughed.

"Hideo?" Ben said.

"Even since the first day, swimming to the Jesus Rock, all the Jell-Os at the Dish . . ."

Ben waited and was just about to speak again.

"Tommy and Graham and . . . They are the first to treat me like it is better for me to be around. Like an asset."

Ben wished he could say words out loud without Ahmed's being able to hear them—What about me?—and only after hearing them choose whether to transmit them. Would he speak more clearly if there were no money between them? "But that doesn't mean you have to smoke."

Ahmed sighed. "It is the only time I feel relaxed. Everyone looks at me. All the time I am supposed to be calm and prepared for everything. All the time there are more things I should be doing, more I should be trying to be. When I am nimbo I get to sit back."

Ben had never heard the word "nimbo" before, and not knowing it rattled him.

"But, I mean...what if you get caught?"

Ahmed didn't answer right away. "Mr. Markson, he gave you 'Decision-Making' to read?"

"We've talked about this."

Ahmed paused for long enough that Ben wondered whether he had lost the thread of the conversation. "Well," said Ahmed, "when I was home, in Dubai..." He paused again.

"Yeah?"

"Well...my family lives in a complex. A group of buildings with a pond in the middle. And another complex is being constructed next to ours. We were driving home, waiting behind several cars at the gate, and we were stopped near the construction zone.

"And I looked over to watch the workmen pouring concrete. I have always been fascinated by concrete, how it will not harden if it always moves, and so I watched the barrel spin on the back of the truck. There was a large spout attached to the end of the barrel, and out of the spout came concrete, a great deal of it very quickly. Two workers guided it into a narrow trench.

"I looked at their faces and clothes and hands. They were so dusty. Their skin, their pants and shirts, even their hair below their helmets was covered, so it seemed that their clothes and bodies were all dust.

"The concrete was coming very fast, and the spout seemed very heavy, and the men were trying hard to move it to a new position. And then it seemed that the whole truck moved, and the spout swayed into the chest of one of the men, and I saw him fall forward into the trench.

"Just then our car rolled forward, and I tried to keep looking back, tried to see them pull him out, but another truck was in the way. But just before the car pulled forward I could see, and the concrete did not stop coming. Maybe they pulled him out, but still they did not stop the flow. It kept coming."

They were quiet, and then Ben said, "Ugh."

"On the way there," Ahmed said, "on the plane, I had been reading that book."

"The *Companion*."

"Yes." Ahmed was quiet for several seconds. "And when this happened, I didn't know what to do."

"Like should you have helped him? The worker?"

"Yes, that." His tone was almost dismissive. "Yes, I should have helped him. But also, how—" Here Ahmed trailed off again, and Ben felt a pulse of impatience.

"How...?"

"How would that book apply to *him*? To this workman? What would he think, reading that? Those rules seem very good for when you have the time to pause and consider what to do. But does it tell that worker how to live at all? Like Hector, and Benito, who were here to help me move in. I have no idea where they are now, how they are able to live. When that worker is waiting to be hired, when he gets hurt, when he waits for others to consider their choices about him? He doesn't decide. He has to wait. No matter what happens, he waits."

"Yeah."

"And if I live in one of these complexes, no matter what I choose, that workman suffers. I can decide this or that, but just my existence determines his life. Or the life of another workman like him. So I think, whether I sometimes do or do not smoke with Tommy, maybe it is not the most important thing to wonder about."

Ben was quiet. "Yeah, hm.

"But don't—" Ben paused. "Don't Tommy and the rest of them like, make fun of you?"

Ahmed looked at him, amazed. "Why would they make fun of me?"

★ ★ ★

Since before Christmas Ben had been thinking about stopping by Alice's room during intervisitation. He knew what he would write in a note for her if he had the chance.

Hey Alice, I was here. Ben.

Funny in its oversimplicity. Yes he wanted to talk with her, ask her about everything that was happening to him and to Ahmed. But part of him also just wanted to leave a note and get away. The worst possibility was that she would come back to her room halfway through his leaving it.

A note in your room: the token that someone has been in your space without you there. He has gone to your desk and pulled a Post-it pad toward himself, taken one of your pens and noticed what kind of pen it is. Some girls put whiteboards with markers on their doors, but the entire hallway sees a note on a whiteboard.

As soon as he stepped out of his dorm he could see Paige House across the snow, behind the Dragon. Who would be in the common room to see him come in? Ben walked along the path and reached the bottom of the Paige terrace and wished he could have met someone on the way over to legitimately divert him from what he was about to do.

Ben prayed for her not to be there. He wanted to perform his courageous act and not have to endure the moment when she looked in his eyes and recognized for certain what he intended and how much she could decide about his immediate future.

He wished he could stop time and just go inside and look at the inside of her room. Where would she be sitting? Would there be a delay that he had to walk around? What if her roommate— did she have a roommate?—was there too? What color would the couch be? What if she had a thousand stuffed animals, or boy-band posters—and god, as he thought about stuffed animals he thought about her sitting on her bed as they talked, and the idea of seeing her there...if that could ever possibly come to pass— all of it was too much, and before he could reach the Paige steps, he stopped and went back. He could always see her later.

Ben returned to his room that night to find a note on his desk.

Yo,

I'm taking those pictures for that independent study. Any interest in being in them?

A

★ ★ ★

"I have no idea what I'm doing," she said.

Ben glowed with discomfort on a gray metal stool.

"What do you want me to do?"

"I don't know, just be there."

As she bent over and looked through the viewfinder of the camera, Alice wondered whether Ben was sick. His color was okay but he seemed shaky, as though he was back to his first day. Alice held a shutter-release device that looked like a syringe on a long cable, but she kept staring through the viewfinder without squeezing it.

The Art Building smelled of paint thinner and clay, and she was too far away now for him to catch her scent. Behind him on the wall of the studio was pinned a large piece of gray canvas that hung in long, shadowed arcs and reminded Ben of fashion shoots from the eighties.

Every time Alice leaned over to inspect the camera, Ben couldn't help looking for a second at her chest covered by a loose-fitting chamois shirt, even though he knew she could see his eyes through the viewfinder. She seemed performatively fixated on the camera.

"That's a nice camera," Ben said.

"Yeah, Ahmed loaned it to me. He said he never uses it. 'There are enough beautiful pictures of the school,' he said."

Ben didn't know if he felt usurped by this. "Who else are you taking pictures of?"

"Bunch of people."

"Why did you ask me?"

Just then she snapped a photo. The camera auto-wound to the next exposure.

"When I was thinking about people to photograph, I just thought that you seem pretty self-conscious a lot of the time, as though you aren't sure"—*snap*—"how you come off to other people, and that difference between how you suspect you might come off"—*snap*—"and how you actually come off is interesting. It gives you"—*snap*—"a sort of vivid look, and I wondered if I could get that"—*snap*—"on film." *Snap.*

A vivid look. Ben didn't know what that meant. He swallowed and began speaking as she continued to take pictures. He had to concentrate hard on saying even a few words to keep his self-consciousness from entangling him, and he remembered this same feeling with Nina, who now seemed decades removed. "How do you think you come off?" he asked.

"Me?" she said.

He nodded and she took a picture.

"Well, I'm pretty self-conscious too."

"Hm."

"Yeah"—*snap*—"so I guess we're"—*snap*—"like partners in self-consciousness."

Ben almost told her everything right then, but it felt good to leave it, and he found that he was laughing with pleasure as she kept snapping photos, and she started laughing too.

"Don't laugh, you're ruining them," she said.

12. Half Unfolded

January verged over into February, and the temperature rose just enough for a grinding rain to start up after classes. Ben had started to skip wrestling practice, but no one called him out. The team itself seemed to be dissolving and they had lost three meets in a row.

Dark puddles formed in the footprints in the snow, and after class Ben came back to the room in soaked clothes and shoes. His Sauconys now had small tears along each toe box. He didn't know how they were going to make it through the semester. He stripped to his boxers in the hallway and carried his clothes into the room, then pulled back the curtain to his closet and dropped everything into the white plastic hamper. Also in the hamper were all of his towels. The one he had used that morning smelled like mildew, but he wanted to take another shower now to warm himself up. He knew he shouldn't, but he pulled back the curtain to Ahmed's closet to find one of those spectacular towels. He would throw it in the dryer downstairs before Ahmed even knew it was gone.

He had never bought Ahmed new towels after throwing up on them in the fall, and it was too late for that now.

At the back left-hand corner of Ahmed's closet, beneath the neat rows of suits and shirts on hangers, Ben saw the Coach satchel, empty now and compressed thin with its strap folded over the top edge. Next to that was an L.L.Bean shoe box that looked like the one Ben's slippers had come in. Had Ahmed bought slippers without consulting him? Ben had a strange urge to turn and make sure his own slippers were in his closet.

Ben took a half step farther in, squatted, and pulled the box toward him. It was light, too light to hold shoes, but not so light that it could be empty. Ben lifted the top. The loose vacuum of the box resisted for a moment. Then the top came away, and Ben caught the smell before he saw a gallon-size Ziploc bag full of dark green pot. Ben wanted to put the top back on and open it again to see if there would be something different there the second time. He kept looking at the bag, at the buds that were each so verdant and so dense that they didn't completely flatten against the transparent plastic. Carefully he replaced the lid and slid the box back into place.

That night Ahmed came back to the room at eleven, and Ben was reading on the couch. Ahmed began to go through his rituals of getting ready for bed. Finally Ben got himself to speak.

"Ahmed, why do you have a box of pot in your closet?"

Ahmed turned and looked at him without any surprise in his face.

"Tommy said no one would guess it was in my room," Ahmed said. "Which is true, if you think about it."

"In our room, Ahmed. No one would think it was in our room."

"Which is true."

"But I didn't decide to take that risk. And if they do find it here, I get caught too."

"You will not get caught because you did not know it was here."

"But they won't make that distinction. You're responsible for whatever's in your room, and now I know it's here."

"But why were you looking in my closet?"

"That's not the point."

"What?"

"That's not the important issue here, Ahmed."

"I think it is the important issue. Why were you looking through my things?"

"I saw the L.L.Bean shoe box and I knew you didn't own L.L.Bean shoes."

"But the shoe box was not out in the middle of the room. It was down at the bottom of the closet. Why were you looking in my closet?"

"People talk. It might be safe right now to hide drugs in your room—"

"Lower your voice," Ahmed said. Ben startled, and Ahmed continued. "And never go into my things again."

Ben went on in a lowered voice: "It's safe to do it now because you don't have a reputation yet, but people talk, and soon people know that you're the kid who keeps drugs in his room."

"No one knows. No one will find out if you stay quiet. So stay quiet."

"But people see you hanging out with Tommy. He smokes constantly, and people see you hanging out with him, which means that you smoke too, or you sit and watch him while he smokes, which no one does."

Ahmed stood still, looking at Ben, and didn't say anything.

"Please take that shit back to Tommy," Ben said.

"No."

"Trust me, it's a bad idea."

"Thank you for your advice."

"Doesn't it affect your squash, though? Doesn't it make it harder to play well?"

Ahmed didn't answer.

"Please, Ahmed, I really don't want it in here."

"I understand that you don't want it in here. It will not be a part of your life in the room."

"What does that mean?"

"It means that if you stay in your parts of the room, you will have the situation that you want."

"That is not a satisfying answer."

"It is the answer you are getting."

★ ★ ★

Ben found a slip in his PO box: it was time to schedule Spring Term advisor meetings. Markson held three consecutive evenings open and invited each advisee to his faculty apartment in Calder House.

Markson's door was propped open, and when Ben came to the threshold and looked in, he saw Tyler Reichenbach sitting in one of the armchairs near the door and Markson facing him from the couch. Tyler looked up and Markson turned and then smiled and held up one finger.

When it was Ben's turn to come in and sit down, he looked at the open door and heard other kids in the hall. He stood up again.

"Do you mind if I close the door?" Ben asked.

"Ah, we're actually required to keep the door open. Faculty can't have students in their apartments with the door closed."

It took Ben a moment to realize what Markson meant, and when it came to him he blushed and shook his head and sat back down. Markson laughed.

"So?" Markson said. Ben so badly wanted to talk about Ahmed paying his tuition and now starting to hang out with Tommy.

Instead he said, "Wrestling...It's not..."

"Ah ha."

"Yeah."

"Okay, well, worth a try."

Ben didn't want it to be resolved that quickly.

"I'm also..." Ben could use the kind of problems that were possible to talk about. "Like the work, and the routine, it's all— like I get to Saturday night, and before I can recover it's already Sunday afternoon and I've got to do all my Monday work."

"You feel burned out."

"In a way."

"And are you interested in the work? In the courses you're taking?"

"I guess."

"Hm. Do you know Alice Morehead?" Markson asked. Ben nodded. "She's working on a photography project. She had me come sit for a portrait. It seemed like she wanted to do it regardless of whether it would count."

"Yeah, I've sat for her."

"So can you find something to do that doesn't count?"

"I'll try."

They talked about how he might try to get work done during Friday free periods to make Sundays a little easier, and even though Ben didn't say any of the other things he wanted to say, he didn't want to leave, either.

* * *

Into mid–February the thaw continued. Water ran down the paths and turned around the storm drains. Kids defiantly shivered in polo shirts and shorts above their wellies and Bean boots. The ice over the pond became cloudy, and long puddles formed in its depressions.

It stayed warm for several more days, and a small hysterical fever broke out among the students. There was no way the warmth was going to last through spring. Until now everyone had securely braced themselves against the cold and dark, but suddenly they saw how much better life could be when it didn't sting to go outside, and the dread of having to descend back into winter caused a spasm of unhappiness.

Gray kept annihilating number ones at other schools. The *Colony* wrote two more articles about him, quoting another player coming off the court saying to a teammate, "I never want to play again." The crowds at home matches became known as the Gray-lanx. Ben finally just stopped showing up to wrestling practice, and in his restlessness he started going to the courts to hit by himself when he knew for sure that the team was at an away match.

At the beginning of the third week of the thaw, Henry Carter, a fifth-former in Gordon and the hockey goalie, was getting a blow job from his girlfriend, Hannah Burke. He pulled out and came on her face without telling her first, and they had never done that before. Hannah was a fifth-former in Paige, and, in response, she and the other Paige girls decreed a hookup ban on campus: if any girl was caught doing anything with her boyfriend, the Paige girls would make sure she either had a nervous breakdown or withdrew from school, or both. The ban would end whenever the Paige girls said it would end.

Faculty felt that something had gone wrong. It took long minutes for Chapel to quiet down before morning announcements, kids began to miss classes, and there was even a shouting match in the Den over a game of pool.

The kids who already hadn't been hooking up with anyone felt delicious schadenfreude for a few days, but as the clammy humidity went on, even the teachers and staff began to bristle over little nothings.

One afternoon before Seated, Ben came back to the room to find a note on the little table in front of the couch. His chest felt light for a moment and then it wasn't for him. Across a piece of the buff stationery Ahmed used to write to his father, someone had written in blue ballpoint,

The 27th works for everybody. Cool?

That day was February fifteenth, a Tuesday, so the twenty-seventh was two Sundays away.

The weather stayed warm, and over the next two weeks Ben saw three more notes, all with the same handwriting. He imagined Tommy in their room, looking at Ben and Ahmed's things.

We're all set with the guy. Come by.

There's no problem having it all together, right? Let me know.

We're gonna do bus instead of car.

On the Tuesday afternoon before whatever was being planned for the twenty-seventh, Ahmed swung open the door and strode into the room. Ben was there reading the Tintin comic book, *The Seven Crystal Balls.*

"Mr. Twombley gave me a high grade on my English paper!"

Ben looked at the outstretched page and saw that it was an Honors, the equivalent of a B. Ben made himself see the friendliness of the exchange after their pot standoff.

"Ahmed, that's so great."

"And look at the passage he circled here." Ahmed flipped two pages and moved beside Ben. "This was the one I asked you about, the one I could not get to go correctly."

Ben looked. Ahmed's father loved falconry, and Ahmed had wanted to draw a comparison between hunting with falcons and hunting for chestnuts in Wordsworth's "Nutting," but he hadn't been able to make the sentences parallel until Ben had straightened it out.

"That makes me so happy, Ahmed. I'm so glad."

"Thank you, Ben. I appreciate it very much."

Maybe it wasn't too late.

"We should celebrate," Ben said. "Want to go into town soon? Get some dinner?"

Ahmed smiled. "Yes, I would like that."

"Great. How about Sunday?"

Ahmed's smile changed. "Ah, Sunday. I can't."

"What are you up to?"

"I am signing out to go to Boston with Tommy and Graham."

"Oh, cool," said Ben. "Getting dinner or whatever?"

"Yes," Ahmed said.

They stopped talking.

"How has squash been?" said Ben.

"Everyone is thrilled and nervous about Gray. But I've been in the same place for a while. Still players on the team think I should lose to them. As though I am lucky every time I beat them."

"But you beat them."

"Some. But I am still on JV. Peter Rutherford, he always gets me by three or four points. And Price, he seems to never remember that I'm on the team. He seems to look at me as a visitor every time, someone visiting for every practice and every match."

"Would you want to play varsity?"

"Of course."

"Well, let's go hit."

"I'm sorry?"

"Why don't we go to the courts? Maybe I can see something you don't see."

Ahmed smiled a more guarded smile than Ben had seen before.

"You would want to hit with me?"

"Listen, head over there and start warming up and I'll come in a few."

Twenty minutes later Ben came quietly up behind the court and for a few seconds watched Ahmed. Ahmed took his racquet back with some extra ceremony, but otherwise his strokes were simple and relaxed, and Ben saw the rhythm of the smack off the front wall and the long slide against the side wall and the one-two bounce off the floor and the back wall and the new stroke falling easily through him. Maybe smoking pot didn't harm his game; maybe it made it better.

Ahmed shanked a ball and turned to pick it up, and in seeing Ben, gave a restrained smile. Ben's smile looked true to Ahmed; not patronizing or reluctant, or like Ben was doing something owed.

Without saying anything Ben changed into his court shoes, stepped through the door, and closed it behind him. Ahmed could see Ben showing off slightly, relishing the crisp volleys back to himself, but before going on for too long he knocked the ball gently over to Ahmed.

"Want me to feed you rails?" Ben said.

Ahmed nodded, feeling as though this would be beneath Ben but not wanting to contradict him.

And so they hit. Ben placed the ball a foot out from the wall two steps in front of Ahmed, and Ahmed stepped in and hit the forehand simply, and Ben put the ball back in the same place. They did it on the backhand side.

"Try bringing your racquet back even farther," Ben said.

Ahmed did, and it was awkward for two strokes.

"Not just your arm; turn with your body a little more."

And Ahmed did, and they both could feel the ball spring to the front wall with new life.

At that moment Ben remembered being on court with his dad so many years before. They were having a bad session. Ben felt like there wasn't enough time to get his racquet back for each ball, and every part of the movement felt like a separate thing dropped into a sack and shaken, and he was near tears.

"Ben." His father held the ball and looked at him. "Don't worry about being good. It's fine to be having trouble. Just do the thing we talked about—try to hit the ball with the butt of your racquet and then turn your wrist like a doorknob—and don't even expect the ball to get to the front wall. It's not your job to hit a good shot. Your only job is to make that movement."

Ben was still young enough to think that his dad was the best squash player in the world. More than that, he murkily thought that his dad *was* squash, was the original source of the game. This act of releasing Ben from hitting a good shot had seemed vast.

At some point later Ben suddenly understood that his dad was actually a fairly middle-of-the-road player, and then they played their first match where his dad wasn't totally in control, and then inevitably and with some sadness Ben beat his dad, and then beat him while hardly ever losing control of a point.

But the sadness was only ever on Ben's side. Harry had never strived with such pleasure as when Ben finally pulled away from him. His son's play became so much more complex, more creative and surprising. It was to Harry as though he had been paddling on a shallow river by unremarkable trees in midday light, and then that river had begun to deepen, and it deepened and deepened until toward dusk its movement had gained an ancient living gravity. Ben had sort of forgotten how much delight he had felt from his father on court.

"All right," Ben said. "Hit twenty more like that. Right, that twist. Good."

Ahmed felt his body moving in this pattern, and he felt some of the gratitude and belonging that he had always expected to feel with Ben. But he also tried to sense whether Ben was trying to move him away from Tommy, to take that from him.

They switched sides back to the forehand.

"What if you took the racquet straight back."

"Straight?"

Ben held Ahmed's racquet and moved it into the right shape. "Just quicker, simpler. See?"

"I think so."

"Hit a couple."

He did, but this one seemed not to take as easily, and Ben could sense Ahmed getting slightly frustrated. Pushing him through this would maybe feel like getting even, but he tried to resist.

"We'll work on it next time."

"Next time, yes."

★ ★ ★

The next day after fifth period, Ben caught sight of Tommy's loose-knit rust-colored winter hat heading down the stairs of the Schoolhouse and went down the same stairs after him. Tommy was by himself, pushing through the heavy outside doors, and without really knowing what he was doing, Ben went through the same doors and started following him from a distance through the slush.

Ben wanted to walk up beside Tommy and say something, but he had never spoken directly to an upper-former without being spoken to first. So he kept following. As he passed the Den, he saw Helena Rusk coming toward him, and he realized that she was one of the cusp-beautiful girls he had seen the first day, but now he knew her name, knew her reputation as really good at the oboe but not so bright otherwise. Very clearly she now knew more about how to regulate the attention that she acknowledged and paid out.

Tommy walked behind the quad past the squash courts (already the Dragon was developing a patina over its bright grinder marks), and it was clear that he was heading along the tree-covered path back to Gordon, where he lived.

As Tommy came out onto the lawn in front of Gordon, Ben paused at the edge of the woods and watched him go inside. He jogged up to the door and pulled it open. He had no idea which room was Tommy's, but he heard gritty footsteps on the stairwell above him and so he climbed up two steps at a time, trying to make his footfalls as quiet as possible. On the second floor he was just able to see Tommy's back foot as it disappeared into the last room on the right. Ben was quietly disappointed. He had half expected Tommy to be living in an unknown turret or gigantic basement somewhere instead of in just a regular room.

Ben walked down the hallway toward the door Tommy had gone through. Taped to it was a postcard of the Vietnamese monk consumed by flame. Ben almost knocked, but then he caught himself—only faculty knock—and he was stuck standing there in the hallway, not prepared to go in but not able to leave.

Then he heard footsteps coming up the stairs and he didn't want to be caught there just standing in the hall, so he turned the knob and went inside. Tommy had a delay bookshelf immediately behind the door with a black-and-white poster of Jack Nicholson's ecstatic face pressed up to the chopped-open gap in the wood.

"Tommy?" Ben said softly after the door had closed behind him. There was no answer. Ben stepped around the delay and into the main part of the room. It was empty.

The windows faced away from where the sun had started to set, and so in the late afternoon with no lights on, the space was gray-blue and very still, as though whoever lived there had been sent home.

"Tommy?"

Tommy wasn't there. Ben looked over the room, and even though he could see the whole place in one view, he looked back and forth from the unmade bed to the pink stuffed couch over and over again, as though looking for misplaced keys. The stereo was on, but it was a McIntosh tube amp, and guys never turned them off because it took a while for the vacuum tubes to warm up properly.

But there on the oval braided rug were Tommy's dark brown docksiders with white soles. Ben wanted to kneel down and put the back of his hand up to the insides of the shoes to see if they were still warm. Then he did get on his hands and knees to check for Tommy under the bed. Four wide plastic storage bins.

"Tommy?"

Had Tommy gone out the window and climbed to the roof? Had Ben imagined seeing him come into the room? Ben got strangely afraid, as though the rules were different in this room; because Tommy was known to do so many drugs, maybe the room itself was inducing an altered state of mind. Ben looked at the books on the room side of the bookshelf: *Cat's Cradle, The Hitchhiker's Guide to the Galaxy, The Tale of Genji.*

Ben was about to leave when he thought to look in the closet. The couch was set across the closet opening, which a lot of kids did to maximize wall space and to leave a convenient place to set a bong out of sight. Tommy had hung a New Zealand flag over the closet opening, and Ben put a hand on the couch's backrest and leaned over to pull the flag aside.

As he did, a hand grabbed him around the wrist and shoved his arm away. Ben let out an embarrassing whoop and sprang away.

"What the fuck?" Ben said.

"What the fuck, you?" The flag still hung flat. "What the fuck are you doing in my room when you can see I'm not here?"

Ben decided to be the kind of person who persists. He took off his backpack and set it on the floor. "Come out of the closet, Tommy."

"I'm not here."

"Seriously, Tommy. I'm not leaving, man."

"Well, I'm not coming out, so you're going to have to come in."

"What?"

"Get your ass in here, before someone comes in and wonders what the hell you're doing in my room. Stop flailing."

Ben paused. Then he lifted his foot and was about to set it on the couch when Tommy said, "Are you stepping on the couch with your shoes on, man? Take that shit off."

Ben took off his shoes, climbed on the couch and straddled the backrest, then hopped his weight over, getting half jammed in the opening and tangled in the flag.

"Jesus, what a flail."

Ben pulled himself clear of the flag and looked around. There were no hanging clothes inside the closet, and all the walls had been painted dove-gray. Tommy sat on an armless stuffed chair at one end, looking up at Ben with hard eyes under his black hair.

The space was lit by a short string of Christmas-tree lights stapled along the molding.

"Sit," Tommy said.

Ben turned around and there was an identical chair behind him at the other end of the closet.

"Where do you put all your clothes?"

"Under the bed. Why hang when you can fold? Now sit."

Ben sat.

"What do you want?" Tommy said.

"I want you to leave Ahmed alone."

Tommy laughed. "No. Why do you even care?"

"He can't keep up with you guys," Ben said. "You, Graham, Morgan—you guys can handle your shit and still pass your classes and like function in front of faculty, but Ahmed can't. He hardly goes to class anymore." Ben knew he himself wouldn't be able to keep it together if he started doing any drugs, and he wanted to ask Tommy how he had learned to do it.

"You don't give Ahmed enough credit."

"What?"

"You don't see what he's good at."

"All right, what's he good at?"

"You'd know if you were his friend."

Ben was too exasperated to speak for a long second.

"Why would you even hang out with Ahmed at all? You're cool. He's not cool." Ben was embarrassed to have said it this plainly. "And he got Ennis kicked out."

Tommy laughed again. "I hated Ennis. When I was a newb, Ennis hit golf balls at me with a tennis racquet. And it wasn't even Ahmed's fault. Ennis would have gotten kicked out for hazing some other newb."

"Seriously," Ben said, "there's no reason for you to take him up."

Tommy shook his head. He was amazed and half impressed that Ben, this antenna of a person, had ventured into his closet. But Ben was also so owned by what the school had told him to be. "You don't see him."

"What?"

"Ahmed's not ashamed of himself. Everyone else here, their worry makes every move for them, just the fear of putting a foot wrong. But like, my Chapel seat is near Ahmed's? And he sings the hymns. He sings them loudly. No one else does that."

With a sudden filling of his throat Ben saw Ahmed, blazing with unselfconsciousness, walking flat-footed to the bathroom in his robe, carrying his shower caddy. Hutch arrived in Ben's mind, and he knew that it was exactly this that affronted Hutch so thoroughly: Ahmed's original, unveneered lack of shame. But now the marks of guile had started to appear.

Then another idea came to him and was out of his mouth before he could stop it. "Is he paying for all the weed?"

"Ha!" Tommy's eyes went wide in disbelief. "You—of all people—you're the one coming to my room, accusing me of using Ahmed for his money? That is just amazing."

So it was out. Of course Ahmed had betrayed him.

Ben didn't say anything. He expected Tommy's face to turn mocking, gleeful, for him to leave the room now and pull aside everyone he saw on the paths, telling them about Ahmed's paying for Ben. But Tommy's face stayed solemn, and then turned heavy, as though he were holding up some familiar weight of his own.

"Listen," Tommy said, "no one's going to hear it from me. Me and Ahmed got nimbo one night in here and he was telling me about this paper he got an H on, and he said he was glad you were still here. And I asked him what he meant and he told me."

Each of them seemed to be by himself for a few moments. Ben tried to get used to this new loss of control.

"Listen, we're his friends; we're not going to let anything bad happen to him."

★ ★ ★

The hookup blackout had been on for three weeks. But Henry Carter, the goalie whose abuse had caused the ban, was playing better than ever, and he wasn't planning on apologizing until after the season was over. Everyone knew the ban was being broken here and there, but overall it had been much more effective than the school's own no-sexual-contact policy. The Paige girls started to prowl through dorms during intervis, bursting into the rooms of known couples to try to catch them scrumping. Miraculously they had only caught one couple, but they then spilled maple syrup in the girl's hair in the dining hall and stopped her every time they passed in the halls and measured her waist with a tailor's tape.

And still, if years later you asked people what they remembered about that time, many would say it was the most intensely romantic period of their lives. To have another person's body so off-limits seemed to make everything, all sense experience, almost painfully keen.

A boy and girl know a place, the Trophy Room, where the Paige girls can't find them. So after dinner she packs notebook paper into the strike plate of the gym's side door. They wait in the Den until an hour before check-in, ostentatiously sitting apart from each other.

Each of them gives a different reason for leaving: work for physics, friend with something to talk over in the dorm. She leaves first, and he slowly finishes the game of air hockey.

They meet up again behind the gym instead of at the side en-trance, and they kiss there, sure they won't be seen. They slip around the outside of the building toward the door, the most ex-posed they'll be, each with delicious fearful impatience to get inside out of sight, each exaggerating the danger to goose that feeling.

Into the inner hallway glowing under the EXIT sign, through the double doors to the Trophy Room. Burgundy leather couches sit against three of the walls, and they choose the one farthest from the door. He sits, she kneels astride him. They have already decided, and they keep their precipice-feeling as he puts on the condom the wrong way and then laughs jaggedly and turns it over and rolls it down with fast graceless pushes.

Now both of them want to postpone it. But already he's tying off the condom and she's making sure she finds the wrapper, and they want to kiss goodbye, but outside in the air they can't, and then it's time for them to go along separate paths toward their dorms, and she clings to his arm and he pulls her into his body almost as hard as he can, both of them walking in the warm-cold trying to tell the other silently that they are still in love, even though they're too embarrassed to look at each other and too embarrassed to say the other's name.

★ ★ ★

After talking with Tommy, Ben went to dinner, then came back to the room and found Ahmed cleaning his ears with a Q-tip. Ahmed wore an expression of listening intently for a sound just out of range, and he spun the swab slowly between his thumb and fore-finger. This person, this defenseless person cleaning his ears, was now fully enmeshed in the most hidden, tender parts of Ben's self.

Ben looked away from Ahmed and thought about the woman

who came to clean their house at home, Marisol. Whenever Ben discovered his swim trunks neatly folded on his neatly made bed, he would imagine Marisol in his bedroom alone—with her carefully dyed hair and the darknesses between her teeth—cleaning. Ben imagined her imagining him: a little boy who left his swim trunks on the floor and had been given an entire room to himself. You could imagine a person like Marisol—what she saw and what she thought of you—but you could also let that person fade away. And then when you came back to your clean room, it was the room itself that had become neater in its own course, and the trunks had appeared there folded like that because that is how swim trunks end up.

Maybe this was supposed to fade in that same way. Maybe tuitions are paid because that is how tuitions end up.

But now as Ben walked to Chapel in the fevery mornings, he couldn't keep these thoughts out of his head. He came inside without taking his scarf off his face. He passed Aston's seat. For the hundredth time he passed Markson, and Dennett—Price was all the way down at the other end of the nave; thankfully he didn't have to pass Price—and the rest of the faculty, all of them looking out over the students. How long before the news spread? Again, the inevitable litany: *druggie, stress case, kid with the rich expat paying for him, anorexic, smug jock, slut* . . . How long until all the students knew? It would be so much worse than being on scholarship and having people find that out, so much more abject a disgrace if Russell knew he had had to resort to this.

★ ★ ★

That Saturday a cold front started east across the Great Lakes, and early Sunday morning Ahmed was out of the room. The temperature kept going down all day, and by sunset it had reached sixteen degrees. Coming back from the Dish, Ben was under-dressed in his khakis and the North Face with just a sweater underneath, and he shuffled fast down the path toward Hawley. He lifted his head at the quiet scratching of wheels on ice, and beyond the rerusting Dragon he saw Tommy, Ahmed, and Graham getting out of a cab in the gym parking lot. They were all underdressed too, in khakis or jeans and sweaters, and Graham had a wide, heavily loaded hockey duffel over his shoulder.

Ben slowed down as the group looked both ways and crossed the Two-Laner. Ben didn't want to be seen, and he kept moving down the path to Hawley. The three walked quickly, visibly hurting in the cold. Then a movement caught Ben's eye and he turned and saw the near-elderly history teacher and football coach, Mr. Turow, emerging from around the side of Paige. He was heading toward the gym. He would pass Ahmed and Tommy and Graham on the path right next to the Dragon. Turow had his hands deep in the pockets of his buckskin jacket, and he wore a red buffalo plaid hunting cap pulled down over his forehead.

Ben watched as the group of boys and Mr. Turow approached each other. He saw how it would happen. Graham would set a run-ning shoe on a patch of ice and go down, and one of the bottles in the duffel would shatter against the blacktop, and Mr. Turow would ask to look in the bag and find not only alcohol. All of them would be busted and Ahmed would be gone and he would be gone.

Ben knew he could start walking more quickly, pretending he was going to the gym too, and intercept Turow. He could ask him a simple question about the football off-season and just start talking, and Ahmed, Tommy, and Graham would pass at a safe distance in front of them. But Ben stopped. He remained where he was. He let them all coast into each other.

But Graham didn't slip, and he waved in cold-weather fellow-ship to Mr. Turow, and Turow nodded wearily in reply. With simple haste, Graham, Tommy, and Ahmed continued to walk the path to Gordon until Ben couldn't see them anymore.

That night Ben checked in again with Mr. Tan. The temperature dropped to seven degrees, and someone poured a travel mug of dip-spit in Henry Carter's hair as he slept. Hannah Burke forgave him the next day, the sex ban came down, and the school's malaise was gone. Everyone left the windows open to the cold, sleeping well for the first time in weeks.

13. Wait for a Real Eclipse

Aᴴᴹᴇᴅ ɴᴏᴡ ᴇxᴄʟᴜsɪᴠᴇʟʏ sᴀᴛ ᴡɪᴛʜ Tᴏᴍᴍʏ ᴀɴᴅ ʜɪs ꜰʀɪᴇɴᴅs ᴀᴛ lunch and non-Seated dinners, and huddled on the padded chairs near the sixth-form couches after Seated. Eventually the last ship-ment would run out, and they would go and buy more, and even if they weren't caught bringing it back on campus, some teacher would catch them smoking and then look in someone's closet and find the sheer volume of what they had, and it would be impos-sible not to know they were distributing at school.

Ben and Ahmed played squash a few more times, Ben trying to keep him from being completely pulled into Tommy's orbit, tending Ahmed's hopes to play number 9—the last spot on varsity—for maybe one match by the end of the season.

"You should play with Gray," Ahmed said during one of their sessions.

"The Brit?"

"Yes. He and I speak. I think he's lonely. He's sort of bored with killing kids from other schools. I think the two of you

269

could play together. What we're doing when we come to the courts, it's okay, it's good and I'm very glad, but we're not to-gether in trying."

"Together?"

"You don't have to wonder if you can get to the next ball when we play. You and Gray need that."

Ben was tempted. Back in seventh grade, when everyone was still playing hardball, Ben had drawn Marcus Drew in the first round of Nationals. Everyone knew Marcus was al-most definitely going to win the tournament—he had in fact gone on to win it—but instead of being intimidated, Ben had felt relief stepping on the court so overmatched. From the first few points Ben had given Marcus a run; even on the points he lost he was almost there. Ben remembered the joy of just being a little piece of steel in the gears of some-one else's machine, knowing everyone else was watching some more marquee match and so feeling that he and Marcus were away playing in some elemental wilderness. Only one of his Um Club friends had come by to watch and was amazed it had gone to four games.

"Not me," Ben said now to Ahmed. "Come on, let's hit a few more."

"Maybe when the season's over."

"Let's hit."

★ ★ ★

After Seated, Hutch held a cup of coffee and just looked at Ben as he approached.

"What are you doing, man?"

"What?"

"Kyle saw you at the courts with Ahmed." He took a slow sip of the coffee. "Why are you at the fucking squash courts with Ahmed Al-Khaled?"

"Come on."

"You know we can't do anything while he's behind Tommy. But the least we can expect from our kind is to hold the line. We thought you were holding the line in your room, we thought you were with us."

"I am with you."

"I don't think you really care about the kind of man the school is supposed to create. I don't think you really worry about a day coming when everyone follows the rules, and is polite to everyone no matter what, and newbs have more rights than the hardest sixth-formers, and it's summer camp for rich kids."

A clamp of rage ejected the words out of Ben.

"Dude, I'm Teddy Weeks's brother. I come from a heritage of that shit. My family fucking established the codes you're just discovering."

"Sorry?"

"You think I don't know how to do that? Is that what you're saying, that I can't carry on that heritage?"

"I don't—"

"Next Sunday, we're going to Boston to buy. We're going to get people seriously wet. Get money together from your Woodruff crew for what they want, and we'll go."

"All right." Hutch had always hoped that Ben would be a conduit to the legendary. "You'll know where to go?"

"Of course I know."

"All right."

★ ★ ★

271

Ben called home, and exhaled with relief when his mom answered. Each of them reported that everything was fine. Ben let a pause arise.

"Listen, I know money's..."

"Ach, I know. I'm sorry."

"But would you be able to put a hundred dollars in my account?"

She was quiet before she could stop herself from being quiet.

"Sure, of course. I know, it must be hard not to—" she began.

"I want to take a girl out to dinner."

"Oh my gosh, little bird, that's so exciting! Tell me about her!"

"She's a class ahead of me."

"Look at you! Okay, so what's she like?"

"I mean, she's cool."

She laughed. "Cool how? Give me something concrete."

"Just... You just don't have to act around her. She's really good at photography. She's learning Japanese, and she's just really cool." Ben thought about Alice's smell, and whether in his life he would ever try to describe someone's smell to another person.

Helen asked what she looked like, and she could hear in Ben's response about her hair and height that he wished she hadn't asked, and it was as though she could see his shoulders turn from her.

Ben said, "Remind me how you and Dad met again?"

Her laugh crossed a span of so many years. "He was just out of business school. I worked typing papers for some of his business school friends." She paused to consider whether Ben was too young. "I was actually engaged to one of his classmates. We met at a party my fiancé was throwing."

"Really?" Ben laughed.

"I had made deviled eggs." She remembered again all the aspects of the party she always remembered—the grooved aluminum-edged serving table, the worryingly fancy punch bowl, those quick eyes behind thin glasses that belonged to this man who introduced himself as Harry. "We talked in the kitchen, with everyone all around us." They traded jokes so quickly. "And we were married less than a year later."

"No! The other guy must have been so pissed!"

"He got over it like that. Grant Hart, my god. He was married before your father and I were."

"Really?"

"Really. I think he thought I wasn't so smart. I had just graduated from secretarial school; that seemed more practical than trying for college. And Grant, I remember him coming home in the evenings and finding me typing these papers, and he always had a smile as though I had been made for just this, and everything in the world was as it should be with me typing out other people's thoughts."

Ben didn't know if he had ever heard her talk so much at one time, especially about herself, and he wondered whether she hadn't been talking very much to other people recently.

"And at that party, your father . . . We were talking about things we had both read, right by the finished drinks, and I think he was probably just trying to make conversation, but he said, 'What else might you want to do other than secretary work?'

"I guess I could have taken that as an insult. That he thought what I was doing was trivial. But I think that question was almost enough for me to decide to marry him. And after we were married, almost everyone else I knew stopped working to raise kids, but he asked me if I'd like to go back to college. And I said, yes, I really would like that.

"And when I told him I was thinking about getting a master's, and a PhD . . . I couldn't have even *said* the word 'scholar' with a straight face when I met him. Let alone 'anthropology scholar.' But, he just always seemed to think, why couldn't I do those things."

"Yeah, of course."

"I haven't thought about that in a while."

Ben remembered again his father's encouragement on the squash court. But also with tenderness Ben remembered the change in his father's face as he fixed his hair in the mirror: a slight arch in the eyebrows, a compression of the lips, a set of the eyes—his unconscious act of trying to convey handsomeness. He had taken on this look when talking to another person's fiancé!

"So what's her name?" his mom asked.

Ben briefly considered lying. "Alice." He paused. "Unlikely we'll be married in a year."

His mom laughed, and Ben closed his eyes with the pleasure of hearing that laugh.

"All right, we can put something in your account."

"A hundred?"

"Yes, a hundred."

★ ★ ★

Ben couldn't believe how easy it was to get ahold of Teddy. He had thought it would take days and only happen at four in the morning.

"So where do I go in Boston?"

"Where?"

"Yeah, like is there an easy place?"

"Little Benny boy, trying to get wet!"

"Shut up," laughed Ben.

"Lemme see... Yeah, right, there's a good store on Beach Street. Hold on."

Teddy told him how to navigate once he left South Station.

"Just act like you fucking own the place, man. Think to yourself that it's yours the entire time you're in there, while they watch you choose stuff, just think that you're doing *them* a favor by letting *them* be in the store while you're in the store too. You already own the vodka, they've just been keeping it for you. It's your fucking store. They only get to be there because you say so."

Ben nodded there in the basement, wanting to soak in this confidence and prevent it from draining out again.

"How's it been going out there?" Ben asked quietly.

"What, now that we're broke?"

Ben laughed.

"Yeah, now that we're broke."

"It's good, I guess. I've found some cool guys."

"Cool."

Teddy heard through the phone that Ben was missing the opportunities for life hidden in the curtains of St. James.

"So how are you dealing?" said Teddy. "They put you on aid, right? And you're still not going back to squash?"

"Nah. I mean, you stopped playing, right?"

"Yeah."

Ben let the silence go on. "I mean," Teddy said finally, "Price wanted me to keep playing, he made the pitch to me so many times, but I just had other things I wanted to do."

Ben felt protective now. He wondered if his brother had made himself believe it.

"Just—" Teddy went on, "by the time sixth form came around,

275

if I had been up the night before scoring beaver and getting wet, I always wanted to be able to take a nap before Seated. That's how I wanted to arrange my afternoons."

"Makes sense."

"So—"

"So how did you work it out there? Did Kenyon put you on aid?"

"No, dude."

"Then what?"

"They paid Kenyon."

Ben wanted to ask him to say it again, but he didn't speak.

"They had to pay Kenyon. I mean, Kenyon doesn't know who we are. You know? We *are* SJS, but here, I'm just another..." Teddy remembered the basements of the quad dorms, sitting there alone talking to their parents. "Put yourself in their shoes, Ben. What would you do?"

"Yeah."

"How do you think they're doing?"

"Hey, Teddy, someone's been waiting for the phone."

"Good luck in Chinatown, little cub. You own that store. It's been in our family for generations."

★ ★ ★

On the map, Chinatown looked like every other neighborhood. They sat on one of the long wooden islands in South Station, Ben holding the tourist map in front of him, Hutch and Evan looking on from either side. It was strange for Ben to be in a place with so many people suddenly, and under the high ceilings of the station it sounded like an aquarium.

"All right, so Teddy said Beach Street, which is here..." Ben ran his finger down the street to show them. They hadn't realized how close Chinatown was to the station.

"All right. All right, cool," said Evan. "So like, do we go in all at once or do we each go in one after the other?"

Ben went to answer but Hutch answered first. He thought the store would get more suspicious about the sheer volume of alcohol if the three of them had everything on the counter at once.

Ben said, "I think they'll catch on by the third fifteen-year-old in a row who comes in to buy five handles of vodka. Let's just go in and get it done. I mean, we're college kids buying for a party, right?"

All day they had been checking incessantly to make sure they had their IDs, and now they checked again. Ben had borrowed the ID of a fifth-former in Woodruff, Jamie Mason, and he thought that he actually did look a lot like the picture. They headed out. Just this much farther south the air contained the clammy hopes of spring now.

Right away they saw the concrete gate to Chinatown with the green pagoda roof. They passed under the arch and saw nests of signs in Chinese on every building all the way down Beach. Ben wished the sidewalks were full enough to conceal them. They passed a couple neon restaurants, but then there was a Subway, too, and Chinatown seemed not all that different from the rest of the city.

Almost immediately they were at the place. Ben had worried that he would be leading the other two around for hours, but now he somehow wished it had been more of a search. A yellow sign with red letters announced PACIFIC LIQUORS, with red Chinese characters underneath that presumably said the same thing. Three boxes of Veuve Clicquot were faded to yellow in the window display, and the glass of the door was clouded with adhesive and paper residue from dozens of stickers attached and removed. They all checked to see if they still had their IDs.

Hutch pushed the door open and brass bells on a string clattered, and they all walked in with their heads up, each of them with his empty duffel bag over his left shoulder. Ben tried to exude his ownership of the store. He tried to wear Teddy's body as he looked at the person behind the counter—a Chinese boy almost their age, it seemed—and got a bad feeling; kids left in charge of things follow the rules.

Ben remembered the different times he had been into liquor stores with his dad, and there was almost the same smell now—a high, slightly sour cork odor, but he could tell that a cat also lived in this store. The different kinds of liquor were grouped together, whiskey and gin and vodka and rum and tequila, each with its own bright wire shelving unit, various brands from top to bottom, and then two shelves with a scrum of liqueurs and other nonsense. Along the other two walls and on a small island in the middle of the store were various kinds of wine. Ben, Hutch, and Evan focused on vodka, their backs turned to the cashier, and Ben could feel how, with no one else in the store, the full weight of the cashier's scrutiny lay over them.

So. They looked at the different kinds. Brand names and prices in black marker on notecards taped to the metal shelves. English on top and then Chinese characters underneath—Ben wondered whether the characters on each label just listed the price, or whether they were transliterations of the words "Smirnoff" and "Absolut." Those brands were off the table, obviously. Quickly they arrived at Randolph's, which came in a plastic bottle with a hand grip molded into the back, and whose label featured a horse-drawn stagecoach. $8.99 per.

They had money for fifteen bottles. They had promised five different guys that they would buy for them. In Hutch's room as the others watched, Ben had taken out his own three twenty-dollar bills—the check for his new balance cashed at the bookstore—and slid them into the envelope. But here at Pacific Liquors there were only twelve bottles on the wire shelf. In two loads each, they brought all the bottles up and set them on the counter, white melamine worn down in patches to the dark brown underlayer. The floor behind the counter was slightly raised like a pharmacist's platform; the boy looked down at them.

"Hi," said Evan, "do you have more of the Randolph's in the back?"

"There's no back." Ben had expected him to barely speak English. Around his neck were the biggest pair of headphones Ben had ever seen, with plush leather earcups that reminded Ben of Ahmed's couch.

"Sorry?"

"There's no back room in the store. Our deliveries come through this door and we stock the shelves with the cases still on the floor."

Hutch said, "But do you have any more of the Randolph's?" Ben heard a pleading in his voice.

"Because there's no back, that would mean that we only have what's on the shelf."

Hutch said, "Are you sure?" and the boy looked at him with ancient boredom.

"We can just get another kind," said Evan.

"All the other kinds are more expensive," said Ben, not turning away from the Chinese boy. "We said we'd get fifteen."

"It's fine," said Hutch, "we'll just go somewhere else for the other three."

"But this is the place," said Ben. The two of them turned and looked at him. "This is the least expensive place."

Evan said, "Listen, we'll get these twelve and two Beefeater, and so we get fourteen, not fifteen, it's fine." He retrieved the two additional bottles and put them on the counter. They turned back to the cashier. The boy's hair was so black and smooth that it looked polished. "So we'll just take these."

"Can I see your IDs?" It arrived in Ben's mind with the authority of a closing gate: one of them should have come in and bought it all.

They all handed up their IDs. The kid looked straight at Evan.

"When were you born?"

"Nineteen seventy-two."

"What month?"

"...January."

"Why did it take you so long to answer?"

"I knew it. It's my birthday."

"If you were twenty-two, you'd be annoyed that I was asking so many questions."

"I'm just trying to ans—"

"Do you want our money or not?" said Ben. "We can just go to the place near the Common."

"So why didn't you?"

"Like he said, you've got the best prices."

"That costs the same everywhere," he said, glancing down at the bottles.

"Hey," said Ben. He counted softly as he pointed to pairs of bottles. "One hundred and thirty dollars: Yes or no?"

"If our store loses its license, a hundred and thirty dollars— Who cares?"

"We're twenty-one!" Hutch said. "You're not going to lose your license!"

The boy laughed.

Out on the street, Evan put his hands on his knees. "Fuck! Fuuuuuck! What the fuck are we going to do? We can't go back to school unwet."

"We got unlucky," said Ben. "There are other stores in China-town."

"You said *this was the place*," Hutch said to him quietly. "You said this was the place."

"Teddy said this was the place."

"I guess it doesn't matter what he said."

Ben looked up at the bright stripe of sky between buildings already in dusk. He had so few chances left. He knew Alice wouldn't care if he was able to buy, but he wanted this to impress her anyway.

Evan said, "I don't know, another place?"

Hutch tsked. "No one's going to think we're older than that guy thought we were, dude."

"But maybe someone will care less about taking fake IDs," Evan answered.

"Exactly," said Ben. "That kid was the problem. The regular owner would have totally sold to us."

"You said that was the easiest place," Hutch said to Ben. "That was the place anyone could knock over."

They chewed sandwiches in Au Bon Pain. The employees were without affect. There was a hectic family next to them and several people eating alone and reading or just looking out the window onto the train station.

Ben felt the other two figuring out what they were going to say when they got back to school.

"Look," Ben said.

"What?"

"That guy." He had to do it before he could stop. "Hey, 'scuse me," said Ben. "Hey, man."

281

The man had his head resting on the wall behind him, and he didn't lift it off as he turned his eyes to Ben. The other two came up just behind Ben and he could feel their reluctance.

The smell of the man came to Ben: his sweat was different from sweat at the gym. The man's eye-whites were the color of year-old newspaper, and his Southpole puffy coat had white wavy rings on it, as though it had dried after soaking in salt water.

"Hey, listen. Could you help us out?"

The man seemed wary, as though trying to anticipate how the boys were going to move.

"Could you help us out?"

"Yeah?"

Ben lowered his voice. "Can you buy us alcohol?"

The man passed his eyes over all their faces again, and then he smiled. His teeth were lighter than his eyes.

"You want me to walk in somewhere and break the law for you?"

They laughed fearfully and nodded.

The man didn't move, didn't lean toward them, and his smile didn't change. Ben wasn't sure if he had understood.

"Nah, I'm good here." He closed his eyes again.

"We'll pay you," Ben said.

The man opened his eyes again and looked at Ben. Ben held his gaze.

"Where're you thinking to buy from?" the man asked.

Hutch started but Ben cut him off. "Chinatown's right here."

The man lifted his head off the wall. Ben expected him to spit on the table.

"The birthday party got canceled without me, huh?"

Ben tried to change his expression to seem like he got some

joke. The man laughed and then coughed, a sound like shucking corn, and in unison all three boys leaned away.

Outside they all stood underneath the Chinatown arch. Everyone passing them, white and Chinese, looked at them in the expiring light. The streetlamps came on. They approached Pacific Liquors, but then Evan said the kid would recognize the duffel bags.

"Don't have all night, fellas."

"All right, it's fine. Just let him use one of them," Ben said.

They told the guy what they wanted: just the twelve, keep it simple, and he could have the money left over.

The three boys started to spread out. Hutch's hand went into his jacket pocket to take out the money, and Evan walked past the entrance to the store and stood on the other side. Ben walked to the edge of the sidewalk. Ben realized as the money came out that he was the last barrier in case the man decided to take the cash and run. Just as Ben realized it, he saw that the man understood what he was thinking too.

Then he went into the store. Ben was immediately convinced that there was a back exit he hadn't noticed and that they would never see the guy again. But a few minutes later he came out with the duffel loaded down, and without looking at them he walked slowly farther into Chinatown. They followed as nonchalantly as possible and then they all turned a corner and the guy lowered the bag to the ground. Evan knelt down and unzipped the bag, counted the twelve bottles, and nodded.

The guy pointed to the bag.

"Careful with this," he said.

"Sorry?"

"This is sadness waiting for you."

"Okay," Hutch said. "You got your money, right?"

The man pressed his side pocket. "So I apologize. For making you all unhappier."

"That's all right."

He walked away toward the arch, and Ben thought they should have asked his name, but he hadn't asked their names either.

★ ★ ★

On the way back to school, with the bags safely underneath their feet, Hutch finally seemed to look at Ben with durable esteem. When Evan was in the bathroom at the back of the bus, Hutch said quietly, "That was right, man."

They decided to take everything to Ben's room to divvy it up because that was closer to the cab drop-off than Woodruff. When they walked in through the back entrance, unseen as far as they could tell, Markson was there coming the other way.

"Hey, Ben. I've been looking for you. Hey, boys."

The three of them were still, and Markson looked at the big duffel that Evan Pingree was carrying, and instantly the knowledge of what was inside became plain in everyone's eyes. Markson smiled and looked down.

"So come by when you have a second. All right?"

Ben kept nodding and had a hard time stopping. Finally they were up in his room, and none of them were in the mood to drink, and Ben played "Blue Sky" on repeat as the three of them sat with their eyes closed, Hutch and Evan on the beautiful couch, Ben in his hard desk chair with his elbows on his knees.

★ ★ ★

Alice asked him to sit for portraits again, and Ben had the beginning of a new not-caring that made him feel like maybe he could try for her. Why should her refusing prevent him from saying it?

And then they were in the studio together again. He felt the mass of all the things he wanted to say to her, but instead he sat in that room and stayed quiet.

"Now the college consultant guy loves that I'm taking photos," Alice said. "'This is great for your narrative' are actually the words that came out of his mouth. 'This is what sets you apart from all the Asian kids with sixteen hundreds on their SATs.' Why couldn't he just leave this alone?"

"They should know you're good at it," Ben said.

"What if I'm not any good? Why is it important that I'm good? As soon as he said it, the drain opened up under my enthusiasm."

"But here we are."

"Here we are, still."

She started taking pictures, and he imagined going to her room. He would walk to her door and come in without knocking, and she would look up and immediately put some textbook aside and pat a space next to her on the couch—no, nobody pats the space next to them. Maybe instead she would come to his room, and her coming would put him at ease because it would mean she was interested in him, and he would make a joke and she would laugh. He wouldn't have to strain to smell her smell. He would lean and kiss her, and instead of him making the decision about whether to put his hand on her breast, she would take hold of his hand and pull it there. And then when Ahmed got caught and kicked out, Alice would go to Aston's office and appeal for a second chance, for aid, but Ben would stop her—his family's pride—and Alice would never forget him.

"Um, can you do something else with your face?"

"Something else?"

"Yeah, you've been looking the same for a while."

Ben didn't move his face.

"I'm worried about Ahmed."

She stood up from behind the camera. "Hanging out with Tommy and those guys?"

"Yeah, exactly."

"I sort of like Tommy, actually."

"Yeah, but you can handle yourself. You know how to, like, stay yourself while you're with him."

"Who is Ahmed's self, though?"

"What do you mean?"

"Why can't Ahmed be figuring out what he wants to be like with them?"

"You really think that would be a good version of him?"

"Who decides 'good'?"

Ben sighed. "Couldn't we take some pictures outside?"

"Nah, I don't know how to do natural light."

"Do you ever think about leaving, Alice?"

Alice stayed hunched behind the camera, now remembering the spring before, when she had seen Joanna Alpert walking from the quad toward the Schoolhouse by herself. Alice had to do it.

"Hey, Joanna?"

They were a little too far away from each other; Alice had to raise her voice as Joanna headed down the slope toward the Den. Joanna turned around and didn't show any recognition as Alice half jogged the distance between them. Joanna was wearing a tan shaggy Patagonia fleece, tight blue thin-wale corduroys, and dark-brown clogs, and somehow it all looked sophisticated on her.

Alice knew it was just as hard for pretty girls.

"Hey, I'm Alice."

Joanna nodded, but Alice couldn't tell whether Joanna already knew who she was. They turned to keep walking toward the Schoolhouse together, and Joanna didn't ask Alice what was up or what was going on. Joanna's hair wasn't blond, as Alice had remembered it, but rather very light brown.

"What are you up to?" Alice asked.

"Going to yearbook."

"Ah ha."

They kept walking, and Alice knew she had to bring it up now so that they wouldn't get to the Schoolhouse before they were done talking.

"So listen," Alice said. "Your mom."

"Yeah."

"Um, I heard that—I'm not sure where I heard it—but, she's a surgeon, right? Like a plastic surgeon?"

Joanna kept looking straight ahead. "Yeah, she is."

"And so, do you know a lot about the stuff she does? Like, what her work is?"

"You know. She does stuff a plastic surgeon does."

Alice resummoned her persistence.

"Right, but does she like specialize in, I don't know, doing stuff for people after an accident, or like nose jobs, or whatever? Or do all plastic surgeons do everything? Sorry, I just don't know anything about this."

"Oh, totally." Now it seemed that of course Alice wouldn't be expected to know the ins and outs of it all and had gone overboard with apologizing. "Yeah, she mostly does reconstructive stuff, nose work. I think she rebuilt someone's ear after an accident."

They started climbing the hill, and the roof line of the School-house appeared through the trees.

"Does she ever do breast reductions?"

Joanna's posture seemed to soften, and she kept looking forward and down at the path.

"I think so."

"So, like,"

" . . ."

"Do you think I might be able to talk to her sometime? Like could I call her at her office?"

"Sure, yeah, I think she could definitely do that."

They kept walking, and Alice's neck felt warm with relief. But then she wondered whether Joanna knew that Alice didn't already have her mother's phone number.

They reached the south entrance, and Joanna swung her bag off her shoulder and set it on the low wall at the base of the stairs. She looked in, separating her textbooks and notebooks, and came out with a slim black address book. Still not looking at Alice she opened it and flipped through, then reached in again for a pen. She folded down a corner of one of the address book's back pages, tore it off, and carefully wrote the 212 number on the scrap of paper and handed it to Alice. Her face looked clear, and Alice could see an open smile in her eyes.

Alice smiled but worried that too wide a smile would scuttle the deal. She turned it into a nod, folded the little piece of paper, and worried about where to put it so it wouldn't get lost. She took off her own bag and slid the number into the inside sleeve of the spiral notebook she used for English and Spanish.

Joanna turned and walked into the Schoolhouse. Alice could feel the secret slip of paper in her bag as her legs propelled her back to her dorm, where she was twenty minutes late for her meeting with Ms. Corbierre.

Alice got ready for Seated that night feeling full of hope. She had a test the next day in Spanish but she was ready for it.

At Seated, though, everyone's eyes seemed to stop on Alice for a moment longer than usual, and at the table the conversation seemed only half about itself. Alice left the Dish as soon as the table was excused, and when she got back to her room, someone had written on their whiteboard:

DON'T DO IT, ALICE!!!!
Sincerely,
The devoted males of St. James School

Alice wiped off the whiteboard, went into the room, and lay down on the bed without turning on any lights.

"Sure, I've thought about leaving."

She snapped a photo of Ben.

"How come?"

"Well," she said, "you're not going to be surprised when I say I think a lot of people are trying to look at my chest." Ben blushed up from his neck and laughed, but she shrugged. "And that obviously makes"—*snap*—"me pretty uncomfortable, and"—*snap*—"so I think people"—*snap*—"can tell how uncomfortable I am."

Ben started nodding. She took two more photos of him.

"I mean, why do you want to be friends with me?" she asked with a sudden hardness.

Ben blushed again, harder this time, and now even twisted slightly away from her on his chair. She took another photo.

"I like talking with you," he said. "We talk about things I can't talk about with anyone else."

"Really? Is that really why?"

He wanted to say, 'Even if you were completely flat, Alice, I'd still come and see you.' He hoped that was true. Telling her about her smell wouldn't help. "Do you really think that I think I have a chance with you?"

She laughed. "This place is teaching you: always with the graceful thing to say." Abruptly she seemed close to tears.

She wasn't touching the camera now, and instead was looking down at the floor.

He got off the stool and went over to where she was standing, and through torrents of resistance put his hand lightly on her shoulder. She took in a breath and gave a ragged exhale. As they stood there, he looked past her to the table where her binder and equipment sat, and saw several prints spread out in a sloppy grid. Among several instantly identifiable faces he saw a photo of Hutch: that lion's head was looking down and to the side, all his swagger gone. Ben remembered Hutch starting to jump up and down after Chapel the first night, how invincible he seemed then, how fully in the stream of self-assured knowingness. He looked young in the photo.

"Wow, Alice, these are really good."

"Stop."

"I'm not kidding. These are good."

And there was Gray, too. Alice hadn't been able to break through his smiling for the camera; he just looked like a boy hoping to please his parents.

Ben said, "What if I took some of you sometime?"

"I've already been taking self-portraits. Those you will never see. And you're not allowed to see yours until the exhibit."

"I can accept that."

"Let's take a couple more."

He went back to sit on the stool.

★ ★ ★

And then Ahmed got caught, exactly the way Ben had expected him to get caught. Tommy's advisor, the junior faculty member in Gordon, had come to talk to him at eight p.m. about a quiz he had failed, and Graham hadn't been able to put the bong away fast enough. Ahmed was there on the couch, also clearly high. When the advisor asked to look in the closet, he found almost a pound of marijuana.

Ben wished something more spectacular had happened: that they had been caught by the state police, that they had run afoul of some syndicate that then sent a couple guys onto campus, that there had been a system of wiretaps. Instead it was bong water on the braided rug. Ben asked Hutch to hold on to his vodka in case the administration searched their room.

Ben felt cold when he saw Ahmed's face as he came into the room from the meeting in Phelps's office. Ahmed didn't seem to notice Ben at all; he went to his desk and sat down in the chair facing the inside of his loft enclosure. Still there from the day before was Ben's Tintin book, *Prisoners of the Sun.*

Ben looked at the fold of skin at the base of Ahmed's head and wondered if it would turn into two or three as Ahmed got older.

"You okay?" Ben asked. He felt as though he were asking an empty room.

"Ahmed?"

Ahmed set his elbows on the desktop and put his forehead on the heels of his hands.

"Come on, say something," Ben said.

"I don't know what to say. Don't worry, they are not going to find any in our room."

"Turn around. Come on, what happened?"

Ahmed slid the chair back slightly and turned his body toward Ben with his arm along the back of the chair. He glanced at Ben but then lowered his eyes again. Ben saw that he had been crying earlier and was trying not to cry now. The idea that Ahmed could cry hadn't really ever occurred to Ben.

"What happened?"

"I will go before the Disciplinary Committee."

"Did they say anything else?" Ben imagined the committee with the *Companion* open, pointing at the rules that the boys had violated.

Ahmed shook his head. "My father will know. Tommy says we will be expelled." He looked at Ben again, this time with a supplicating face.

"I told you. See? I told you," Ben said.

Ahmed's face closed again, and Ben felt immensely sorry he had said this.

"So when's the DC?" Ben said finally.

"Tomorrow night."

Then, without looking up, Ahmed said, "Will you be my advocate?"

Ben said, "What, in the DC?" but he knew immediately that Ahmed meant this. He imagined Hutch's face.

"You have not been breaking expectations," Ahmed said.

Ben felt proud to be asked, and to have kept his own rule-breaking discreet, and then came a twinge at his hypocrisy. But also the relief that Ahmed wouldn't have him at such a disadvantage. Or was this actually to be Ben's employment, to earn back what he owed?

"Maybe I shouldn't."

"Would you do it if there was no money?"

Ben paused, but then nodded.

"So, please."

Ben tried to nod again.

"You're not sure," said Ahmed. He seemed suddenly ready to cry. "Why do we even want to be here?"

Ben constantly held this question away.

"What are we all trying to be? My father is just as a man should be, and he never came here."

"But you can't go back and grow up poor in the desert."

Ahmed nodded. "So," Ben said. "Let's figure out what we're going to say in the DC."

14. And Now

It was dark when Ben got up, dark when he showered, dark when he pulled his wool hat on. He braced himself for the cold and pushed out the door. You'd get busted if you were caught out of your dorm at two a.m., but Ben wondered at what time of morning it became not against expectations to be outside— six a.m.? Five? He walked out along the main road to the chapel. The melting snow and the overcast sky formed a single field of gray that the dark buildings and trees stood against.

His footfalls scraped quietly on the grit. The bracken on the banks of the Lower Pond waterfall bobbed under the falling water, and the branches were no longer frozen into long bright arcs.

Ben passed the front of the PO and moved under the trees that lined the road, then came up to the vast chapel lawn. He stopped even though the slush was starting to soak through his cared-for Sauconys. The black chapel had the proportions of a sitting sphinx, its spired head triumphant over its paws in front.

The air that morning had just the slightest swaddling texture against his face. Ben could sense the trees gathering their strength to push new buds out into the world.

Ben kept walking to the chapel's front entrance. The wind started to gust, and with gloveless hands Ben pulled back on the main door's giant iron hoop and stepped inside.

The door closed behind him, and the long echoing of wood against wood gave the immense dimensions of the space. He walked without ceremony to the little door at the back of the ante-chapel, slipped the key in, and after the key wouldn't turn, he pulled it out slightly and tried again. Still it stuck, and he endured a moment of supreme disappointment, but then he slid it in again, not as far as before, and the key turned surely. Ben pushed the door back and smelled the colder air of the chapel-tower staircase.

He stepped inside. The bottom step was so close to the threshold that he almost tripped. He climbed the first stair and pulled the door closed behind him. It was almost totally black. There was a weak glow from a slit window in the stairwell above, enough for him to barely make out the curving walls around him. The stairwell turned inside the circumference of a very large Hula-Hoop.

The inside of the chapel tower had been described to him by Marco Salatino, the varsity crew coxswain, who had bragged about catapulting water balloons off the top of the tower until one of the balloons shattered a lamppost light and twisted its metal enclosure and Marco realized what would happen if a balloon actually hit a person. Marco had loaned the keys to Hutch, who wanted to bring his girlfriend Lily up here when it got warmer. Hutch had vowed to let Marco hit his pinky toe as hard as he could with a hammer if he ever made a copy of the keys. That's how too many people would start going to the chapel tower, and then the lock would get changed. But Ben had seen the keys go into the pencil drawer of Hutch's desk.

To keep his balance Ben decided to climb with his hands down on the stairs in front of him, and so he started up like that, twisting around the stone spindle of the staircase with his hands in the cold dust and tiny loose pebbles.

Very quickly he lost track of his progress. He had a while before Chapel would start—two and a half hours, maybe—and so he didn't move too fast. He got tired of crawling and lifted one arm to stroke the outside wall to try to find a railing, and for a moment it seemed that he would fall back into the twisting space behind him.

But his outstretched hand met a rope, and as he took hold he heard it lift the many iron loops that anchored it into the wall. He stood and began to climb.

He imagined the substance of the tower disappearing and his body hovering exposed in the air. He stopped briefly to recover from the dizziness of going around and around.

And then the rope railing stopped with one last iron hoop, and he came up from the floor into the carillon room, which was about the size of a two-car parking garage and lit by vertical slatted windows. The wooden apparatus of the carillon itself looked like an enormous mantis trying to conceal itself as a loom.

He walked over to the player's seat and looked down at the keyboard of wooden dowels. In the light now he could just see his breath. The bells for the carillon and for the clock weren't in this room, and Ben guessed they were one or two levels above.

He turned away and looked to a flat-runged ladder rising up to an arched opening high in the wall that looked like the mouth of a brick pizza oven. He set his hands on the vertical beams of the ladder and set his foot on the first rung. As he shifted his full weight onto it, the wood and metal of the tower began to move, and quickly the entire structure vibrated higher and higher toward the point of collapse. Then it was a clapper striking the first bell in the Westminster Quarters. The sound of the bells cracked around him, and he gripped the ladder until the five tolls were done.

His heart began to slow down and he kept climbing. When he reached the opening at the top of the ladder he looked out along the length of the chapel roof's interior: mammoth wooden rafters above and the dark panels of the chapel ceiling below. From the roof beam a gangway on steel cables hung down a foot above the wooden spine of the chapel ceiling.

Each sloping panel beneath the gangway had a frame around the edge, with an iron eyebolt embedded in it. A clothesline tied to the eyebolt ran up over a pulley anchored into the roof and back down, and was secured to the side of the gangway with multiple wraps around a metal cleat. To clean the chandeliers, the maintenance men opened these panels, pulled the chandeliers up by their chains hand over hand, cleaned the bulbs and wrought iron, then lowered each one down again. For the first twenty years of the chapel's life, this had been done every day to light the candles in each chandelier.

Ben went to his hands and knees and crawled out onto the gangway. It was expanded metal lath with treaded edges and it was painful on his palms and kneecaps. He imagined himself as a Spartan warrior, for whom this pain would be nothing. He thought of Alice getting up now, sleepy, careless of the fact of her body. He crawled out only a few feet because he wanted to make sure he heard Aston's voice, and the Rector's podium stood at the near end of the chapel.

He unwound the rope from the first cleat to his right, and with a slow, steady pull, tried to open the panel. It resisted for a moment, then opened with such a loud crack that Ben was terrified he had broken it. But the echo subsided and the panel rose smoothly when he continued to pull on the rope. After he had raised it about two feet, enough to give him a six-inch-wide opening to look through, he wrapped the clothesline back around the cleat. Ben leaned over and could see straight down five stories to the rows of seats that seemed from here like toy railroad tracks. Looking down from this height turned his body rigid. But it was so truly beautiful; if this kind of beauty had arisen, then the force that made it couldn't be entirely wrong. Ben could see the podium from which Aston would speak.

Now all he had to do was wait. Ben turned over and lay against the metal, already cold through his coat, bringing his hands along his sides. He could feel the tread of the gangway through his wool hat.

Ahmed had told him that because Tommy and Graham knew they were going to be kicked out, they had decided to say that Ahmed hadn't known what he was getting into, that he was trying to fit in, that he had come under their sway without realizing what the consequences could be. They were saying that they had never known Ahmed to use drugs or import them.

For their DC the previous evening, Ben and Ahmed both got dressed in jacket and tie. Ahmed's clothes looked just right for this.

And later, after the DC, Ben had sat on one of the couches at the far end of the Den and described what had happened. The whole Den was arrayed around him. Hutch was there too, now looking at Ben as though having represented Ahmed was the most distinguished possible deed. Ben said that, according to plan, he had argued to the DC that Ahmed hadn't known what he was getting into, that he was trying to fit in, that he had fallen under the sway of his charismatic new friends. Ben stated that he had never seen Ahmed use or import. The faculty were buying it.

"And then Ahmed started shaking his head. He said that he was just as responsible as the other two, that he had been to Boston a bunch of times already and had helped plan how to get there and where to go, that no one had pressured him to put in more than his share of money, that Tommy and Graham said he could stay behind if he wanted to, but that he had volunteered to go.

"And no one knew what to say. They just thanked us and let us go."

Ben didn't tell them about the walk back to the dorm.

"So then why did I lie for you?"

"It was absurd to keep doing what we were doing. Everyone knew it was a lie."

"Will you just thank me for doing it, though?"

"After I leave, we can keep paying." Ahmed regretted saying this.

"That's not why I represented you. You wanted to stay." They were quiet for several steps. "And I don't think St. James is going to seem worth paying for. For your dad."

Ahmed didn't answer right away, but then he nodded.

And so now, from up in the chapel ceiling, with Ahmed back in the dorm excused for the day while his punishment was read, Ben was going to witness the end for both of them, even if the end would come for him a little later. And once Aston read out Ahmed's expulsion, Ben would climb back down to the carillon room and bring his hands down onto the giant keyboard. He wouldn't stop the noise until they found another key, came up there, and kicked him out too. In his mind he could already feel the long vibrations hanging over the campus.

Another two turns of the tower clock bells and then the soft churning sound of voices roused Ben. He lifted his head and looked around at the attic-like place he was in and had a vivid image of living up here—disappearing from campus, withdrawing without any responsibility for anyone or anything, hoping that Alice would wonder where he had gone. He seemed to be in the supporting cast of Ahmed's life now.

Ben went to lean out over the opening in the ceiling, but now along with his fear of falling came a fear that someone would look up and see him there. He tried to find where Alice was sitting but it was too far down the length of the building. He wondered what his face might look like; a little white polyp in space. For the first time in months, he heard the faint, familiar sound of a bulldozer beeping in reverse. Construction had resumed on Ahmed's father's pool.

The organ began heaving through some hymn that Ben didn't recognize, but he couldn't tell whether it was something he had never heard before or some familiar melody that was being muddled in the massive space. All the heads that had been moving around each other came to rest and formed into rows. The first organ piece closed and a new one began, and the sound of bodies standing up from wooden pews reached Ben. They began to sing, but Ben still couldn't hear what the song was.

After the hymn closed, there was a long pause. Usually this was when some student would give a speech about study abroad or an a cappella group would perform, but now it was just empty. Ben got impatient and felt foolish for being up here. Would it be so

300

hard to hear this news next to other people? Was his tiny act of rebellion so urgent? The long building stayed quiet.

He saw the top of Aston's blond head shift and move the two paces to his podium. His voice came from so far away that it sounded delayed, as if it had spoken some time ago.

" do not take discipline lightly.   student admitted to St. James deserves to be here and each offers   unique and valuable. Never   ess a student proves him or   self   adhering to the school's contract.   student tears the fabric that binds school   must   consequences.   term health of the whole must prevail   the short-term   of any individual student.   not easy decisions necessary."

Aston didn't speak for several seconds.

" using drugs   bringing   campus, Graham Lasseter asked leave the school."

"For   drugs and bringing drugs   campus, Thomas Landon has   asked   the school."

"For   in presence of   drug use,   Ahmed Al-Khaled   pro-bation   one year and will   days work duty."

Aston paused. Ben rolled over and lay back on the gangway again. It seemed that whatever had laid itself over him would press his body down through the gridding. He wanted the roar of the carillon. He wanted the school to apply its rigor, to enact some bracing justice. But, too, he was relieved for his friend. He saw Ahmed savoring the forest walk to Seated Meal. And maybe the sheik still had some patience left for him.

But the school. The school's ethics were a scrim over its animal need to survive. Just manners over its unforgiving appetite.

" us pray."

★ ★ ★

Ben waited for everyone to leave before he came down. He locked the door behind him, walked out across the chapel lawn in the first-period quiet under a flat overcast sky. He couldn't bring himself to go to class, to go to lunch, to practice, to do homework, to sleep, any of it. He regretted locking the door to the chapel tower, so dutifully following the little rules of schoolboy mischief.

Across the chapel lawn Ben saw the small brick PO, so appealing still, and from force of habit he went in to check his little window there. An L.L.Bean catalogue with a thoughtful couple in shorts walking across a sand dune.

Ahmed was on the couch with his eyes closed when Ben came back to the room.

"Are you all right?"

"All right," said Ahmed. Mr. Dennett had relayed the news to him.

His father had still sent him a box of dates—lemon, almond, plain—to mark the end of Ramadan. He was going to ask the school to set aside a place for him to pray. He couldn't imagine praying in their room if he knew Ben could come in and discover him, or wake up and look down at him in prostration.

"What did your parents say?" Ben asked.

"My father is quite heartbroken. After all that preparation, for me to take those decisions, and be known publicly for doing that. What my father said was, 'Would he have done this?' He puts so much power into this stranger, this person he knows nothing about. Maybe Underhill drank with his friends here, maybe he cheated on tests. Maybe he went on and lied to his business partners, to his wife."

Ben didn't answer.

"It will be hard for me again after this, like after Ennis," said Ahmed.

"Maybe," Ben said.

"I will miss Tommy and Graham, also." He paused. "It was nice to have friends."

Ben couldn't hold his gaze. Eventually he asked, "Do you not want to stay?"

"I don't know." Ahmed laughed briefly. "I never thought I would say *that*." He looked at Ben. "Do you?"

"Well . . . Has Alice Morehead taken your picture?"

"Yes."

"Yeah. I want to be here at least to see her show."

★ ★ ★

Green peeked out from the blazing snow. Ben walked out along the Two-Laner in the direction of the crew boathouse, and every few steps he closed his eyes to briefly bask in the sun without stopping.

He came up to Number 40—a white two-story colonial with a garage to one side. He had run through countless scenarios of discovering what the inside of the house looked like, but as he passed a large bush that was budding in the same blush-gray as a female cardinal, he saw Manley Price there in his driveway, kneeling at a jack next to the front driver's side of his car, a dark green Volkswagen Jetta. Ben didn't want to wait for Price to find him this time.

Price squinted up at Ben, and Ben saw rare surprise across his face—like smelling something acrid. But then Price smiled and came stiffly to stand. The front of his blue oxford was marked with new grime and many colors of old dried paint. Ben approached and Price nodded but didn't extend his hand to shake.

"What a surprise about your roommate," Price said, and laughed. "But you knew all along he was safe."

"I actually thought the school wouldn't make an exception." Ben expected Price to laugh again, but he seemed suddenly chastened, as though tasting the bitterness of what he had said.

"You wish they had lived up to their own standard," Price said.

"It seems like the whole point of St. James."

Price nodded. "Even at the school's beginning, not many were leaving here and giving their lives over to orphans. 'To serve man and to glorify God.' The beds are a lot softer when you drill oil."

Ben thought about when he would see Markson again, undertaking the rewrite of "Decision-Making." *Above all else, a St. James education teaches a boy to look out for himself.* Markson would say there was more humanity to it than that.

"What keeps you here?" Ben asked.

Price didn't respond for a long time. "It's a time of no escape. That's what I like. Seeing what happens when you're trapped with your experience."

Ben looked up into the safe sky.

"So play Gray, Ben. I can't make you, and I know I can't really even move you in that direction. But don't miss the chance to find out what's on your inside. And you can give that to him, too. You can let Gray find out what's on his inside."

Ben laughed. He looked in Price's eyes.

"Make him bleed for it. Let yourself bleed."

★ ★ ★

An hour later, after telling Rory to set up the match for that night, Ben dialed the calling card number from memory and held the receiver to his ear with his eyes closed. He imagined her wiping wet hands on the towel hung over the bar of the oven door as she moved for the phone.

She answered with the same voice as always, but her breath had a ragged edge. They asked each other if they were okay, and Ben told her about the DC and Ahmed's decision. He told her he was fine.

"What's happening there?" he asked.

Now the raggedness gave way to a short sob.

"I don't even know why I'm upset!" she said with a laugh through her crying throat. "It's good, not having to keep waiting. So. Dad's property deal—the local board—they voted to keep the land zoned as is."

"So they can't turn it into retail."

"Right."

"Did he not plan for that?"

"He says his partners told him it was a *fait accompli*."

"I mean . . . did someone take advantage of him? Did they sell it to him knowing it wouldn't be changed over?"

She didn't answer right away. "I hadn't thought of that."

Harry was out in the trees splitting wood. He lifted the maul and let it fall through each standing piece. Inside the house Helen was telling Ben, and he needed to go inside and take responsibility, to look in her face again.

But instead Harry stood there in the last snow, trying to accept that this was his real course, that all the branching decisions had shunted him here. He had expected himself to do so much more than make money; just making money and nothing else was a failure. But before you can lead or give back or spread excellence or let culture thrive, you have to earn. He stayed there and waited to lift the maul again and to feel the pleasure of it falling.

Helen and Ben let the phone be quiet between them.

"Okay," Ben said.

"I'm just glad it's done with. So let's talk about what's best: staying up there on aid, or . . ."

Ben told her about the arrangement he had made. She couldn't say anything for several seconds.

"Mom?"

"We should never have waited so long! Oh god! I'll never forgive myself, forcing you to *this*. We just, we've never met them, we know nothing about them, and they're extending this much? I knew we left you exposed but, augh, it kills me to think—"

"It seemed like the best way."

"We can't keep doing this, though. I mean, your father will never agree to it."

"When is it not his decision anymore?"

"It's just so *embarrassing,* Ben. I'd never be able to look Ahmed's father in the face, ever."

"What if we don't have the luxury of looking everyone in the face?" He paused. "We don't have to decide now."

"No. We do have to decide. You'll just go on financial aid."

"What if I came home and went to Leaford High?"

She paused. "We're not asking you to do that."

Ben went back up to his room. He ate half a PowerBar. The light was fading across the walls, and as he looked out the window at everyone under their backpacks coming back from dinner, he had to remind himself that he had come down from the chapel tower earlier that same day.

He left the dorm with his long bag, and as he came up to the courts he saw heads through the lit windows and heard the tremor of a crowd. He opened the vestibule door into the sound, and walked down the stadium steps through all the people, through Hutch's gaze and Price's gaze, and Ahmed's gaze and Alice's and Teddy's and Russell's and Thomas Weeks's, through all of them, through his own, and on the court he saw Gray's tall form turn. He went through the glass door into that incinerating brightness.

Acknowledgments

This book has many authors.

Before anyone, my parents and sisters, who saved my life and whose love was never contingent on results.

The brilliant and determined Asya Muchnick, who drew the best out of this book. The rest of the Little, Brown staff: Cynthia Saad, Michael Noon, Allison Warner, Ashley Marudas, and Alyssa Persons, who prove that people still do things better than they need to.

The subtle and terrifyingly effective Kathy Robbins, who signed on before the main character really existed and gave me the time and structure to find the book's voice. No one could ask for better representation. Janet Oshiro, Jane Arbogast, and Liza Darnton at the Robbins Office are expert and extremely kind.

Susan Rieger, who led this book over the narrow path to an audience.

Many teachers: George Carlisle, David Newman, Katharine Weber, Kate Walbert, John Crowley. Ellen Bryant Voight, Pete Turchi, and Debra Allbery, who created and sustain the outstanding Warren Wilson writing program. Diana Wagman, Victor LaValle, Maud Casey, T. M. McNally, and Rob Cohen, who transformed my writing. Amy Grimm, who kept it all together.

At the D. E. Shaw group: Erin Granfield, Kari Elassal, Eugenie

Kim, Drew Ashwood, Isaac Bauer, Claire Muldoon, Trey Beck, Alexis Halaby, and David Shaw, who let me survive in a kind of slow-motion writing retreat for eleven years.

The MacDowell Colony: David Macy, Karen Keenan, Kyle Oliver, Cindy Fallows, Courtney Bethel, and Blake Tewksbury.

Laura O'Loughlin, Greg Snyder, and the community of the Brooklyn Zen Center, who reminded me that it takes as long as it takes.

For help, love, reading drafts, and food: Josh Barenbaum, Nazli Parvizi, Sam Breslin Wright, Amdé Mengistu, Katy Dion, Amanda Filoso Schreyer, Nick Yap, Sarah Stehli Howell, Pete Light, Carl Bialik, Dave Goldenberg, Shamus Khan, Terry Bowman, Thackston Lundy, Marco DeSena, Jennifer Barros, Ben Kulo, Hannah Toporovsky, Lauren Dewey, Sarah Von Essen, Josh Billings, Victoria Blake, Mónica Palma, Calvin Burton, Ashley Powers, Erik Simpson, Christoph Janke, Megan Hustad, Ben Loehnen, Aria Sloss, Brigid Hughes, Ben Ryder Howe, Scott Adkins, Erin Courtney, Nathan Pinsley, Khaled Al Hammadi, Patrick Granfield, Kelly Granfield, Rachel Beach, Richard Sennett, Cullen Stanley, Julie MacKay, Leila Kazemi, Alan Donovan, Rachel Karpf, Sammy Tunis, Moe Yousuf, Nancy Hughes, Owen Hughes, Doug Kaden, Meg Weeks, Chris Weeks, Tyler Sage, Rachel Crawford, Jonathan Lee, Kate Scelsa, Deji Olukotun, Lindsay Edgecombe, Allison Lorentzen, David Herskovits, Jennifer Egan, and GPH.

And most of all, Sarah. My oasis, my love, and my full-on collaborator, who never wavered through all the bad versions. I wouldn't have come close without you.

About the Author

Alexander Tilney received a BA from Yale University and an MFA from the Warren Wilson College Program for Writers, and has been a fellow at the MacDowell Colony. His writing has appeared in the *Southwest Review*, the *Journal of the Office for Creative Research*, and *Gelf Magazine*. He lives in Brooklyn, New York. *The Expectations* is his first novel.